Sheila Norton lives near Chelmsford in Essex with her husband, and worked for most of her life as a medical secretary, before retiring early to concentrate on her writing. Sheila is the award-winning writer of numerous women's fiction novels and over a hundred short stories, published in women's magazines.

She has three married daughters, six little grandchildren, and over the years has enjoyed the companionship of three cats and two dogs.

When not working on her writing, Sheila enjoys spending time with her family and friends, as well as reading, walking, swimming, photography and travel. For more information please see www.sheilanorton.com

Also by Sheila Norton:

Oliver the Cat Who Saved Christmas
Charlie the Kitten That Saved a Life

Sheila Norton

The Vets at Hope Green

EBURY
PRESS

1 3 5 7 9 10 8 6 4 2

Ebury Press, an imprint of Ebury Publishing
20 Vauxhall Bridge Road,
London SW1V 2SA

Penguin
Random House
UK

Ebury Press is part of the Penguin Random House group of companies
whose addresses can be found at global.penguinrandomhouse.com

Copyright © Sheila Norton, 2017

Sheila Norton has asserted her right to be identified as the author of this
work in accordance with the Copyright, Designs and Patents Act 1988

This novel is a work of fiction. Names and characters are the product
of the author's imagination and any resemblance to actual persons,
living or dead, is entirely coincidental

First published in the UK in 2017 by Ebury Press

www.penguin.co.uk

A CIP catalogue record for this book is available from the British Library

ISBN 9781785039959

Printed and bound in Great Britain by Clays Ltd, St Ives PLC

Penguin Random House is committed to a sustainable future for
our business, our readers and our planet. This book is made
from Forest Stewardship Council® certified paper.

MIX
Paper from
responsible sources
FSC
www.fsc.org
FSC® C018179

In memory of our own 'Nanny Peg', my late mum-in-law, whose favourite random phrases will live on in our family conversations forever! Nana Peggy in this story isn't based on her or even much like her, but I thought about her a lot while I was writing it.

PART 1

ESCAPE TO THE COUNTRY

PROLOGUE

It was a beautiful, warm day at the end of May and the countryside on either side of the road was full of the promise of summer ahead. I wound down the driver's window of my little car and turned up the radio so that I could hear the music above the noise of the breeze as I whizzed along in the fast lane of the motorway. Mile by mile, I felt myself relaxing. I felt my worries and uncertainties begin to melt away and my heart lifted with the anticipation of my destination.

Hope Green. The very name made me feel more optimistic. I sang along to the radio, remembering happy family holidays on the Dorset coast when I was a child. Hope Green had hardly changed since those days, its age-old charm untouched by the increased pace of life elsewhere. It was somewhere I could unwind and be at peace, take stock of things and perhaps really find myself at last.

As I steadily increased my distance from my home on the outskirts of London, I could almost feel my old life slipping off my shoulders like a heavy coat that had been weighing me down – the crowded streets, the rush-hour crush on the Tube, the traffic fumes, the stress on people's faces – I was leaving all this behind me, leaving it for a place where life still depended on the seasons, where people still had time to chat on street corners, where people picked blackberries and elderberries from the hedgerows instead of buying them in tiny plastic packets from the supermarket at ridiculous expense. Here I would be able to see the stars at night instead of neon lights. And the only traffic jams were caused by tractors.

I knew I was also leaving behind a few people who thought I'd lost my mind and was making a huge and ridiculous mistake. Perhaps I was, but I didn't think so. This was my opportunity to start again, to carve out a new future for myself. A future that wouldn't be just about me. And I was rushing headlong towards it, never more certain of anything in my life. Hope Green was my hope for that future, and I was determined not to look back.

CHAPTER ONE

Six weeks earlier

It had been a fairly ordinary day at the James Street Vet Clinic. We'd had the usual procession of dogs, cats, hamsters and rabbits, but also a pair of budgies, a little white mouse and an urban fox who had been hit by a car and had been carried in almost lifeless by the kind but distraught lady who had found him. Without exception, the pet owners were all well heeled, well dressed and well paid, settling their bills without a murmur on their Amex cards before rushing back to their large expensive homes and their important jobs.

Not that I resented our clientele, I reminded myself as I pulled on my coat and prepared to set off for my own, not-so-large home in a far less expensive area of the city. They were polite and responsible people for the most part and, after all, they did keep me employed. I loved seeing all the different animals being brought in and I knew many of the regulars by name and personality. I enjoyed the breakthrough moments when sick animals were restored to health and, on sadder occasions, though it was initially upsetting, I took satisfaction in my ability to comfort and console the owners.

I'd always wanted to work with animals, and when I was offered the position of receptionist at this upmarket clinic in the heart of London's West End, I thought all my dreams had come true. However, after four years of the same monotonous routine, I was beginning to feel that it wasn't enough any more.

Adam didn't understand. I knew this because he delighted in questioning me on it every time I brought up the subject. I thought that your boyfriend was supposed to be someone who listens and sympathises, but he had taken the opposite tack. The last time it had come up, when we'd met for drinks after work, he had asked me in his usual weary voice what exactly it was that I wasn't happy with.

'Nothing,' I'd told him, equally wearily. 'I keep trying to explain to you – there's nothing wrong with the job itself, it's just that I feel … kind of frustrated, I suppose.'

'Frustrated with what?'

I sighed. To be fair, I had trouble rationalising it myself. On the surface, my job was everything I wanted it to be. I loved seeing and spending time with all the animals, especially the regulars, but I'd always hoped for something more. I'd never really told Adam how strong my desire was to become a vet myself one day, though of course he knew I'd taken the City & Guilds course in Animal Care the previous year. His view was that I was 'only' the receptionist – as if I wasn't all too aware of this already – and wasn't employed to start 'scrubbing up and interfering in operations'.

I'd taken the course with the intention that it would allow me to help out occasionally at the clinic. Playing with my favourite pets while they waited in the reception area was nice, obviously, but it wasn't where I saw myself further down the line.

'I just don't have the chance to *do* anything with what I learned.'

'You're not one of the nurses,' he said, with a slight lift of his eyebrows, 'or one of the vets.'

'I'm not that stupid, Adam. I just thought they'd let me help out if they needed an extra pair of hands. Holding a difficult patient or calming them down, that kind of thing.' I sipped my drink, wishing yet again that I hadn't brought up the subject.

'You must have known what the job description was when you accepted the post.'

'Of course I did, but that was four years ago and … well.' I shook my head. This was going nowhere. 'Let's just say I'm starting to feel like I want a change.'

When I'd first moved to London from Norfolk to take up the much longed-for position of *working with animals*, I was perhaps a tad starry-eyed and naïve. The reality of living in London had been a series of shocks, mostly of the financial variety – I rented a tiny single room, no bigger than a matchbox, in an upstairs flat which I shared with two other girls – and the reality of being a receptionist in an inner-city veterinary clinic was not how I had envisioned it. I don't know why I'd allowed myself to assume it would eventually lead to something other than what it was. It wasn't the job. It was me.

'Perhaps you're just in a bit of a rut,' Adam said. 'Maybe you'll feel differently when we buy a place together.'

And that was the other thing. I might have been naïve when I first moved to London, but the scales had long since fallen from my eyes. It amazed me that Adam continued to think it was only a matter of time before we could afford to get a place together – neither of us was exactly earning mega bucks. Adam was living with his parents in Hampstead, claiming to be saving up, and while I couldn't deny the idea of one day setting up home together had once been an exciting prospect, as time passed it seemed more and more unrealistic. In fact, the difficulties seemed to be all I thought about these days, and I'd started to question whether I actually wanted our relationship to last at all.

I wasn't ready to confront these thoughts, though, so I changed tack and gave Adam an apologetic smile.

'OK, maybe I'm just being silly,' I said. 'You're right: I knew from the start what my job was all about, and at least it's better than working in that estate agents' office back in King's Lynn.'

'Exactly. I don't suppose there was much contact with dogs and cats there.' He smiled and took my hand.

'And of course, I do *want* us to move in together,' I went on, ignoring the doubts at the back of my mind. 'It's just so difficult. I wonder how we'll ever manage it.'

'At least we can *try*, though. We can still have our dreams.'

I smiled back at him. 'I do dream about it, actually. A lot, as a matter of fact. I like to fantasise about a pretty little cottage somewhere in the country. It has a huge garden all around it where the dogs can run free, with apple trees where the children can climb and swing from the branches—'

I stopped short. What on earth was I thinking of, sharing that with him? But it was too late. He'd stopped smiling and had taken his hand away from mine.

'More of a fairy tale than a dream, that one, isn't it?' he said. 'I mean, if you're going to be *that* unrealistic, no wonder you think we'll never be able to afford it.'

'I know. I did say it was just a fantasy.'

'We both work in London. It'll have to be a flat. And as for a garden, forget it. Quite apart from the fact that you know I don't particularly like dogs.' And then he added under his breath, 'Or children.'

'Since when have you not liked children?' I asked, taken aback. 'That's a new one to me.' It was one thing he wasn't an animal lover, but I didn't quite know if I could process that he didn't like children either.

'OK, I don't *not* like them, but I've never wanted any of my own. Not for a long time, anyway, if at all. Maybe when I'm about forty I might feel differently ...' He looked at me sharply. 'You're not getting broody or anything, are you?'

'No. Of course not,' I said. 'But I suppose I've assumed we'd have them at some point. When we're ready and … financially stable and everything.'

'And living in the cosy cottage in the country with roses round the door?'

'Don't mock me, Adam. We all need our dreams.'

As I swung my bag over my shoulder and walked out of the clinic, I thought about my 'dream' and whether Adam really was part of mine or not. I'd met him just over three years ago at a birthday party for one of my flatmates, and the attraction was instant – and mutual. Back then, we never seemed to argue. We were like any other young couple – independent and carefree, spending what little we had to spare on fun and frivolity. Ironically, it was only when our relationship became more serious and we started making long-term plans to settle down that the arguments began. Our differences, which hadn't particularly mattered up till then, now seemed to loom in almost every conversation. He positively loved London and never wanted to leave, whereas I'd only ever seen it as a temporary base, somewhere I could enjoy an independent city-dweller life and establish a career, but not a place where I could settle down.

Adam was a trainee accountant and had aspirations of climbing the professional ladder and eventually commanding a big salary, with things like flashy cars and riverside penthouse apartments high on his wish list. I'd have been happy with a pushbike, a couple of Labradors and, well, yes, that fantasy cottage in the country. Were we really even compatible? Or had our relationship simply become a habit?

Easter was coming up and I'd booked two weeks off work so I could spend at least part of it with Adam at his parents' house in Hampstead. I hadn't taken any holiday since the previous summer, and when Adam had suggested it around Christmas time it had seemed like a nice idea. Back in the dark chill of December, when I was spending every evening huddled in my duvet in front of the electric fire in my tiny room, the thought of going for long walks with Adam on Hampstead Heath in the sunshine held a lot of appeal. I liked his parents, I liked their big townhouse on a tree-lined avenue, and I liked his mum's hearty cooked breakfasts, roast dinners and home-made desserts. I'd managed to romanticise the whole notion of the holiday to the point where it was almost irrelevant that Adam and I were quarrelling so often. I'd even convinced myself that, somehow, things would be different during this mythical springtime idyll, and that afterwards, everything would feel better.

Dream on, Sam, I muttered to myself as I swiped my Oyster card at the turnstile in the Tube station. I needed to start facing up to the fact that we weren't getting along so well any more. The longer it went on, the harder it was going to be. And suddenly, I realised that instead of spending more time in each other's company over Easter, what we really needed was a break from each other.

'Darling! How lovely to hear from you! Hold on, let me just put this down and turn off this …' My mum, as usual, sounded like she was in the middle of doing at least three things at once, all of them urgent. 'How are you?'

'OK, thanks.' I hesitated. It was best never to beat about the bush with Mum, so I just came out with it. 'I wondered if I could come home for a couple of weeks?'

'How lovely! Of course you can. When are you thinking?'

'Next weekend.'

'Hold on, let me think. So you'd be here over Easter?'

'Yes, and the following week, if that's all right. It'll be nice to see you both, and catch up with the family, and—'

'I thought that was when you were going to stay with Adam and his family?'

'Well, yes, it was.' I let the pause become ominous, not really knowing what else to say. 'I don't think I'm going to go.' It was surely the biggest hint that things weren't going well in my relationship, but Mum failed to pick up on it.

'Oh, that's a shame. Dad and I will be away,' she continued in her upbeat voice. 'Didn't I tell you? We're going on a cruise – Venice and the Greek islands. We thought we'd treat ourselves.'

Oh yes. I remembered now – Mum had told me about the cruise. I think she'd counted on me being with Adam over Easter. These days, it seemed as if my parents made a career out of treating themselves, not that I blamed them. They worked hard, and since my two brothers and I had all left home, they had no ties to hold them back and were determined to see the world. I was usually pleased for them but at that moment I could have really have done with their company.

'Oh. Never mind. I hope you enjoy it.'

'So what will you do? Go to Hampstead after all?'

'I don't know. Perhaps I won't take the time off work at all.' The thought of a holiday had lost all of its appeal now. 'Maybe I'll wait till you and Dad are back.'

'Well, don't forget we're going to Madeira in May with Peter and Gaynor. And then at the end of June we'll be in France for a week as usual. And then there's the trip to New York coming up—'

'Of course. OK, Mum. I'll get back to you.'

'Is everything all right? You sound a bit ... down.'

Finally, she'd picked up on it, but it was too late now for her to help, so I brushed it off. 'I just fancied getting out of London for a while, that's all. I'm OK.'

'I don't blame you, Sam. It must be so exhausting, in those crowds all the time.' She paused. 'Why don't you go down to Dorset and stay with your nan? It must be a while since you saw her.'

I hadn't thought about staying with my nan. And it was true: I hadn't seen her since she'd come up at Christmas. I loved spending time with Nana Peggy, and Hope Green, the village where she lived, was the exact opposite of London: just what I needed. I wasn't sure if she'd want me descending on her at such short notice, but there was no harm in asking. And since my granddad had passed away a few years ago I was sure she wouldn't mind having a bit of company.

Suddenly, my day was looking a lot brighter.

CHAPTER TWO

One of my favourite things about my job, apart from the animals themselves, of course, was that it was how I met Claire. Claire was one of the other receptionists, and although we didn't always work together – she was part-time – it was always more fun when she was there. She was ten years older than me, not that you'd have known it to look at her, and was married with a little boy, seven-year-old Harry. Harry was the reason Claire only worked part-time, and he was also the reason she hadn't had any more children. When she'd first told me this, I'd looked at her in surprise, assuming she meant that there had been complications, but she'd immediately laughed and said she meant purely for the cost of the childcare.

I could see how true it was that life wasn't easy for a working mum. But despite my little roses-round-the-door fantasy that had so irritated Adam, I knew perfectly well that children weren't going to be on the agenda if Adam and I stayed together. The very thought made me anxious.

'Have you told him you're starting to have doubts?' Claire asked.

'No. I'm not even sure enough myself. I'm just kind of unsettled, I suppose. But I do think it'll be good to have some space. Now I've made the decision to go to my nan's instead of his parents, I'm really looking forward to it.' I smiled at the memory of Nana Peggy's enthusiasm on the phone. She'd been delighted to hear from me and was looking forward to spending some time together. 'It'll be great. I can take Rufus for lots of long country walks. The fresh air will help to clear my head.'

'Oh yes, Rufus. He's a springer spaniel, isn't he? They're hard work, I'll bet.'

'They need a lot of exercise, but Rufus is getting on a bit now. Last time I went, I noticed he was beginning to slow down. But he's a lovely boy, such a good-natured dog. I adore him.' I sighed at the thought of being in a position to have a dog of my own. 'And I adore Hope Green, too. It's such a pretty little place, so friendly, and close to such a gorgeous part of the coast.'

'It might not be quite as gorgeous in April as it is when you normally go in summer,' Claire pointed out, laughing. 'Nowhere quite as cold as the seaside when there's a biting wind blowing.'

'But if you wrap up well, it does you good,' I said, very conscious of how much I was sounding like my mother.

'Maybe,' she conceded. 'And, speaking of which, I need to pop out for a sandwich. I won't be long, but call me if it suddenly gets busy.'

There was small chance of that, I thought to myself. It had been a very slow day at the clinic.

I'd convinced myself that after a couple of weeks in Hope Green, I'd feel more ready to make a decision about Adam, one way or the other. We'd been together for more than three years now, and I knew it'd be hard for both of us if we decided to split up. We didn't tend to go out clubbing or to restaurants like we used to because we were supposed to be saving up for our future, but there were still good times that I'd miss – cooking together, watching TV together, laughing at some inane thing one of us had said. Those times were the reason I was still with him, why I hadn't ended it yet. *Was I really going to end it?* I thought to myself. My heart felt heavy at the thought. It was bad enough that I'd changed my holiday plans – a fact that he hadn't responded to very kindly – but did I want to end the relationship completely?

The night before, I'd told him that I was going to Hope Green to see my nana instead, and he hadn't taken it well at all. I tried to explain my reasons calmly and thoughtfully, but it was as if we were speaking different languages. Adam's expression quickly changed from calm to perplexed, and then through disappointed to downright annoyed. He stared at me as if I'd grown horns and demanded to know whether it was because of the 'funny moods' I'd been having recently.

'Funny moods?' I repeated, immediately on the defensive.

'You know, about your job. About being in a rut. Does that apply to being with me, too?'

'No!' I lied. I wasn't ready to cause a scene, and the last thing I wanted to do was hurt him. Instead, I told him about Nana – how Mum didn't often get the time to see her, so I felt like I ought to give her some company.

'My parents will be so disappointed, Sam. Mum's been stocking up the freezer with apple tarts because she knows you like them so much.' He shook his head, paused, and then said grudgingly, 'But she'll probably think it's really nice that you want to spend time with your nan.'

It struck me as odd that he seemed more focused on his mother's disappointment than on his own. But perhaps that was just my imagination.

But before I could dwell on this any longer I was brought back to the present by a loud banging noise. The door at the front of the reception had flown open, smacking into the wall violently. I looked up, half-expecting it to be Claire having forgotten her purse or something, but it was a thick-set, worried-looking man struggling under the weight of a large Alsatian lying in his arms, its head and paws dangling lifelessly.

'Can you help me?' the man cried out. 'Please – he's been hit by a van!'

I immediately sprang into action before I'd even had a chance to think about what was happening. Emergencies like this happened from time to time and I was well trained to know just what to do. I jumped to my feet and showed the man through to one of the treatment rooms, at the same time calling out for someone to come and help.

Sonia, one of the nurses, appeared at once and helped the man to lay the poor dog on the table, reassuring him that Mr Fulcher, the vet, would be with them in a minute.

'He got out,' the man said, wiping his eyes. 'There was a fence panel broken. It must have happened in the storm the other night. I didn't notice. Oh my God. Is it too late?'

I stared at the dog as Sonia checked for vital signs. His injuries were terrible. I could barely look – just the sight of the wound sent my head funny. I had no idea whether he could be saved or not.

'There's a pulse,' she said gently. 'But it's very weak. We'll do our best, sir. Here's Mr Fulcher now.' She turned to greet him and caught my eye. A look of concern crossed over her face. 'Are you OK, Sam?'

'Yes. I, er, think so.' My head had started to feel peculiar. Everything in the room was going out of focus.

'Go and sit down,' she said. 'You don't look well.'

But instead, I bolted out to the staffroom, past Claire, who had just returned, and straight into the toilet cubicle, where I was horribly sick.

'What …?' Claire was behind me in a second, holding me and scraping back my hair. 'You poor thing, you look awful. Are you not well? You'd better go home.'

'No. I … I think I'll be all right now. I just came over kind of woozy. There's a dog just come in, he's awfully hurt …' I straightened up and tried to compose myself.

'I'm really sorry, Claire. Could you cover the desk for a moment? I just need a minute.'

'Of course. Typical, I'd only popped out for a minute. I still think you need to go home, though.'

And I had to, of course, even though I was starting to feel better. It was the clinic's policy, in case I had something infectious. I knew I didn't, that I'd just reacted badly to the sight of that poor dog's injuries. But what I couldn't understand was why. I'd witnessed scores of horrible sights during my time here, and although the emotional impact had sometimes been hard to deal with, I wasn't squeamish and I'd never been taken ill like this before.

As I sat on the Tube on my way back to my dismal flat, I thought about what had just happened. Was it just the shock? The emergency had come in pretty suddenly, after all. But I still didn't really get why it should have affected me so violently. Maybe I was overtired, working long days and worrying myself silly about Adam. Perhaps I really did need my holiday.

Now I thought about it, there had been a couple of times recently when I'd felt a bit dizzy and nauseous for no apparent reason. Perhaps I was anaemic or something? I remembered one of my flatmates had fainted halfway through making herself an omelette one evening, and had eventually found out that she needed iron tablets due to her heavy periods. Whereas my periods were—

Well, actually, come to think of it, I hadn't had—

I sat up straight. It *couldn't* be that, surely? My pulse suddenly racing, I fumbled in my bag for my diary and had a quick check of my dates. I was over a week late. How had I not noticed? I must have been so caught up with my worries about Adam and what I was doing for the Easter break. A wave of panic overcame me, but within minutes I'd talked myself round. No, there was probably another explanation. Like stress. Yes, that'd be it. I was probably late because of the stress of all the recent arguments.

But the next morning, there was something about the sight of my boiled egg that gave me the same feeling as the poor Alsatian's injuries had, and after being thoroughly sick again, I went back to the kitchen, feeling shaky and anxious, wondering what I could eat or drink that wouldn't make me feel ill. I automatically went to put on the kettle, but changed my mind. The last thing I fancied was a cup of tea, which was strange in itself as it was always my favourite lifesaving pick-me-up. And then I remembered how Claire had joked with me a couple of days before when I told her I didn't want one.

'You're not pregnant, are you?' she'd teased, making me laugh through my firm denial. 'There's got to be something up for you to say no to a brew. Loads of pregnant women go off tea or coffee, it's a really common sign.'

At the time, of course, I thought nothing more of it. But now …

'What's up?' Helen, one of my flatmates, gave me a curious look. I was sitting at the table, staring into space. 'Did you overdo it last night or something? You look well hung-over.'

'No. I'm OK.'

'Well, you don't look it. Not going into work, are you?' She shook cereal into a bowl and poured milk over it, which made my stomach lurch with nausea again.

'No. I've got the day off.' I'd been told to stay home for forty-eight hours in case I had a bug. I got to my feet and headed back to my room. 'See you later.'

Within minutes I was dressed in jeans and a jumper and heading for the pharmacy on the next street. All the way there and back, I kept telling myself there must be some other explanation. But there wasn't. Back in the safety of my flat, the result of the test was all too conclusive. I was pregnant – with a baby Adam had made very clear he didn't want, and I wasn't sure I was ready for either.

The shock made me feel weak and nauseous all over again. I spent most of the day lying on my bed, my mind in a whirl. I had no idea what I was going to do. But I had made one very important decision. I wasn't telling anyone yet – not my parents, not Claire or my flatmates and most of all, definitely not Adam. I'd wait until I'd got back from my two weeks in Hope Green. That, at least, would give me some time to think, get some much-needed perspective and make some decisions. Perhaps by the time I came back, Adam and I would have missed each other so much we'd be ready to make a fresh start, and perhaps then, his reaction to the pregnancy would be better than I was imagining.

CHAPTER THREE

When I left for Hope Green, the wind was bitterly cold,
but at least the sun was shining, making it feel comfortably
warm inside my ageing little Polo as I headed down the
M3. I'd waited until the nausea had settled before setting
off. It seemed that now it had started, it was going to be
a regular thing every morning. In the last few days at work
I'd really hoped that I wouldn't have any further episodes,
or I'd have had to come clean about the pregnancy sooner
rather than later. But fortunately my morning sickness was
limited to just that – the morning – and I left London
feeling at ease, if a little hungry. I turned on the radio and
sang along with the music, trying to get myself into a
happier frame of mind for when I arrived at Nana Peggy's.
I was supposed to be there to keep her company, and I
wasn't going to be very good company if all I kept thinking
about were my own worries.

I realised Claire had been right when she'd said Hope
Green wasn't going to be quite the same at this time of

year as when I normally visited in the summer. Then, it always looked like a picture postcard, with every little pink or white thatched cottage sporting hanging baskets of brightly coloured summer flowers – geraniums, lobelias, fuchsias, petunias. Front gardens were full of roses, marigolds, dahlias and sunflowers; grass verges were sprinkled with forget-me-nots and wild basil. The village had either won, or been runner-up, in a Best-Kept Village contest for as many years as it had been going, and the residents worked hard to keep their lawns immaculate, the paintwork of their houses spruce and their roadsides litter-free.

I'd never visited outside of the summer holidays – for other family occasions, Nana was usually brought up to the family home in Norfolk – so I was used to the village having a festive atmosphere, with tourists strolling along the main street taking photographs of the church, the duck pond and the ancient stocks on the village green, and families relaxing in the pub garden or outside the tea room. Luckily, Hope Green never got completely overwhelmed with visitors as, although it was only a mile from the sea, that area of the coast was inaccessible except by footpaths. The nearest seaside town was several miles away and the one road in and out of the village consisted of a long, winding and very narrow hill, which was enough to put off all but the most intrepid drivers if they weren't familiar with the area. So, despite the village pub and only guest house usually being fully booked for the season, a large proportion of the visitors were walkers, and none arrived in coach parties.

It'll probably be really quiet and a bit dreary at this time of year, I told myself as I eventually turned off the main road on to the lane that climbed up to the village. The sun had suddenly gone in, and there was a spattering of drizzle on the windscreen. *But that's OK. It'll suit me to be quiet and dreary at the moment. I just need a bit of peace and a chance to get my head together.*

But coming into the village, I was welcomed by bright, colourful daffodils and grape hyacinths clustered around the village sign on the green. Despite the weather, the village still seemed to exude a warm, welcoming feel and I let out a huge breath that I had unknowingly been holding.

Nana got hold of me in a fierce hug the moment she opened the cottage door. Rufus was just as keen and circled us enthusiastically, barking and sniffing at my legs.

'Come in, come in, quickly now, it's raining! You can fetch your bag in later. I've got the kettle on, and a nice fruitcake just out of the oven.'

She held me at arm's length and studied me with a slight frown on her face. 'My Little Sam!' she said affectionately, kissing me on both cheeks.

I'd always been 'Little Sam' to my family. The youngest child, I had always been short for my age. My two very tall older brothers liked to tease me about being short, blond and curly-haired, as if this somehow made me a silly airhead. Since growing to the grand height of five foot three and regularly straightening my blond curls, I'd forgiven them. But, although she was exactly the same height as me, Nana had never got out of the habit of my pet name.

She was in her late seventies now and getting a bit stout, but her short, curly grey hair was still regularly highlighted with glints of copper or silver (depending on her mood) by the local hairdresser who did home visits, and the sparkle in her bright blue eyes and frequent bursts of hearty laughter made her seem at least a decade younger.

'You look worn out, love, and no wonder, all that rushing around in London, and standing up on those damn Tube trains every day with your face in people's armpits – so unhealthy.' She shook her head in disgust and laughed. Nana had a countrywoman's instinctive distrust of cities. 'Go and sit down and put your feet up. There's a nice fire going in the sitting room.'

I laughed. 'But Nana, I've come to look after *you*.'

'Who said I need looking after?' she said indignantly. 'Don't you go listening to your mother. Nothing wrong with me, young lady, nothing that a couple of new knees wouldn't put right anyway, not that I'm considering having any of those *replacements* everyone keeps harping on about. Not natural, that, having bits of metal stuck inside your body, not natural at all. I'd rather use my walking stick, thanks very much, it hasn't let me down yet.' At this point, almost in a bid to prove her wrong, the dog jumped up at her, placing his paws on the aforementioned knees. 'Rufus! Pack it in, before you send us both flying!'

'He's OK,' I said, squatting down to give him a thorough stroking and belly rub. 'I'll take him out for a walk in a bit.'

In truth, it looked as if his exuberant greeting had worn him out, as he immediately laid himself by my feet, grinning up at me and panting from all the exertion. His big soulful eyes were fixed on mine, waiting for my next move, and I smiled as I scratched him behind his floppy ears. I wondered what went on in his little head; he was probably thinking about when he would next be fed or walked!

At least you don't have my worries, Rufus, I thought to myself ruefully, and he turned to lick my hand tenderly with his big rough tongue. It was as if he'd read my mind and felt sorry for me.

Ignoring Nana's instructions to sit myself down in front of the fire, I followed her into the kitchen and obediently cut two slices of warm fruitcake while she poured the tea.

'I'll just have a glass of squash, actually, Nana,' I said without looking at her, 'if that's OK.'

'No tea?' She stared at me. 'That's not like you.'

'I know.' I smiled, and quickly thought of a fib. 'I've given it up for Lent.'

'Hmm. Well, good for you. Not too long till Easter now, at least.'

And then I'd have to think of another excuse, unless I'd started to like it again by then. I had a feeling it was going to be difficult to keep my situation hidden from Nana, but as tempting as it was to confide in someone, I was determined to keep the news to myself for a bit longer. She seemed to have twigged that I was worried about something, though. By the time we were sitting on either side of the fireplace with our slices of cake and Rufus's head on my feet, she was already demanding that I 'tell her all about it'.

'All about what?' I said, feigning innocence.

'Whatever it is you've run away from.'

'Run away?' I said. 'I didn't say I was running away from anything, did I?'

'No. But for the last – what, nine, ten years, maybe? – ever since you've been old enough to drive yourself down here, I've had the pleasure of your company every July. Now suddenly I get a bonus visit at Easter? And very nice it is, but I'm thinking there must be a reason for it.' She gave me a sympathetic look. 'Still, you don't have to tell me if you don't want to. It's nothing to do with me. I'm only your grandmother.'

I smiled. This had always been Nana's stock phrase. When my brothers and I were younger she'd often sit us down and give us interminable (but good-humoured) lectures on subjects like the length of our hair, the suitability of our friends, our choice of clothes and school subjects, and these would always finish with: '*But I'm saying nothing, it's nothing to do with me, I'm only your grandmother.*' We never minded. It was different from being lectured by our parents, and although we never admitted to taking any notice of her, somehow we usually did. She had a knack for knowing just the right thing to do in any situation, though at the time we hated to admit it.

'I just wanted to see you,' I tried. But she gave me a look of disbelief, so I smiled and added, 'I had two weeks' holiday booked from work, and, well, Mum and Dad are off on their cruise, so I thought it'd be nice to come down here instead.'

'Right. Instead of going to stay with that young man of yours and his family.'

I sighed. Mum had obviously told her about my cancelled visit to Hampstead, and Nana being Nana had joined up the dots.

'Yes,' I said. 'Instead of that. We changed our minds about it.'

'Fair enough,' she said, taking a sip of her tea. 'We all need time apart from them occasionally.'

'Them?'

'Men. Husbands, boyfriends, partners, whatever you want to call them. However much you love them, they can drive you round the bend if you spend too much time with them.'

I laughed. 'I can't believe you ever felt like that about Granddad.'

'Of course I did,' she said. 'Why do you think I used to pack him off to his allotment after he retired? How else do you think we survived over fifty years together?'

'But you miss him now,' I said gently, reaching out for her hand.

'That's different,' she said, her voice only wavering slightly.

'I know.'

We ate our fruitcake in companionable silence together.

I slept well that first night in my cosy bed in Nana's spare room, and the next morning I managed to nibble a piece of toast and sip a glass of fruit juice without being ill.

'Hope you're not on one of those ridiculous diets,' Nana commented, looking disgruntled as she put away the frying pan, sausages and eggs. 'You look too pale and pasty already. You need some good solid food inside you, girl.'

'Sorry. I'm not on a diet, don't worry. I just don't really fancy cooked breakfasts these days.'

'No, you've got too used to rushing off to catch those damn Tube trains every morning, I suppose.'

'Yes, you're probably right,' I said quickly, anxious to avoid any more discussion of armpits. I got up from the table and busied myself washing my plate and glass. 'Now, would you like me to go to the shop for you? I thought I'd take Rufus, give him another try now that he's well rested.'

The evening before, I had tried to take Rufus for a walk, but because of his excitement of my arrival and his old bones, we hadn't made it very far at all. Warmly wrapped up in my coat, scarf and hat, and with Rufus on his lead beside me, we had headed up the village street to take a brisk walk across the fields. Well, *brisk* was the intention, but after just five minutes Rufus had begun to lag behind me.

'What's the matter, boy?' I said, turning round in surprise to see him plodding along, tongue out, panting slightly. 'Not tired already, are you?'

He looked up at me as if to say it was my fault for walking too fast. I hung back, and he immediately sat down to give himself a good scratch. While I waited, I had a sneaking suspicion that he was merely using this as an excuse to have a rest.

'OK,' I said, when he staggered back to his feet. 'We'll just make it a quick walk round the village today, shall we? Perhaps we can go a bit further tomorrow.'

'Trouble is,' Nana had said when I arrived back home and watched with some concern as Rufus headed straight for his water bowl and then flopped into his bed, 'he's slowed down because of me. It's my fault, see, because of my knees. I can't give him the amount of exercise he needs – you know how lively he's always been.'

'But he's fourteen now, Nana. I don't think it's just because of you that he's slowed down.'

She shook her head. 'He'll soon get his energy back now that you're here to take him for walks. It'll do him good, poor old bugger.'

I didn't have the heart to contradict her. I hoped she was right, but it wasn't hard to see that, although he was still the same loveable, happy character he'd always been, physically Rufus had aged considerably since I'd last seen him.

But now that he'd had a full night's sleep I thought he might be able to take a slightly longer walk. I went to grab his lead from where it hung on the wall, much to his delight.

'I'll come with you, Sam. I need my exercise too.' Nana laughed. 'Just wait while I get my boots on.'

The shop was only a short walk away, but we made slow progress, with Nana holding my arm but also leaning heavily on her stick, and Rufus plodding and panting just in front. I couldn't imagine how the pair of them did this on their own every day. But here in Hope Green, time wasn't an issue, and fortunately so, as everyone we passed wanted to stop and say hello. I'd got to know most of the villagers over the years, and they all greeted me with excitement, almost as if I were a celebrity. It soon became clear that most people were already aware I'd be coming for an unscheduled visit. Word got around fast here.

'You remember my granddaughter, Little Sam, don't you?' Nana introduced me to them all in the same way, and we had similar conversations over and over as we made the short walk to the shop. 'Down for a break from that dratted London.' They all commiserated with me as if I'd escaped from hell itself, sighing and shaking their heads at the thought of the crowded streets, the drugs, the criminals lurking on every corner, the traffic, the threat of being blown up by terrorists, and of course, the Tube trains.

'Not that I've ever been there, myself,' the girl serving us at the village shop said, as Nana finished another diatribe about the evils of the city. 'Thank God.'

'It's actually not that bad,' I tried to tell her, but she just laughed and said she admired me for making the best of it.

The village shop was a bright, cheery place where everyone congregated to chat as well as make their purchases. It was a million miles removed from the type of shop I used in London – usually a busy, impersonal branch of Tesco or Sainsbury's – and nowhere else had I ever seen such an assortment of things for sale under one roof. Whether you needed tea bags, dental floss, a pair of socks, colouring books or a hammer and nails, you'd find it somewhere on those shelves. And, in the rare event that what you wanted wasn't stocked, they'd order it from elsewhere and have it in within a day or two.

I hadn't met Izzie, the girl serving us, before, but I guessed she was probably a little younger than me. Slim and attractive, with long glossy dark hair in a ponytail and a sprinkling of freckles across her nose, I imagined her being fun-loving and carefree, as well as having a host of male admirers. So it was quite a surprise when Nana explained, as Izzie helped us pack our bags, that she'd lived in the village all her life but that I probably hadn't met her before as she'd been *stuck at home, busy with her babies.*

I wondered how she could see this as a better life than in London. Sure, the commute on the Tube is awful, but it must be better that staying at home all day, a young mother with *children*. But of course, I kept this to myself and gave her a sympathetic smile.

'How many children have you got?'

'Only three,' she said.

Only?

'But they're all under five. So it's been hard work, you know, what with their dad buggering off before the last one was born.'

'How on earth do you manage?' I asked her. 'I mean, with working and everything.'

'Luckily my mum lives just down the road,' she said. 'And she absolutely loves having the children. Otherwise

I'd probably go bloody mad. I couldn't really leave them much at all until I'd stopped breastfeeding the littlest one.'

I was feeling faint with exhaustion just at the thought of all this. I couldn't even begin to imagine her lifestyle, but despite saying how hard it was, she seemed perfectly calm and collected. It made me feel stupid for worrying about how I was going to manage with *one* baby. It'd be interesting to get to know her a bit better and find out if she had any tips. God knows, I could do with someone outside the family who'd also been through it.

Walking back from the shop took even longer. We didn't stop to talk to quite so many people this time, but it was uphill and both Nana and Rufus were struggling. I was surprised when, as soon as we got back to the cottage, Nana commented: 'Well, he managed that walk fine today, didn't he?'

I smiled and nodded for her benefit. But thinking about the long walks down to the coast and along the beach that Rufus and I had always taken before, I felt sad and worried. Perhaps Nana was right that he'd get fitter again with more exercise. I resolved to keep on taking him out at least twice a day. I hated to imagine Nana losing Rufus as well as Granddad, however much she liked to pretend she was fine on her own.

CHAPTER FOUR

Nana decided she wanted to take me out for lunch. I looked at her in surprise.

'I want to treat you,' she said. 'Fish and chips, a meat pie, or at least one of those big ploughman's lunches and a pint of Guinness, to put some colour back in your cheeks.'

'That's nice of you,' I said, fighting the nausea at the picture this conjured up. 'But honestly, I'd be quite happy to just have a sandwich here at home.'

'Nonsense. I insist. It's a poor show if I can't treat my granddaughter on her holiday away from that dratted city. Get your coat on, we're going to the Horse.'

The Horse – nobody ever seemed to give it the benefit of its full title The Old Black Horse, because according to Nana it was too much of a mouthful – was a typical country pub. It had a thatched roof, crooked whitewashed walls and lead-light windows. Inside there was a massive fireplace and cosy inglenooks, with horse brasses and ancient sepia-tone photos of the village hanging on the wall. Next to the bar, there was a collection of jugs (no one seemed to know why) lined up along shelves. It was the only pub in the village and for miles around and, along with the shop, was the hub of the community. If I was expecting to find the bar half empty on this cold, damp spring day, I couldn't have been more mistaken.

The heat from the fire almost knocked me out as we walked in and, if that wasn't welcome enough, dozens of voices seemed to be singing out a disorderly chorus of 'Hello, Peggy!', 'Hello, Sam!' and even 'Hello, Peggy's granddaughter!' Before we'd got our coats off, people were leaping out of their seats and insisting that we sat in the most comfortable chairs or at the best table (nearest the fire, away from the draft), as if we were royalty at the very least. While we deliberated, Rufus plonked himself down in front of the fireplace with his head between his paws contentedly, and Ted the landlord yelled at the barmaid to give him a bowl of water.

'What a welcome!' I laughed as we finally settled ourselves at a table Nana decided was neither too near nor too far from the fire.

'The usual, Peggy?' Ted called out, his hand already on the pump ready to pour her a small glass of stout. And to me: 'What'll it be, Sam?'

'Just an orange juice and lemonade, please,' I said without looking at Nana. 'Thanks.'

'You driving?' he joked, but I could feel Nana staring at me.

'Given the booze up for Lent too, have you?' she said lightly.

I just nodded. It looked like it might be even harder than I'd imagined, keeping my secret from her, but I'd just have to do my best. I was wondering what further excuse I could make when Suzie, the barmaid, a sullen woman of about forty whom I'd never credited with much personality, never mind tact, came over to place our drinks in front of us.

'Staying sober so you can help your nan get home, are you?' she asked.

'I don't need helping home, thank you very much,' Nana replied tersely. 'And when you're quite ready, we'll have a look at your menu, please. Not that I don't know it off by heart,' she added half under her breath as Suzie sauntered off. 'Ted hasn't changed the menu since about 1974.'

No sooner had we ordered our ploughman's platters than we were being pressed by various friends of Nana's to have another drink.

'Have one on me, Peggy!' people were calling out. And 'Come on, Peggy's granddaughter – what's the matter with you? A little glass of wine won't hurt you.' Or 'How about a nice drop of sherry – even the vicar drinks *that* during Lent, you know!'

This last comment came from a red-faced, bearded little man who was so bent, gnarled and wrinkled he reminded me of a garden gnome.

'You remember old Billy Henderson, don't you?' Nana said as he shuffled back to the bar. 'He lives down the lane near the school. Used to be the blacksmith back in the days when we had such things. Must be getting on for a hundred now but still manages to toddle down here every day for his couple of pints. Nice old boy but a bit too fond of the ladies, if you get my meaning.'

I nearly choked on my drink. *Really*? Nobody could have looked much less like the village lothario! I made a mental note to steer clear.

A stern-looking woman with grey hair pinned up in an untidy bun was the next to stop by our table.

'Nora from the post office,' Nana reminded me in a whisper as she approached.

'How are you, Sam?' she asked, and without waiting for an answer went on to tell me in no uncertain terms how difficult life was for her now that her 'staffing levels' had been reduced, so that she was obliged to 'work all the hours that God sent, for less than a pittance'. It was no wonder, she went on, that she needed a drink or two in order to survive the stress of her work. And while she was on the subject, what was all this about me refusing drinks from all and sundry, was this some new fashion in London – going teetotal, as well as following ridiculous crash diets invented by anorexic supermodels? Because if so, she was glad she'd never been to London and she had no intention of doing so.

'Miserable cow,' Nana muttered to me before Nora was even out of earshot. 'Stress, my backside! The post office is only open three mornings a week – and "staffing levels"? They got rid of her assistant, Frances, because there's hardly enough work for one, never mind two. Shame, really. Frances worked a damn sight harder than Nora does, I can tell you, and a lot more cheerfully. We'll all be glad when the old bat retires. The only good thing about her is her green fingers.'

'Her what?'

'You know. Gardening, planting things. She's good at it – she does hanging baskets for everyone for the Best-Kept Village judging. Charges an arm and a leg for them, mind you, but it's worth it if we can keep the title again.'

Just then a burly young man in jeans and a waxed jacket brushed past us on his way to the bar, very nearly knocking over Nana's glass of stout. He seemed to be in a hurry, but Nana put out a hand to stop him and he looked at her with undisguised irritation.

'Here's someone you might be interested to talk to, Sam,' she said, ignoring his obvious reluctance. 'He's in the same business as you. Our new vet, Joe Bradley.'

The young man turned to me and gave me a shockingly rude glare.

'This is my granddaughter, Little Sam,' Nana went on unperturbed. 'She's in your line of work, Joe.'

'Really? Where do you practise?' he asked, sounding completely uninterested.

'Oh, I'm not a vet myself,' I said with a little laugh of embarrassment. He remained stony-faced, and I really didn't want to go on, but he wasn't saying anything and I felt like I had to fill the silence. 'I'm a receptionist ... at a vets in London,' I added quietly.

'Right. A receptionist. I see.' His tone of voice made it sound like the most despicable career choice imaginable.

'She always wanted to be a vet, though, didn't you, Sam?' Nana said, nudging me so that I nearly dropped the forkful of coleslaw I was holding. 'Right from an early age. I remember when you were only about six, you found that bird with a broken wing—'

'Well, interesting though your childhood *undoubtedly* was,' Joe Bradley interrupted, 'I'm afraid I haven't got all day to indulge in trivial chit-chat. Some of us have work to do.' He looked very pointedly at his watch. 'I've just got time for a quick sandwich and a coffee, so if you'll *excuse* me …' He'd moved on before we could say whether we were excusing him or not. As he pushed past, he brushed up against me, leaving my arm wet from the rain outside.

My face was burning with humiliation. 'What a rude man!' I exclaimed. 'He could have at least feigned interest in the blackbird story. Oh wait, I forgot, I'm "just a receptionist".'

'Probably just a bit busy,' Nana said, shrugging. 'You can tell him all about it another time.'

Hell would probably freeze over first, I decided, if Joe Bradley's frosty manner hadn't already done it. What an obnoxious, arrogant man. If I ever saw him around Hope Green in the next two weeks, I decided to make a point of ignoring him. Some people just aren't worth your time.

The following day I attempted a slightly longer walk with Rufus, testing Nana's theory that all he needed was someone fit enough to give him a little more exercise.

We'd just left the house and already the walk was doing me good. I'd been worrying so much about the pregnancy and Adam, and even Rufus being so old he couldn't walk very far, that I'd worked myself up into a state. I'd been close to tears and decided that a walk with Rufus would help calm me down. Lost in my thoughts, with Rufus plodding along slowly beside me, I was halfway down the main road when I stepped straight into the path of a tall, slim man wearing a bright pink anorak. He was running after two large dogs who were pulling him along on their leads.

'Whoops! Sorry!' I said, stepping quickly aside.

'My fault,' he said, to me, with an apologetic grin. 'Mabel! Tess!' The dogs had been heading at a fiery pace down the lane, pulling him away from where we stood. They eventually turned and trotted back to where we were, one jumping up at my legs, tail wagging excitedly, the other giving Rufus a suspicious sniff. 'These two don't get out often enough, you see, so when they do, they give me a right old run for my money. Are you OK?'

'Yes, of course. I should have been looking where I was going.' I bent down to pat the dogs' heads. 'What breed are they?' They were both brown, one darker and slightly larger than the other.

'Cross-breeds – probably a bit of retriever in Mabel here.' He pointed at the fairer dog. 'But God only knows who Tess's parents were.' He laughed. 'They're not mine, by the way. I just walk them for their owners – they're at work all day.'

'That's nice of you.' I was trying not to stare at him. Despite his floppy dark hair and boyish smile, I guessed from the laughter lines around his eyes and the appearance of a few streaks of grey that he was probably nearer to forty than thirty. I just wondered why he'd thought the pink anorak – which looked far too small for him – was a good idea. Perhaps he was gay. That might explain it, though I did think that that would be quite progressive for Hope Green.

'Oh, no, I'm not being kind!' He laughed again. 'It's my job. Well, one of my jobs. I walk dogs for people like the Crowthers – Tess and Mabel's owners. Partly because I haven't got a dog of my own. And, more to the point, partly because I haven't got a proper job at the moment either.'

I smiled at him, a bit wistfully. It sounded like a lovely job to me. Walking dogs for a living, out in the fresh air, with no cares or worries … how nice that must be. But before I had time to indulge this little dream any further, he'd gone on to explain that he was only doing the dog-walking to help with his rent and bills while he tried to get started as a freelance copywriter. He'd been made redundant from his previous job.

I sympathised. 'That must be hard.'

'Well, luckily I'm on my own. It would've been far worse if I had a wife and kids to worry about.'

'Yes. That's true.'

So maybe not gay, I thought.

I looked down at Rufus, who was taking the opportunity for a rest, lying flat out on the pavement at my feet now. Typical Rufus. I smiled. 'Well, I'd better get started on this walk before he decides to take a full-on nap!'

'I'm heading back into the village. I'll walk with you, if you don't mind? Sorry for boring you with my life history.'

'Not at all. I love dogs too. I'd like to have one of my own, eventually.'

As we set off again, I was conscious of him staring at me. 'Are you new around here? The dog seems familiar, but—'

'Oh, Rufus is my nan's dog. Peggy – she lives in the pink cottage, Meadow Croft, just past the village green. I'm Sam, her granddaughter. I'm just here for a holiday.'

'Of course, I know Peggy. Lovely lady. Well, pleased to meet you, Sam. I'm David.' He paused, trying to offer me his hand, which was impossible as the dogs were almost pulling him over. We both ended up laughing again, and I found myself thinking: *he's nice.*

For a few minutes we walked on in silence, and then he blurted out: 'Tell me I'm being nosy, Sam, but are you OK? Only you seemed to be miles away, back then when we nearly collided with each other. Probably none of my business. Sorry.'

I sighed. I didn't realise my upset was so clear on my face. 'No, it's all right. It's nothing really. Just that I'm worried about poor old Rufus – he's really struggling to walk now, as you can see. I know it sounds silly and I should just take him to the vet or something, but …' I trailed off, not wanting to mention Joe, the vet whom I'd met in the pub.

'Oh, our new vet. Right.' There was an edge to his voice. I turned to him in surprise. It seemed like I wasn't the only one who wasn't impressed by Joe Bradley. David gave a little cough, smiled at me and went on: 'Sorry, take no notice of me, I'm just not too keen on the guy.' He hesitated, and then added with more feeling. 'In fact, I think he's a complete pig.'

I giggled. 'I must admit, I got the same impression. He doesn't exactly seem to have much in the way of charm, does he?'

'He's good with animals, I'll give him that. And I suppose that's what matters. It's just people he can't deal with, apparently.'

'So it seems.'

We'd reached the church. I stopped at the entrance to the lane that led to the meadow and said, 'Right, we're heading this way.' I turned to walk up the path, only turning back to say, as an afterthought, 'Do you just *like* pink?'

'Sorry?' Then he looked down at his coat and laughed. 'Oh, this! It's Mrs Crowther's old one. I didn't think it was going to be cold out today, and once I realised it was, I didn't want to go back home so I just borrowed this – it was hanging on the back of the door. I don't suppose she'll mind.'

I laughed with him, it all made sense now. On closer inspection it was clearly a woman's jacket.

'Well, it was nice to meet you, Sam,' he said, and continued on his way.

I'd decided to take the footpath across the meadow from behind the church, but having made slow progress thus far, Rufus only made it as far as the stile which separated the churchyard from the meadow before he plonked himself down, panting heavily and giving me the most disdainful look, as if to say I ought to know better than to expect him to climb over it.

I stood there watching him and wondering whether we should just call it quits, but thought I'd make one last-ditch attempt at continuing with our walk. I patted the step of the stile encouragingly and sang out a few hopeful suggestions of 'Come on, up, boy!'

Then I heard a voice behind me mutter, 'I don't think you'll get him to agree to that.'

The voice made me jump at first, but as soon as I recovered I recognised whose voice it was and a part of me groaned inside. *Him.*

'I know that,' I said, which was a bit ridiculous, really, as I was still patting the stile.

'He looks done in,' Joe Bradley added. 'If you want him over the other side you'll have to carry him.'

'No, we're just going home,' I said, giving Rufus a gentle tug on the lead. 'Come on, boy, home now.' I had no particular wish to spend any time in conversation with the only unfriendly person I'd come across in Hope Green.

But as I turned to walk back through the churchyard I was surprised to find that he followed me. I couldn't help myself from commenting. 'I thought you were headed in the other direction.'

'No. I just saw you from the roadside and thought you looked like you might need some help with the dog. Rufus, isn't it?'

'Yes,' I said, thrown off track momentarily. 'Well, thanks, but I'm fine.'

'I'm just saying, he looks shattered. You should probably leave it for the day.'

'Thank you for your advice,' I said through gritted teeth. 'But I can perfectly well deal with this. I do work at a vets, you know.'

'Well, yes. But you did say you're just a receptionist ...' There was a glint in his eye that I couldn't quite read when he said this. He was smiling too, which made me seethe.

He thought he was so clever. And here he was with his whole 'just a receptionist' talk again. I really wanted to say something cutting, but when I went to speak, to my dismay, I suddenly felt tears welling in my eyes again. Not because this hateful man was being rude – no, I'm much stronger than that. It must have been because Joe was reminding me that Rufus was old. He was just sitting there by my feet looking so helpless, with his patches of grey fur on his face, the heavy way he was panting and the imploring look he gave me which almost said 'Please, can we just go home?'

Damn it, I thought to myself. My hormones were definitely all over the place. Was this how I was going to be for the next eight months: getting overemotional and crying about everything? I swiped at my eyes with my gloved hand and looked away, hoping Joe hadn't noticed, but perhaps not quickly enough, because he said: 'Are you sure you're all right?'

'Yes.' I sniffed. It was particularly embarrassing to be snivelling like this in front of someone like *him*. 'It's nothing. Just ... my nan would be so lost without him. If anything happened to Rufus ...' I swore to myself crossly. Why on earth had I said that? Like he would care anyway. He probably didn't even like animals. His whole manner showed him to be a completely unsympathetic, insensitive person; a profession that requires a certain level of care seemed like a terrible career choice for such a man.

He walked beside me silently for a moment, and then said in a quieter but still offhand way, 'I could give him a check over in the surgery if you like. If your grandmother agrees. Tomorrow morning at ten?'

'Thank you,' I stuttered.

'And look,' he went on, 'about that *receptionist* comment. Well, let's just say I haven't had much luck with reception-ists lately, at least, not with my current one.'

'Thanks,' I managed to get out again.

Why was I thanking him? I hated myself for sounding so apologetically weak. All he was doing was touting for business. It wasn't charitable or thoughtful in the least. And that comment about receptionists? If it was meant to be an apology, it was a pretty poor one!

By the time I got home I had stopped crying, which was something. I thought back to the conversation with David, which had felt like a breath of fresh air. It had put me in a happier frame of mind. For a few minutes, at least, until I had the difficult encounter with Joe Bradley. But even though the two meetings had been markedly different in tone, they had been similar in one way: I'd almost forgotten my worries about the pregnancy. And, although I didn't really want to admit it to myself, I'd almost forgotten about Adam too.

CHAPTER FIVE

Daisy-May, the receptionist at Hope Green Vet Clinic, was sixty if she was a day, despite her incongruously childlike name and nature. When I arrived for my appointment at ten o'clock the next morning, an unhappy Rufus whining softly beside me in protest at the smell of antiseptic, she was dealing with a client whose pet rodent she clearly didn't like the look of. She kept giving its cage anxious glances as if she were expecting it to make a break for freedom at any moment. I watched her idly for a few minutes, wondering how she might have coped with the gravely injured Alsatian that had made me throw up the week before. Admittedly, she couldn't have been much worse than me.

Suddenly the door to the consulting room flew open and Joe appeared in the doorway. 'Come on, then,' he barked at me. 'I've fitted you in as an extra, I can't have you keeping me waiting.'

'Excuse me!' I said angrily. 'I was here on time!'

'Sorry, Mr Bradley,' Daisy-May said, her face growing pink and flustered. 'I was busy with the rat, and I didn't notice your ten o'clock had arrived.'

'Right. Well, come through, then,' he said in only a fractionally less hostile manner, holding the door open for me.

Not even a bloody apology. If it hadn't been for Nana worrying about Rufus, I'd have walked straight out. As it was, I had difficulty controlling my annoyance. But to my surprise, the moment the consulting room door closed behind us Joe Bradley seemed to undergo a personality change.

'Hello, boy,' he said to Rufus in a soft and reassuring voice. He laughed and squatted down on the floor, rubbed the top of the old dog's head and scratched him behind the ears. 'How are you doing, old chap? Starting to feel your age a bit, are you? Let's have a look at you, come on.'

And with only the slightest help from the young nurse, who I'd noticed looking at him from under her eyelashes in a very obvious manner, he heaved Rufus up on to the examination table and started to check him over. He reached for the stethoscope around his neck and listened to his heart.

'There doesn't seem to be any more wrong with him than you'd expect of such an elderly dog,' he said and hung his stethoscope back around his neck. 'He doesn't seem really breathless now like he was yesterday –' at this he gave me a pointed glance '– and if you haven't noticed a cough, I'd say it's just his age that's tiring him rather

than anything more worrying. Though he is a bit overweight. But if you think the panting and slowing down
has got considerably worse recently, we could do an ECG
or a chest X-ray. Ask your grandmother, and bring him
back if she'd like us to do that. Meanwhile, make sure she
isn't overfeeding him. And his back legs are a bit stiff, so
one or two short walks a day will be better for him than
long ones. Definitely no stiles,' he added, with the merest
hint of a smile.

I waited for the sarcasm, but there didn't seem to be
any coming.

'You're a lovely old boy, aren't you, Rufus? You're doing
just fine,' he went on, giving the dog's head another rub
and – yes, *smiling* down at him. Rufus was grinning back
happily in the way that only spaniels can, his tail swishing,
his tongue out, wanting to have a good lick of this new
human who seemed to have taken such a shine to him.

'Shall I help you down with him now, Mr Bradley?' said
the simpering nurse.

I glanced at her again. She looked about eighteen,
although she must have been older, and had pink streaks
in her hair. He hardly seemed to be aware that she was
there. *Poor girl*, I thought, *she's got a crush on him*. And
then I glanced back at Joe himself, wondering what on
earth she saw in him. He was tall and broad-shouldered,
true, but without the romantic hero type of dark rugged
looks. His hair was a light mousy brown, short and
messy, and he was either sporting designer stubble or
hadn't had time to shave. But as he looked up from

giving Rufus a final stroke, I couldn't help being struck by his deep brown eyes – they had a surprising warmth to them. The warmth quickly disappeared, though, when he met my gaze, as if he was annoyed to find me looking at him.

'Daisy-May will take your payment and give you a diet plan you can follow,' he said abruptly. 'Feel free to come back if you or your grandmother have any further concerns.'

As I walked back to Nana's I wondered what the hell I'd done to upset him again, but at the same time, I felt stupid for even caring. Didn't I have enough to worry about without being distracted by Joe Bradley's moods? Why did it matter whether he was being a surly grump or . . . showing this other side of his character, the gentle giant dealing with the animals he so clearly loved? It was a puzzle, a strange mix of a personality, but why should I even be interested, unless it was to distract me from my equally mixed feelings about Adam?

As I'd hoped, being down here at Hope Green was slowly soothing my worries – the quiet country burr of people's accents, their welcoming smiles and chatter, the gentler pace of life. Even my undercurrents of anxiety about Rufus and about Nana herself – whose repeated assurances that she wasn't lonely without my granddad didn't fool me – were, in a way, helping to take my mind off my bigger worries. But I knew they weren't going to go away. I was only taking a holiday from them, after all, and when I returned home they were still going to be there. What was I going to do about the baby? And what about Adam? We'd been in contact, obviously, while I'd been away, but our conversations had been stilted, as if we were distant relatives who weren't too sure why they were still tethered to one another. And that was my own fault. The effort of *not* telling him about the baby was making it difficult to talk to him at all.

'What do you think about it all, eh, Rufus?' I whispered into the old dog's ear as we sat down for a breather on a bench on the side of the road. His head was in my lap, his tail wagging, his lovely trusting eyes staring into mine. 'Can you imagine me being a mummy? Would I be any good at it?'

He wriggled even closer and gave a little whine as if he understood. I stroked his head and he nuzzled my knees. As a puppy, he'd been a holy terror – refusing all my grandparents' efforts to train him, regularly chewing up their shoes, cushions, rugs, anything he could get hold of – a bundle of mischief who could only be satisfied by the long romps they were able to give him back then. Sometimes now when he was asleep, giving those little grunts and twitches like all dreaming dogs do, I wondered whether he was remembering those days. Those days when his energy was boundless and he'd run ahead of us through the fields, diving through streams, bursting through thorny undergrowth in pursuit of a rabbit or a pheasant, coming home covered in mud from nose to tail and ready to demolish however much food was put in front of him – including the inevitable tidbits and treats Nana could never resist giving him.

We'd have to look after him better from now on. No more treats and leftovers from our mealtimes. We would put him on a diet, take shorter walks – anything to give him more time with Nana. I only hoped it was going to work.

With Rufus's new exercise regime in place, I took him for a short stroll to the village shop the following day. Nana had gone to her regular 'Knit and Natter' group at the church hall, so she and all her friends from the village would be keeping themselves busy making knitted toys, hats and baby clothes to sell at the village fete in the summer. She'd asked me to come along – 'It'd do you good to learn something useful' – making me wonder if she saw my entire life in London as being completely idle as well as dangerous and unhealthy. When I told her I thought it'd take a lot longer than two weeks for her to teach me to knit, she tutted and tossed her head, giving me a half-serious lecture about girls these days – not learning to cook properly, knit, make curtains or even sew on buttons – ending as usual with: 'Anyway, I'm saying nothing, it's nothing to do with me, I'm only your grandmother.'

I was thinking about this as I looked along the shelves for the items on Nana's shopping list. The shop housed everything under the sky, and one of the many things they stocked was knitting wool, piles and piles of it. One sign caught my eye: *Baby Double Knitting*. White, of course. And blue. And pink.

A stab of panic made me gasp to myself. This little life inside me – it wasn't just a random collection of cells, some unimaginable developing *foetus*. It would be a little girl: someone to name Amelia or Violet, or a boy: a Noah, perhaps, or a Charlie. I stared at the patterns, with pictures of old-fashioned bonnets and bootees, on the shelf next to the wool. Did babies still wear those? What did I know? I knew nothing whatsoever about babies. How could I possibly go through with this? I couldn't even knit my baby a bonnet!

'Are you all right there?' A voice made me jump and turn round. It was the young shop assistant, Izzie. She'd been stacking jars of baby food on the shelf behind me and I realised I must have gasped out loud. 'Was there something you wanted?' Her eyes went to the piles of baby knitting wool and back to me. 'Or did the knitting wool say something to frighten you?' she joked.

I laughed. If only she knew how close to the truth she was, I thought.

'I'm fine, thanks. I was looking for toothpaste. I obviously don't know the first thing about all this stuff.' I waved my hand vaguely in the direction of the knitting patterns. 'It's more my nana's province – she's at her knitting group today. And your province too, I suppose,' I added, 'what with your three little ones.'

'Me? God, no, I've never bothered with knitting – far too difficult!' She grinned. 'I leave that to Mum. Most of my kids' clothes are lovingly made by Tesco.' She pointed down the aisle. 'The toothpaste is over there, look. Top shelf. Let me know if there's anything else you can't find.'

'Thanks, Izzie.'

It was funny, but I felt better just from having that short exchange with her. It was infinitely reassuring to know that someone with three small children could be so cheerful and … well, *normal*. Perhaps having one wouldn't really be so hard?

It was cold again that evening, with a strong wind blowing blustery showers against the windows, so I decided against taking Rufus for a second walk. Nana and I settled down in front of the television, laughing at one of her favourite shows, and the old dog lay at our feet, dozing contentedly.

'Good Friday tomorrow,' she commented, as she took a sip of her hot chocolate. 'I've got some hot cross buns in for our breakfast.'

'Lovely.' I smiled. I liked the fact that Nana kept to all the old traditions. It would have been unthinkable to her to bite into a hot cross bun before Good Friday, to eat Christmas pudding or mince pies at any other time than Christmas, or to pass Shrove Tuesday without having pancakes. She hated the fact that everything was now available all year round. 'They'll be having Easter eggs in the shops before Christmas next!' she'd said a few days earlier in a scandalised tone.

'It's a shame poor Rufus can't have a bun, though,' she added sadly. 'Our old vet, John, told me years ago that they're very bad for dogs. You'd think just a little bit of one couldn't hurt, wouldn't you?'

'No, Nana,' I said. This was one piece of veterinary wisdom I'd never forget. 'He really can't have things like that. It's the raisins and currants and sultanas – they're all very toxic for dogs. We had a terrible case once of a little poodle who scoffed a whole packet and—'

'Oh, don't tell me, I can guess,' she said, shaking her head. 'I know, I'm not daft, I won't let him have any. But it's so sad, he looks at me with that mournful expression if he sees me eating one, whining for me to give him a bit. They smell so delicious.'

I smiled and gave Rufus a pat as we went up to bed.

'Never mind, eh, boy? We've got to watch your weight anyway. Treats like that wouldn't do you any good.'

And as it turned out, neither Nana nor I ended up wanting our hot cross buns that Good Friday at all.

CHAPTER SIX

I woke up to the sound of a terrible wailing. For a minute I couldn't even think where I was – then almost at once I realised it was Nana, crying as if she'd fallen. I jumped out of bed so quickly, my head spun and I had to hold on to the wall for a moment to wait for the dizziness to pass.

'What's the matter?' I yelled, as I raced down the stairs. 'Have you fallen? Are you OK?'

But as soon as I stepped through the kitchen doorway it was all too obvious. Nana was kneeling on the floor – God only knows how she'd managed to get down there on her poor knees – with both arms around Rufus, her face pressed into his fur.

'He's gone, Sam,' she cried. 'It's too late, he's gone, he's cold. Oh, Rufus! I wasn't with you. I couldn't help you!'

Choking back my own tears, I joined her on the floor and held her in my arms.

'He must have died in his sleep,' I managed to say. 'It would have been peaceful, Nana. I'm sure even if we'd been awake we wouldn't have been able to do anything. He will have just slipped away.'

'But he's only just been checked over by the vet!' she sobbed. 'He said he was fine, nothing wrong with him apart from being a bit overweight, didn't he? Is it my fault, Sam? Should I have put him on a diet before? Oh, poor Rufus!'

She started to cry loudly again. I helped her to her feet, sat her in a chair and made her a strong cup of tea.

'You mustn't start blaming yourself, honestly,' I said. 'You've looked after him amazingly well all these years. Nobody could have done better.'

While Nana sipped her tea and gradually calmed down a little, I slipped back upstairs to get dressed. Tears were pouring down my cheeks but I wiped them away and blew my nose. I needed to control my own emotions so that I could be of more support to Nana. I'd loved Rufus too, and I knew I'd miss him terribly, but for her it was nothing less than the loss of her best friend – her only constant companion since my granddad died. In my job I'd seen plenty of people devastated by the death of their pets, but this was different. This was my beloved nana, and I couldn't imagine how she was going to get over it.

As it was Good Friday I doubted whether the vets would be open, but I found their phone number anyway, hoping they'd at least have the line directed to an out-of-hours emergency service. To my surprise, a distracted-sounding voice answered: 'Hope Green Vets.'

'Oh.' I swallowed. 'Um – hello, Joe. It's Sam, Peggy's granddaughter.'

'Hello.' He didn't sound the slightest bit pleased to hear from me. I waited for him to ask how he could help me, but apart from the rustle of papers there was silence. 'Well?' he said eventually. 'Was there something …?'

'Sorry. Yes, it's … my grandmother's dog.' I swallowed again, struggling to go on. 'Rufus. He—'

'Yes?' he snapped. 'Is it an emergency?'

'Well, no—'

'Then I'm sure this can be dealt with in the morn—'

'I'm afraid he died during the night,' I said in a rush before he could stop me again. 'I know it's Good Friday, I didn't expect you to be open, but if there's an emergency service, I wondered if—'

'Oh, no – I'm so sorry.' His tone of voice had completely changed, and before I'd even finished explaining he said, 'I'll come straight round.'

'Thank you, but I wasn't expecting—' But he'd already hung up. I was left staring at my phone, wiping away the tears from my face.

Nana and I sat and waited. I held her hand and tried to soothe her as she talked sorrowfully about how she should have given Rufus more exercise, or different food, or more care and attention, and nothing I could say seemed to help.

Within minutes, there was a ring at the door and there stood Joe Bradley, red-faced and dishevelled as if he'd rushed out in the middle of something. I immediately wondered whether he was in a hurry to be somewhere else and was irritated at having to make this unexpected call.

'Thank you for coming,' I said, holding the door open for him. 'I didn't think you'd be open today, though.'

'We're not. I just went in to try to sort out some of the chaos in my admin work while Daisy-May's not there to make matters even worse.' He stopped, shook his head and then gave me a look that, to my surprise, seemed to be actually, genuinely, sympathetic. 'I'm so sorry. Sorry for your grandmother's loss, and yours too. Where is poor old Rufus?'

'In here.' I led the way to the kitchen. 'He must have gone during the night – in his sleep, I hope.'

He squatted down and touched Rufus's head gently and respectfully, before checking his vital signs and agreeing with what we already knew.

'Do you think he would have suffered, Joe?' Nana said, her voice breaking as she spoke. 'Is it my fault? Should I have let Sam bring him straight back for the X-ray and heart thing? I was going to start him on the diet today. I was only saying to Sam last night ...' She shook her head, and then added in a whisper. 'We didn't let him have any hot cross buns. Not even a crumb. I kept them on the top shelf of the larder, see? Because we knew about them being poisonous.'

Joe straightened up and put an arm around Nana's shoulders. The expression on his face was so unexpectedly kind, I felt tears rush to my eyes again.

'Of course it's not your fault, love. The poor old chap had quite simply had enough. He didn't appear to have any underlying disease, he was just old and tired. And I know quite well you'd never have done anything to harm him. He was a happy boy. You must have given him a wonderful life.'

'Thank you. But I don't know what I'll do without him,' she said, still in a whisper.

'I do understand how hard it is. But in some ways, you know, it's better that he's gone like this, peacefully in his own bed, without going on to get sick, or really incapacitated, so that you'd be in the situation of having to decide when he'd had enough. Your memories of him won't be spoiled by seeing him suffer.'

'That's true,' she admitted, making a noticeable effort to pull herself together. 'I do have lots of lovely memories. Thank you again, Joe. You've been very kind.'

'Not at all.' He paused, and then, looking from one of us to the other, asked in a quieter voice what we'd like to happen to Rufus now. 'I've brought the Jeep. Would you like me to take him? I can arrange a cremation, or do you have any other preference? Would you like time to think about it?'

'No.' Nana sighed, shook her head and swallowed hard. 'Take him now, Joe, if you don't mind. He's gone – I know some people feel differently, but I was never one for weeping beside graves. Like you said, I've got my memories. I don't need a burial site in the garden to remind me of him, that'd just make it harder.'

'If you're quite sure, then.' He glanced at me. 'Are you happy with that, Sam?'

'Of course. Whatever Nana wants.'

Joe waited outside in the hall while we both said our goodbyes to Rufus, and then I took Nana into the lounge and held her hand again so that she didn't have to watch Joe taking him out to the Jeep.

'What do we owe you?' I asked him at the front door afterwards.

He shook his head. 'Pop into the surgery sometime and settle up with Daisy-May. She'll make out your bill to include the cremation fee. Will she be all right?' he added, nodding towards where Nana was in the lounge.

'Yes. I'm glad I'm here with her.'

'And are *you* all right?'

I gave a little start of surprise at his unexpected concern. 'Oh, I'll be OK, thanks. I see a lot of these situations at work.'

'But it's not the same when it's your own family.'

'No, it's not.' I managed a smile. 'You're quite right.'

'Your grandmother said you always wanted to be a vet,' he said suddenly as he turned to go. 'What happened? Did you change your mind?'

'No.' I sighed. 'It was ...' I hesitated. He wouldn't want to hear the whole story. He'd been dismissive enough when it was first mentioned, the other day in the pub. And anyway, I always found it hard to talk about. So I just shook my head. 'I didn't get the grades I needed in my exams.' I was conscious I'd made it sound as if it didn't matter, as if I wasn't talking about the biggest disappointment of my life.

But with Rufus lying lifeless outside in the Jeep, and Nana still quietly weeping in the lounge behind me, I wasn't really in the mood to discuss it any further.

'I see.' He looked at me thoughtfully for a moment as if he were going to say more, then glanced at his watch and said, 'Well, I'd better be off.'

'Thanks again for coming so quickly,' I said.

'Not at all. Take care.'

I watched him drive away, then went back into the lounge to comfort Nana. We talked a lot about Rufus that day, looking at old photos of him and remembering him as a mischievous little puppy.

'Remember that time he ate one of your mum's new shoes and just left the high heel?' she said, cackling with laughter at the memory, and then she burst into tears again. 'I tried to tell him off,' she went on, wiping her eyes. 'But he just gave me that look, wagging his tail, like he couldn't believe I was really cross with him.'

'I'll always remember him running through the fields when the corn was really high, so that all you could see were his tail and ears waving,' I said. 'He was such a lovely doggy, Nana.'

It was a quiet afternoon spent in reflection. I found myself thinking a lot about Joe Bradley too, wondering how it was that someone so brusque and offhand could suddenly become so tender and caring when it really mattered. I wondered if that was just his professional manner, and the grumpy, rude version was the real him. After all, any of our vets from my London clinic would have been just as sympathetic and respectful in today's situation. It was part of the job, of course, although they also all loved animals themselves and knew how sad it was to lose a pet. But ... there was something about the way Joe had seemed so genuinely upset for us. I'd found his kindness and patience with Nana particularly touching.

I didn't really want to admit it, even to myself, but I'd actually been quite attracted to the Joe who'd visited that morning. How awful was that, in the circumstances of grieving for poor Rufus? And quite apart from anything else, I had a boyfriend already, not forgetting the fact that I was expecting his baby. I shouldn't even have been looking at another man, or spending so much time pondering the enigma of his personality, let alone secretly admiring him and even ... yes, even fancying him a bit. Especially as he'd previously been so horribly rude to me. Perhaps it was the trauma of losing Rufus that had unhinged my mind slightly. That'd be it. That, or my peculiar pregnancy moods again.

The following day, Easter Saturday, I wandered down to the shop to look for something to take back as a treat for Nana. She'd stayed at home, claiming her knees were particularly bad, but I knew she just wasn't ready to face her usual morning walk without Rufus at her side.

The shop was decked out with festive Easter garlands of yellow and white. Fluffy toy chicks jostled for space on the crowded shelves with reduced-price Easter eggs, hot-cross buns that were about to pass their sell-by date and garishly packaged chocolate cakes decorated with sugar eggs.

'Sorry to hear about your nan's dog,' someone said as I hesitated over a display of cut flowers near the till.

I looked up. It was Nora, the 'miserable' postmistress. I thanked her, wondering how she'd heard about Rufus, but almost immediately there was someone else offering commiserations, and then two more, and before I'd chosen my bouquet, at least half a dozen people had patted my arm or taken my hand and asked me to pass on their sympathy to Nana. One of those offering their condolences was the dog-walker, David, without the pink anorak this time. He made a beeline for me as soon as he saw me and, somewhat to my embarrassment considering I hardly knew him, enveloped me in a hug.

'It's so sad,' he said. 'Your poor nan must be distraught. You too. Is there anything I can do?'

'That's kind of you, but no, we're OK,' I said. 'Thank you.'

'Things get around, you know. It's such a small community,' Izzie said, giving me a sympathetic smile when I eventually went to pay her. 'Daisy-May from the vets told me about it. I guess that's who most people have heard it from. Some people might call it gossiping, but I think it's genuine caring.' She put her head on one side, looking at me. 'I don't suppose you get that kind of thing so much in London.'

'No.' She was dead right: I didn't. Apart from my flatmates, I didn't think anyone living in my street even knew my name. There were always stories about poor lonely people being found dead in their flats, nobody even aware that they hadn't been outside for weeks or even months. I couldn't imagine that kind of thing happening around here.

As the vets was just over the road from the shop, I decided to call in and see whether Daisy-May had sorted out the bill yet. The waiting room was crowded and I stood patiently to one side while she dealt with a man paying for some worming tablets and then took a call from someone trying to book an appointment.

'I've come to settle my grandmother's bill,' I said when she was finally free. 'For ... for Rufus.'

'Oh yes.' She looked at me sadly. 'I was so sorry to hear about that. Now then, where did I put that invoice?' She started rifling through a pile of paperwork. 'I'm sure Mr Bradley put it on my desk just this morning. Oh, drat, there's the phone again. Excuse me ... sorry, I'll be with you in a tick.'

I stepped away from the desk while she took the call, pretending to read the posters on the wall, but I couldn't help overhearing Daisy-May's stuttered excuses and apologies on the phone.

'Difficult client?' I asked sympathetically as she hung up, looking pink-cheeked and flustered.

'Oh dear, I seem to have got myself a bit muddled,' she said by way of reply. 'I've sent a letter about cat vaccinations to a client who hasn't got a cat any more. Which means his reminder about puppy-worming has probably gone to the cat's owner. Mr Bradley will be furious.'

'He doesn't have to know, does he?' I said.

'The client was cross. He says it's the second time I've sent him appointments for his cat and it's upsetting his wife because she still hasn't got over losing him. I think he's going to make a complaint about me.'

'We all make mistakes,' I pointed out gently. The poor woman looked like she was on the verge of tears and I remembered what Joe had said the previous morning about the admin being in chaos.

'I seem to keep making them, these days,' she said, sniffing. 'I'm beginning to think I'm getting too old for this job. This new computer system keeps crashing, for a start, and Mr Bradley thinks it's my fault. I can't get to grips with all this new technology. And it's so busy today! I don't usually work Saturdays but the weekend receptionist is ill, so I had to rush in at the last minute. I haven't even had time to try restarting the computer and I've got no idea what appointments are booked.'

'Would you like me to have a quick look at it?' I offered. 'I work at a vets in London, and your system might be similar to the one we use.'

'Oh, would you mind?' she gasped. 'It'd be so kind. Could you just see whether you think I'm doing something wrong when I enter the appointments? Oh, drat, there's the phone again.'

'You answer the phone,' I said, slipping round to her side of the desk, 'while I have a little look at your computer.'

I'd already started doing a quick scan of the appointment system before it occurred to me that I might get Daisy-May into more trouble by doing so.

'Actually,' I said as she finished her phone conversation, 'I probably should check with Mr Bradley before I—'

'Check what with me?' said a voice from behind my shoulder. And then, 'Oh, it's you. What are you doing to our computer?'

'I'm sorry,' I said, almost falling over in my haste to get back on the right side of the reception desk. 'It's not Daisy-May's fault – I insisted on having a look in case I could help her – not that I thought she'd done anything wrong, she hasn't, the system was trying to do an update, that's all, there's nothing wrong with it.' I paused, feeling my face burning with embarrassment. Why was I making such a big deal of it? 'I just thought I'd try to help, that's all,' I finished more quietly. 'I came in to settle my bill, and Daisy-May happened to mention there might be a problem.'

'You use the same system at your practice?' Joe said, frowning.

'Yes. Sorry for interfering,' I said again. 'I'll come back another time to pay the bill, if it's more convenient.'

'It's fine, you can do it now if you'd like to,' Daisy-May said, smiling at me. She'd evidently uncovered the paperwork.

'Right. I'll leave you to see to that, then, Daisy-May,' Joe said. 'I've got to go and look at that horse at Dunelm Farm.' He headed for the door, and then turned back to me, still frowning. 'Ms Martin, if you could return to the correct side of the counter and let my receptionist do her job ...'

And then he was gone. For a moment, Daisy-May and I both stared at the door. Then she turned to me, her eyebrows raised.

'I thought he was going to be cross.'

'That wasn't cross?' I asked, surprised.

'You really don't know Mr Bradley, do you?' she said, sounding slightly sad. 'He must like you. And that's quite unusual. He doesn't like many people. He always says he prefers animals.'

I laughed. 'Oh, I don't think he likes me much, either. Probably just didn't want to shout at me until I'd paid my bill.'

I was being flippant, of course. The truth was that I was secretly a little bit thrilled that she thought he liked me. And a little bit shocked that I felt thrilled. And then a little bit exasperated with myself for being so shocked. On the way home to give Nana her flowers, I wondered to myself how it must be for him, as the sole vet in this small village practice. Was it stressful? Was that why he had such inexplicable mood swings? Could I really allow that as an excuse for his bursts of rudeness? Surely not. In fact, to me the idea of working in a surgery in a little rural village like this, where life was slower-paced and where everyone knew each other, seemed positively idyllic. If I were lucky enough to live and work somewhere like this, I thought to myself as I walked, I was sure *I* wouldn't be so damned moody.

It wasn't until later that I realised how closely this perceived idyll of country life matched my roses-round-the-door fantasy that had so irritated Adam. And how completely it differed from our lifestyle in London.

CHAPTER SEVEN

On Easter Sunday, Nana persuaded me to go with her to the village church for the service, doing a very good job of making me feel that I couldn't say no. From the way she'd described it, I gathered it was the social event of the year, when everyone – 'even young people like you who don't normally bother with church' – turned up. I got the feeling she'd probably like to show me off to the other old dears at the service. I supposed it wouldn't kill me to go, especially as she'd looked so pleased when I agreed.

I helped her along the road to the cheerful sound of church bells ringing. It was a chilly but sunny morning, and the village was looking bright and pretty. Daffodils were nodding their heads on the green, the ducks inhabiting the pond were preening themselves and airing their feathers by the side of the water, and seagulls were swooping and calling high in the sky.

'Beautiful day, isn't it!' Nana called out to everyone we saw. To my surprise, she had pulled herself out of her grief surprisingly easily. When I'd returned from the vets the day before, having paid the bill for the cremation, I had found her in the kitchen, furiously mixing the batter for some cakes.

'They're to go with the refreshments after the Easter service tomorrow,' she'd said, closing the oven door with a decisive bang and rubbing her back as she straightened up.

'Don't overdo it,' I'd said gently, fully aware that she was keeping herself busy to avoid giving in to the sadness.

'Huh,' she responded, giving me one of her looks. 'It's no good sitting around feeling sorry for yourself, is it?'

I had to admit I admired her attitude. Nana's generation of women had a lot to teach us about strength and fortitude. We might think we're clever because we combine careers with raising families, because we expect to be treated the same as men and 'have it all'. But when it came to picking ourselves up and dealing with life's sorrows and difficulties, I doubted many of us were as tough as those who'd had to live through the war.

As I helped with the washing up, I told Nana how many people in the village had sent their love and sympathy. 'I sorted everything out at the vets as well.'

'He was very kind, that Joe, wasn't he?' she said. 'I don't know why people are saying he's rude.'

'There must be two sides to him,' I offered.

'Well, we all have our problems,' Nana said. 'No doubt there's a woman and a broken heart behind it.'

It had made me laugh. Trust Nana to come up with a solution straight out of a romantic novel. But I couldn't help wondering if she might be right.

On the way to the church we stopped to talk to so many people I lost count. I was hoping that Joe might be one of them, but they were mainly Nana's friends wanting to talk about the Best-Kept Village competition.

'What I want to know,' said a tall lady with bright red hair who'd been introduced to me as Maggie Stammers, 'is why Nora takes on the job of the hanging baskets if she's so bloody stressed. She's happy enough to take our money but she does nothing but moan about it.'

'I know.' Nana nodded in agreement. Maggie was walking along with us, holding Nana's arm on the other side. We were a slow little procession, with two more of Nana's friends following behind us and joining in the discussion. 'What happens if she doesn't get them all done in time for the competition judging?'

'She won't give us our money back, that's for sure,' Maggie said grimly. 'I've a good mind to tell her I'd rather do my own this year. Trouble is, I'll suffer for it in the long run.'

'Yes, you will,' agreed one of the other ladies. 'Remember when she fell out with old Billy Henderson? She refused point blank to serve him in the post office afterwards – he had to take the bus into town to get his pension.'

'That was at least twenty years ago, Ellen!' Nana exclaimed. 'And it only happened once – she had to give in and serve him because we all threatened to report her to the post office bosses. Anyway,' she added, 'he deserved it, after what he said to her.'

There was a general mutter of agreement, but before I could find out what he'd said to her (which was very intriguing, given his apparent reputation as a *ladies' man*) someone had changed the topic of conversation to 'that strange new vet' Joe Bradley. I got the impression he was a frequent topic of village gossip.

'Yes, he's a miserable young bugger, if ever there was one,' Maggie declared. 'Never a smile or a "good morning" for anyone.'

'Oh, I don't know about that,' Nana said. 'He was very good to us—'

She stopped, shaking her head, and I realised she wasn't going to be able to talk to her friends about Rufus's death without breaking down. For all her good humour and bravery, it was still too soon. Luckily, at that moment we were engulfed by a huge crowd of people rushing to get to the church in time for the start of the service, and with all the shuffling, the subject was dropped.

St Matthew's was an ancient stone church with a squat square tower and thick, solid walls. Outside was a neatly tended graveyard with some leaning, worn memorial stones looking even older than the church, and inside the wooden pews were furnished with home-made cushions. I imagined generations and generations of Hope Green women working on them.

'They'd have been kneelers originally,' Nana explained. 'But they've worn flat now and we just sit on them – they make the pews more comfy.'

I had to amend my ideas about the gathering congregation pretty quickly. Far from being just a bunch of *old dears*, there was a large number of families with children:

toddlers skipping along holding their parents' hands, babies propped up in prams and buggies, school-age kids giggling together, some arriving on bikes and scooters that they left outside the church doors, some of the younger ones bringing their favourite toys with them. Of course the older generation was out in force too, but many of them were accompanying their own children and grandchildren, and seeing this, I was glad I'd agreed to come with Nana.

'It's because it's Easter, you see. Everyone has their families visiting,' she said happily, pausing halfway down the aisle to introduce me to yet another friend.

'So it's not normally like this?' I asked, as we squeezed on to one of the pews.

'Oh, we get quite a good crowd most Sundays,' Nana said. 'People round here like a good old hymn. And it doesn't do the kids any harm, if you ask me, bringing them up with some old-fashioned values.'

The vicar, Paul – who was probably not much older than me, and who bounded into the church with all the exuberance of a young puppy – was obviously loved by all the congregation, especially the children, who laughed at his jokes, and he joined in enthusiastically with the cheerful choruses.

'It's nothing like the services I remember from when I was a kid,' I whispered to Nana at one point.

'Ah, well, things have moved on,' she said with a satisfied expression. 'And a good thing too. There's no need for church to be miserable, is there?'

And it certainly wasn't. During Paul's sermon, which was actually just a nice story with a happy moral ending,

I glanced around at all the smiling faces, at the children who were mostly listening with interest but in no way being made to sit to attention, and babies being rocked in their mothers' arms or pacified with toys and comforters. As the sermon finished, there was a sudden high-pitched shout of 'Wee wee!' from a couple of rows in front of us. Paul chuckled, made a quip about the effect of his story, and everyone laughed. When the child in question was helped out of the pew by her red-faced mother, I realised it was Izzie from the shop. She had her youngest child in her arms and, as well as pulling along the toddler who'd expressed her urgent need, was being trailed by an older boy of about four. Before I knew what I was doing I jumped to my feet and intercepted her at the end of my row.

'Leave the baby with me while you go,' I whispered. 'And the boy too if—'

'Oh, thanks!' she said, quickly depositing the little one in my arms. 'But Oliver had better come with me, he'll only make a fuss otherwise.'

She rushed off, leaving me to sit back down on the pew, holding the baby. She was a little girl, dressed in miniature pink jeans and a purple stripy top, her feet in matching purple socks. No knitted bootees or bonnet, then, I thought to myself with a laugh. How old was she? I had no idea. But she could support herself, sitting on my lap and staring at me with wide-eyed curiosity. Suddenly she gave me a huge smile that lit up her little face, displaying two tiny white teeth, and I found myself smiling back and whispering, 'Hello, baby!'

It felt so natural holding her in my arms I could have happily sat there all day, making faces at her and watching her eyes light up as she giggled back. The congregation stood up to sing another hymn but I stayed seated, holding the little one until Izzie came back with the other two children.

'Thanks, Sam!' she whispered, and to my surprise, I felt something akin to a sense of loss as the baby's weight was lifted from my lap.

They seemed so happy, that little family, despite how hard it must be for Izzie to manage on her own. It must be lovely for them, living in this village, this friendly community where everyone knew and helped each other. It was so different from the way I lived in London. I suddenly felt overwhelmed with the feeling that this was the sort of life I wanted. I wanted to be one of these young mums bringing her children here on Sundays with all the other families, taking them to the village school during the week, joining in with the fun of the summer fete and the Christmas parties and concerts. I wanted a career, of course, but I also wanted to bake cakes in the kitchen of a cosy cottage like Nana's, to romp through the woods with my dogs and play on the beach with my children.

I felt the flatness of my stomach beneath my coat – I wouldn't be showing for a long while yet – and thought about the child I was carrying. I *wanted* this baby, I thought with a sudden absolute certainty. And I wanted him or her to grow up somewhere like this. I didn't want them growing up in London, never being able to ride a bike safely in the street, watch new baby lambs playing in the fields, pick wildflowers or climb trees.

OK, I suppose the atmosphere in the church that Easter Sunday had slightly gone to my head and, yes, I was getting carried away by my own unrealistic fantasy of rural life. But if nothing else, it had made up my mind for me. Come what may, and whatever Adam had to say on the subject, I was keeping this baby. As we stood up at the end of the service, I was almost nodding my head to myself with the satisfaction of having reached this momentous decision. And then, turning to file out of our row, I noticed someone at the back of the church for the first time. It was Joe Bradley, holding the hand of a little girl in a red coat.

He was already in the church hall by the time we entered, standing at the refreshment table with one of Nana's cakes in his hand. He was talking to Paul the vicar while the little girl ran around with the other children.

'Hello, Peggy,' he said as we approached. 'How are you now?'

'Bearing up, Joe, mustn't complain, lots worse off than me,' Nana said at once. I was probably the only one who noticed the slight tremor in her voice. 'Of course I'll miss him terribly, you know, but as you said, he was a good age.'

'Peggy's lovely old spaniel died in his sleep the other night,' Joe explained quietly to Paul.

'Rufus? Oh, Peggy, I'm so sorry to hear that,' Paul said. 'He must have been – what, about twelve or thirteen?'

'Fourteen, actually,' she said with a note of pride in her voice.

'Ah, you'll miss him, won't you? Will you think about getting another dog?'

Paul started to tell her about one of his parishioners who'd recently got a new puppy, and Nana explained that – apart from the fact that she couldn't imagine ever being able to replace Rufus – she didn't think it'd be fair, now that she was so old herself and wouldn't be able to look after a dog well enough or give it enough exercise. I glanced at Joe, who'd turned away to look for the child in the red coat.

'Is she your daughter, or—?' I left the question hanging, wondering what the other possibilities could be. Niece, perhaps? Child of a friend? Goddaughter, even?

'Yes,' he said. 'My daughter, Ruby.'

Well, why should I be surprised? Why wouldn't he have a daughter? And why, after all, should anyone have mentioned it? 'How old is she?' I asked.

'Ten.' He bit into the cake, staring at me. I wasn't sure if he wanted to continue the conversation or not, but something made me plough on, regardless: 'So, do you have any other children?'

'No. Just Ruby.'

'I see. Lovely name.'

We continued to stare at each other. His expression was a mixture of hostility and challenge, almost as if he was daring me to go on, to be nosier still. Why stop there? I *should* have stopped there. But there was something about that challenging look that made me determined to carry on. It was none of my business, but still, I wanted to know. Was he divorced? Widowed? A single dad bringing up his daughter alone? I imagined Ruby's mum having walked away from them both, leaving him to cope with all the worries and financial difficulties. No wonder he was so moody and stressed. Poor guy. He needed sympathy and understanding. And let's face it, isn't there something strangely appealing about a man nursing a broken heart or a secret tragedy? That irresistible combination of strength and vulnerability …

'So is Ruby's mum …?' Again, I left the question hanging, my eyebrows raised, waiting. There were several seconds of silence, during which I felt a hot rush of panic that he was going to walk away in disgust at my blatant nosiness. Or worse, give me a mouthful of abuse for being so insensitive about his (dead/missing/non-existent) wife.

He looked away, swallowed the final mouthful of his cake and wiped the crumbs from the corners of his mouth. I thought he wasn't going to answer. I was just about to make a flustered attempt to pretend I hadn't even asked the question, to say I was in a hurry and grab Nana's arm to hasten her away, when he suddenly turned back to meet my eyes.

'My wife's at home,' he said abruptly, and then called for his daughter, took her by the hand and walked off out of the hall, leaving me standing alone with my mouth open, feeling like a complete idiot. He was married. His wife hadn't left him or died; she was at home, cooking their Easter Sunday lunch while he took the kid to church. I pictured this happy family scenario and felt my face burn with humiliation. What the hell was I thinking of, pressing him for details of his private life – like a besotted teenager, for God's sake! What a fool I'd made of myself. Why hadn't it even crossed my mind that he was married before I started – let's be honest here – having such ridiculous fantasies about him?

I grimly smiled and nodded at all the other villagers who wanted to chat, waiting for the moment when Nana said it was time to leave. I felt so embarrassed. I happily held Izzie's baby girl again while she sorted out drinks and biscuits for the other two children. But I felt like the whole mood of the day was spoilt. I knew it was my own fault – I shouldn't have been so nosy, or got carried away with my fantasy – but did Joe really have to be quite so sharp, quite so abrupt and dismissive? What happened to the tender, caring, side of him I'd seen – and liked – during the previous couple of days?

Well, as far as I was concerned, he could keep his ever-changing moods to himself. I needed to get real, to stop dreaming about a non-existent perfect life in an idyllic rural village where people lived in a kind of happy-ever-after state of bliss. It was all just escapism. I knew it. I just didn't want to admit it. My real life was in London, my real job was at James Street Vet Clinic, and my real boyfriend didn't even like animals, let alone cute babies or cosy cottages in the country.

This was just a holiday. When it was over I was going to have to go home and talk to Adam about the pregnancy and where our relationship was going. I had to stop trying to distract myself with totally irrelevant curiosity about Joe Bradley and his totally irrelevant wife and daughter. And next time I visited Hope Green, I was going to have to avoid him like the plague.

PART 2

FOLLOW YOUR HEART

CHAPTER EIGHT

Back in London, and back at work, it felt even more as though my time in Hope Green had been a silly romantic fantasy. It was good to stay busy – it was helping to keep my mind off everything. I'd been so worried about leaving Nana, knowing how sad it would be for her now, with no welcoming tail-wagging when she got up in the mornings and no warm, furry companion to snuggle at her feet in the evenings. I knew she had good friends in the village, but it wasn't the same as having company at home, especially at night. She'd been in the habit of talking to Rufus all the time. Would she be talking to herself now that I'd left her on her own? My eyes kept filling with tears at the thought of her loneliness. She refused to admit she was lonely, of course, and I knew better than to contradict her protestations that she was 'perfectly all right, just have to keep myself busy, don't you worry about me'.

I'd talked to Claire about Joe – the humiliation was still so fresh in my mind and I wanted an outlet for my feelings – without mentioning the ridiculous schoolgirl crush I'd been in danger of developing, of course. I told her all about how he was the rudest, most obnoxious man it was possible to imagine. I might have exaggerated slightly and embellished some of my encounters with him so that he probably came across more like an evil pantomime villain than merely a grumpy, bad-tempered male. However, in my mind, he deserved every word of it. But when Claire asked if Joe was still moody when I saw him as a client, I suddenly remembered his gentleness with Rufus, the way his whole demeanour had altered as he dealt with him and the kindness he'd shown to Nana and me on the morning of his death.

'No,' I had said quickly. 'No, in fact he was completely different then. So that's something.'

'Good.' She gave me a sideways look. 'So what's he like?'

'I told you! Cross, rude—'

'That's not what I meant. Old, young, tall, short …?' She looked at me even more directly and I felt myself going slightly pink. 'Good-looking? Fit?'

'Not particularly.' I blushed. 'Anyway, he's married with a little girl, and to be honest they're welcome to him.'

'I see. Well, let's just be thankful he doesn't work with us at James Street.'

But I couldn't waste too much time regretting my embarrassing faux pas with Joe Bradley. I was meeting Adam to have *the* conversation, about the baby. He was waiting for me in our favourite bar after work.

'You look well,' he said, pulling me close for a kiss.

I'd already told him about Rufus, and he'd been surprisingly sweet about it, considering he'd never particularly liked dogs. For the first time in ages it had made me feel as if perhaps we were back on track together, and had reminded me of how nice Adam could be and why I fell for him in the first place. So maybe the conversation would go OK after all. Perhaps he'd take the news all right, perhaps we'd actually be able to make a go of it together: Adam and me and the baby.

I needed to ignore my doubts, try to sound positive. Telling him straight away would be best, I thought – he was leaning close to me, holding my hand; I could catch him while he was looking particularly tender and caring. Blurting it out in the middle of a random conversation would probably give him a cardiac arrest.

When I'd accidentally brought up the topic of children during our chat before my holiday, in this same bar, he'd freaked out merely at the suggestion that I might want kids at all. In a way, it felt as if I'd somehow brought this pregnancy on myself by subconsciously wishing for it, although I knew that was ridiculous.

'Adam, there's something I have to tell you.'

'What?' He looked worried. 'Is something wrong?'

'No. Well, yes, in a way.' I took a gulp of my drink he'd bought for me. *Get it over with*! 'I'm … Well, it might come as a bit of a shock …'

'A shock?' he repeated, looking down and fiddling with his beer mat. 'Are you about to say you want to finish with me?'

I hadn't expected that. 'No, that isn't—'

'No? You've been giving me that impression recently.' He was standing the beer mat on its edge, trying to spin it like a top. I wished he'd leave the bloody thing alone. 'What with not wanting to spend the holiday with me – all that crap about needing time apart,' he added sulkily.

So it *was* still a sore point, after all.

'Well, yes, I know I said that,' I admitted. 'We'd been arguing a lot, hadn't we, so yes, I thought we should give each other some space, but—'

'I suppose you think it's all *my* fault.' His tone completely changed. He slapped the beer mat back on the table and looked up at me. 'Just because I'm more realistic than you about the future, about how much we need to save for a deposit on a place of our own.'

'No, that's not what I'm saying at all, Adam – it's nothing to do with that!' This wasn't going the right way at all. I really didn't want us to start arguing before I'd even given him the news. 'Look, I just thought it'd help if we had a break, so that we'd miss each other, and after the holiday we'd feel happier and—'

'But instead, you've decided to call it a day. Or have you met someone else?' he levelled at me. 'Is that it?'

'No!' I stared at him. 'Adam, where has this all come from? For God's sake, I'm not trying to break up with you. I'm trying to tell you I'm pregnant.' The words came out in a rush.

'*Pregnant?*' He couldn't have looked more horrified if he'd tried. He actually pushed his chair back from the table, as if he wanted to make sure I didn't touch him. 'You can't be.'

'Well, I've got two positive pregnancy tests that would beg to differ. I know it's a shock – I couldn't believe it myself at first – but ...'

He was silent for a minute, just staring at me. Then: 'How long have you known?'

'Since just before I went away.'

'And you didn't think you ought to tell me first?' He raised his voice. People were looking at us.

'Not really, no. I needed time to adjust to the idea myself, to be honest.'

'I suppose you told your nan? And your parents? And Claire? I suppose everyone knows except me?'

'No.' I was beginning to feel upset by his tone. 'Nobody knows yet. I wanted to tell you first. I knew you'd be surprised, but—'

'*Surprised*? That's a bit of an understatement! I can't believe you'd do this, Sam. It's a pretty underhand way of going about things, isn't it?'

I stared back at him. 'What are you talking about?'

'Getting pregnant – ha! Just as we're going through a rough patch.' He gave a snort, like it was funny, but neither of us were laughing. 'So what's the idea, Sam? Planning on being a single parent, are you, with me being the bloody mug – the *sperm donor* – who has to fork out for child maintenance for the next eighteen years?'

I gasped and felt my face turning red with shock and disbelief.

'No!' I managed to squawk. 'It wasn't deliberate, for God's sake! Do you honestly think I'd *want* to be a single mum? And anyway—'

'Oh, of course, you said you don't even *want* to break up with me.' He gave another sarcastic snort. 'What, then? You're trying to force me into your little romantic cottage fantasy, I suppose? Getting married, God forbid, and bringing up a whole brood of kids – well, you'll have to find someone else, I'm afraid, because *I'm* not—'

'Adam, stop it!' I raised my own voice, stopping him in his tracks. I wasn't going to cry. I was too shocked to cry, anyway. 'Or I'm walking straight out of here and going home. I knew you wouldn't be pleased, but I'm not listening to any more of this.'

He picked up his glass, scowling, and took a gulp of his drink.

'I *was* hoping we could make a go of it,' I went on, my voice trembling now. 'For the sake of the baby, at least. But if this is how you're going to be—'

'Forget it!' he snapped. 'If that's all you want me for, Sam – just to *use* me, *for the sake of the baby* – when it's quite clear you don't love me any more—'

I'd had enough. I stood up, rummaging in my purse with shaking hands for some money, which I then threw on the table for my unfinished drink. I was burning up with anger – anger and *disappointment* – in him. Yes, I'd been prepared for him to be shocked – and unhappy – about the news, but I'd never, in a million years, have expected him to react like this. I was gutted. Part of me had already felt sure that I'd rather be on my own than carry on with someone who thought so little of me. But on the other hand, we'd been together for a long time and whether he liked it or not, he *was* the father of this baby.

That night I spent a lot of time staring into space, trying to imagine the possibility of being on my own with a baby. Getting up to change nappies and take a child to a nursery before rushing off to work every day. It seemed unreal, impossible, even if plenty of other people did it. Where would I live? How would I manage? My little fantasy about an idyllic life in a village seemed childish and ridiculous now. I tossed and turned in bed, worn out by the upset and worry of the evening, but too cross with Adam to care whether we even spoke to each other again.

It was work that helped me through the turmoil of my emotions. The next morning, a little cat was brought into the surgery by an exhausted-looking young mum with twin babies in a buggy. She explained that she thought the kitten must be a stray, he'd been hanging around her door after she'd fed him a few times and she'd love to take him in herself but – she nodded at the sleeping babies – she had her hands full.

'You certainly have,' I sympathised, suddenly freaking out in my head. The thought of twins had never even occurred to me. 'Don't worry, you've done the right thing bringing him here.'

She looked relieved when I told her that one of the vets would check him to see if he had an ID chip, in the hope he might be reunited with his owner.

'But if he isn't chipped ...?' she said, suddenly frowning again. 'He won't be put down, will he? He's such a cute little thing, even if he does look a bit poorly.'

Not if I had any say in it, he wouldn't. I explained that we always tried everything to find the owners of lost cats – putting their photo on our website and Facebook page – before sending them to the rescue centre in the hope someone would adopt them. The woman went away looking happier, and as soon as she'd left, I opened the cardboard box and lifted out the little black cat. He was very scrawny and didn't look well at all. One of his bright green eyes was very sore and weepy and his ears sat at jaunty angles, making him look puzzled. When I picked him up he gave a faint indignant squeak of protest, and I couldn't help smiling.

'Ah, isn't he a cutie?' Claire crooned from where she sat beside me.

'Yes, but he's very thin, and look at the state of his fur. I wonder how long he's been lost. He seems quite nervous, doesn't he? Like he's not used to being handled.' I scratched the cat's head. 'I hope someone claims him.'

I waited until Mr Fulcher had checked him over, before asking about what would happen.

'It's a girl, for a start,' he said. 'And a timid little one at that. Unfortunately, she isn't chipped, so we'll try an appeal on the website and so on. Otherwise she can go to the shelter – after we've nursed her back to health. She's very undernourished, of course. She'll need deflea-ing, and some teeth removed and we'll have to get that bad eye sorted out.' He sighed. 'Though obviously we can't afford to keep caring for her indefinitely.'

'Surely someone will be looking for her?' I said.

'You'd be surprised,' he said with an air of resignation. 'People move house and don't take their cats with them. Or they just decide they've become too much trouble and turf them out – perhaps because their own circumstances have changed. You said the woman who brought her in had just had twins?'

'Yes, but I'm sure she wasn't the cat's owner. She seemed genuinely concerned. She'd been feeding her.'

'Well, we'll see if anyone comes forward. It's a shame, though. She'll probably struggle to get adopted.'

'Why?' My heart sank for the little thing.

'She's black. Nobody seems to want black cats, unfortunately. They're always the ones left at the shelter.'

I'd heard this before and always found it hard to believe. I thought black cats were supposed to be lucky! I just hoped this little one would be. How could anyone resist her? I certainly couldn't.

During the next couple of days, I popped out to the back of the clinic during my breaks to see how she was doing, and had asked one of the nurses to keep me updated about her progress. There was something so sweet but pitiful about her. She needed someone to love her. Surely someone would come forward. There were already some comments on Facebook from people saying how cute she was, but so far, no one recognised her or had offered her a home.

'It's just a matter of time, little cat,' I whispered as I said goodbye to her after the second day. 'Someone will want you, I'm sure they will.'

I was just hoping and praying it would happen sooner rather than later.

CHAPTER NINE

Looking back, I realise I'd been focusing on the little black cat to distract me from my worries about Adam and the baby – and to stop me thinking about Hope Green too. My embarrassment about Joe had faded a bit by now, but I was still concerned about Nana being on her own, and apart from calling her regularly I didn't know what I could possibly do to help from so far away.

At home, I had the James Street Vet's Facebook page open on my tablet, staring at the little black cat's picture, when my flatmate Helen called up the stairs to tell me I had a visitor. It was Adam, and he was already halfway up the stairs before I could stop him.

'I'm so sorry, Sam,' he said straight away. 'I can't believe I said all that stuff the other night.'

'Neither can I.' I stood in the doorway of my room, my arms folded.

'Can we talk? Just for a minute?'

'I don't think it's a good idea.'

'Please. I know it was unforgivable. But...'

Reluctantly I stepped aside and held the door open, ushering him inside and closing it quietly behind us. I really didn't want everyone in the flat hearing this.

'But what?' I said.

'Well, you must admit, you did spring the news on me. What did you expect?'

'Expect? Well, *not* for you to accuse me of getting pregnant deliberately, to force you into anything.'

'I know. Look, I've had time to calm down now.'

Good for you, I thought crossly.

'We can't leave things like this,' he insisted.

No, I supposed we couldn't.

'It was the shock. I didn't mean it, all right?' he said.

'No, it's not all right,' I retorted. 'I can't believe you were so vile to me.'

'You knew I wasn't keen on the idea of children. You should've broken it to me more gently, at least let me have my drink first.'

I gasped. Surely he wasn't trying to blame me for the things he'd said?

Seeing the look on my face, he went on quickly, 'All right, sorry, there's no excuse. I was out of order. Obviously, we need to discuss this sensibly.'

'Discuss what, exactly?'

I didn't intend to sound quite so confrontational. He'd apologised, I guessed he meant it, I supposed I should be letting him off the hook a bit. But I really couldn't be doing with all of this. My mind was focused on the little black cat, whose picture was still staring back at me from my tablet next to where we were sitting. I didn't even want to talk to Adam, I realised. All we were doing was skirting around the real issue. Were we ending our relationship? One of us had to grasp the nettle and actually say it.

'We need to discuss the future,' he said, giving a moody shrug. 'I don't know about getting married, to be honest, but perhaps in due course—'

'Adam, for God's sake, I don't want to marry you!' I exclaimed.

He looked at me in genuine surprise.

I took a deep breath. 'Look, I don't really know *what* I want, OK? But I don't think that it's this. At least, not any more. Us. Carrying on the way we are: fighting, losing respect for each other. Do you? Honestly?'

He scowled. Too late, I guessed he wouldn't forgive me for being the one to say it. It hurt his pride. Well, tough. He'd hurt me, more than enough, the other night.

'It's not all my fault,' he muttered.

'I'm not saying it is.'

'You can be bloody annoying, yourself.'

'Right. Can we just stop this, now, please?' While we could still salvage a bit of dignity, I hoped. 'I'm sorry, Adam, I really am. I wanted it to work. But it's not going to, is it?'

'No,' he relented. He looked at me sadly, then looked away. 'Will you keep the baby?' he asked after a moment's silence.

'Yes. I can't … I can't *not* keep it.'

'How will you manage?'

Finally, he'd asked!

'I mean, I'll pay,' he added quickly. 'I'll pay whatever I can – I'm not the person who said those things in the bar, you know I'm not really like that.'

'OK.'

So was that *it*? We stared at each other, neither of us sure what else there was to say. It all felt unreal.

'We could at least stay friends?' he suggested.

'Yes, if you like.'

'Well, obviously I'd "like",' he said crossly. 'It's not too much to ask, is it?'

As I opened the door for him and he turned and went, still scowling, without a backward glance, I still wasn't even sure whether I'd done the right thing. How had I ended up feeling like such a bitch?

But equally, I was just glad to go back to thinking about simpler things and the stray cat.

Mr Fulcher had already told me she'd be taken to the shelter the following week. She still wasn't in the best of health, but he felt she mainly needed lots of TLC now. Claire had tried to reassure me that someone would be bound to want her.

'*I* want her!' I'd said, knowing that my hormones were making me overemotional; but even so, it was unbearable to think of this little furry bundle of cuteness sitting in a cage unwanted. I would have liked to keep her myself, but I knew I couldn't: it was impossible, living in my one room, and especially with a baby on the way. But at the time, it had felt like the only thing I really wanted.

Just to make me feel worse, the next day at work was dominated by pregnancies. It had started with a Pekingese bitch who was brought in with complications during her delivery. Then there was a bulldog who was having a phantom pregnancy. Just after lunch, we had an egg-bound budgie. And then in came an elderly lady who refused to believe her little ginger kitten could possibly be expecting at the age of only six months, when the only potential father was its own brother.

'Surely they wouldn't do that!' she'd protested in a scandalised tone.

I'd had to gently persuade her that cats didn't really see things quite the way humans did, and that if neither of them had been neutered it was more than likely she was pregnant.

She looked very shocked when she came back to pay for her consultation. 'If I'd known they were going to behave like that, I'd have kept them in separate rooms.'

I sympathised. 'Well, let's hope you can find good homes for the litter.'

'Yes. What a nuisance, I really didn't want all this fuss. And the vet thinks we should get Fritz neutered straight away.'

'The male kitten? Yes, let's get him booked in, then.'

After the lady had left, I said to Claire, 'Isn't it amazing that people just get kittens or puppies and think that's it, they don't need to do anything else except feed them?'

'Yes,' Claire said with a sigh. 'Although perhaps not so amazing, when you think there are people who have babies without giving it much thought either.'

My stomach lurched at this. I hadn't told Claire yet about my news, as I'd only just told my parents.

Claire's mouth dropped open with shock as I explained, and then she looked hugely relieved when I assured her that no, Adam hadn't *dumped me because of the baby*.

'Are you sure – .about it being over?' she asked sympathetically.

'Yes.' The word didn't come out as emphatically as I'd intended. Sure? Was I ever going to be sure? Was I going to regret it eventually, look back and think I'd been an idiot for preferring to go it alone? 'It hasn't been right between us for ages,' I reminded her, or maybe I was reminding myself. 'I'd rather try and manage on my own … somehow.'

'It won't be easy,' she warned me, looking worried. 'What did your parents say?'

Mum and Dad had only returned from their cruise the previous day. I'd let Mum tell me all about the holiday first, waiting for her to stop for breath before I told her my own news. She was surprisingly animated about how wonderful it was that young women nowadays were perfectly capable of bringing up children without having to have a man around. She gushed on so much, admiring my independence and self-sufficiency, that I couldn't help feeling she was trying to cover up her shock. So it probably didn't help that I then burst out crying, protesting through my tears that I wasn't as strong or independent as she seemed to think I was, that I hardly earned enough to pay my rent as it was, and that I'd have to look for somewhere else to live when the baby was born. I had no idea where I could afford to move to, or how I was going to manage, especially when it came to paying for childcare, and perhaps I'd been crazy to break up with Adam even though I didn't think I loved him any more – in fact, I couldn't even stand the sight of him since he'd been so horrible to me about the baby. When I finally ran out of steam, there was a silence at the other end of the line for so long, I thought Mum must have hung up.

'Yes, I can see it's going to be hard at first,' she said eventually.

I wondered how she felt about the prospect of becoming a grandmother. I hadn't really given her a chance to let it sink in. But when she went on to say that of course, they were there for me and would help and support me, I sniffed back the tears and said: 'Thanks, Mum, but I don't think coming back to live with you is going to be the answer – not long term, anyway—'

'Coming back? What, with a baby?' she gasped. 'Oh God, no, I didn't mean that, Samantha. No, I don't see that as being a solution, not at all, not with our career commitments, my charity work and your dad's golf club – not that we wouldn't be prepared to move heaven and earth to help you, darling, that goes without saying, but I don't think it'd be what you'd want yourself, would it? I know how much you've always loved living in London.

No, I was thinking more in terms of some *financial* assistance. I mean, obviously we could set up a trust fund for the baby, but your father and I had better sit down and discuss what we can do to help you with the initial expenses, and, well, for the first year or so at least – perhaps a regular monthly sum into your account …'

This all came out in such a rush, I could perfectly picture the panic on Mum's face at the thought of me turning up on their doorstep with a baby in my arms. I wouldn't want to inconvenience their lifestyle, now, would I? I was of course hugely grateful though and relieved that they were going to discuss giving me a financial safety net. But it was strange: after talking to my mum I didn't really feel any less alone than I had done before. I'd rather have confided in Nana, but I couldn't because each time I spoke to her, I was more worried about how down she sounded. Every time I tried gently to discuss this with her, she insisted she was OK, putting her barriers back up and telling me off for making a fuss.

Mum had promised me that she and Dad would go down to Dorset to see her 'when we next get a free weekend'. I knew this 'free weekend' wouldn't happen for a long while and I tried not to feel annoyed with her. It wasn't that she was selfish; she'd given up her own life, really, when my brothers and I were born, staying home to look after us and then only working part-time to fit around our schooling until we were old enough for her to pick up her career again. But this was *Nana*, Mum's own mother! If she couldn't find the time to go and see her, then I was going to take on the responsibility myself. I'd go back down to Hope Green for the coming bank holiday weekend and see for myself how she was coping without Rufus.

I was still worrying about the little black cat as well. I couldn't bear to think what might happen to her after she went to the shelter. Would the people there have the time to stroke her and pet her? I was just getting her more used to human contact again. She was eating treats from my hand now, and sometimes even purring when I picked her up. What if she became more timid again, or even aggressive, with the wrong kind of handling? What if nobody wanted to adopt her? We'd obviously taken in stray pets before at James Street, but I'd never become so attached to any of them. Claire seemed to think I was using her to take my mind off the break-up with Adam. Perhaps she was right. But as the weekend approached, the thought occurred to me several times that perhaps I wasn't the only one who would benefit from having her mind occupied with a new little friend …

By the time I left work that evening, preparing to drive down to Hope Green, I'd made up my mind. I knew Claire thought it was crazy, although she tried not to say so in quite so many words. 'Impulsive', she called it. Maybe it was, but I just had a feeling it might work. Nana couldn't cope with another dog, but a cat would be different. It'd be company for her and cheer her up.

I picked up the carrying basket I was borrowing from the surgery, from which the little black cat meowed anxiously.

'It's all right, Ebony,' I said softly – the name I'd christened her with. 'We're going on a journey, but you'll be fine. You'll be safe. And perhaps …'

Perhaps she wouldn't have to come back. I desperately wanted her to be the lucky black cat – the one who bucked the trend and was adopted and loved for the rest of her life. If Nana didn't want her, I'd have no option but to bring her back and watch her go to the animal shelter, praying somebody else would come along who'd care for her. And I knew how incredibly hard I'd find it, now, to let her go.

CHAPTER TEN

The traffic was heavy as I left London that evening and only eased slightly as I headed down the motorway. It was probably a good thing that I had to concentrate on the road; it was taking my mind off my anxiety about how Nana might react to my plan. I hadn't told her about Ebony. I was, of course, hoping she'd love the little cat on sight. I hoped she wouldn't be offended at being presented with a *fait accompli*. I knew she was far too independent, not to say opinionated, just to cave in and accept what I might say was good for her so I'd have to somehow make it seem like she was choosing Ebony herself.

Halfway through the journey, I realised I probably shouldn't have gulped down a full glass of water just before leaving home. Apart from the nausea, the only other symptom of early pregnancy I'd been victim to was a sensitive bladder. I tried to put it out of my mind and listened to little Ebony mewing quietly in the back of the car; thought about other things; turned the radio from a music station to a phone-in programme – that'd give me some-thing to concentrate on – but it was no good; the need was getting more urgent. Surely I wouldn't have to stop?

I kept telling myself I could hang on till I got to Nana's, but in the end, only ten minutes from Hope Green, I knew I had to find somewhere to relieve myself. Luckily, I was just approaching a petrol station. I pulled up with a screech on the forecourt, jumped out of the car and glanced quickly at Ebony. She'd be all right – I'd only be a few minutes. There was nobody using the toilet cubicle or I'd have been in big trouble. I made a mental note to myself with a laugh to be more aware of my body's changing needs in future.

Feeling much more comfortable, I went back outside to top the car up with petrol – to find someone standing next to it, peering in at the window.

'Excuse me!' I called out. 'What are you—'

And then I froze. Because the person had turned round as I approached, and of all the people in the whole of Dorset, it had to be Joe Bradley.

'Is this yours?' he asked in his usual abrupt manner, nodding his head towards the car.

'Yes, it is.' *And what's it got to do with you?* I added inside my head.

'Right. You've got a cat in the back.'

'I do know that, thank you.' I couldn't help the sarcasm. I really wasn't in the mood to see him, never mind getting into conversation with him.

'You left him in the car on his own,' Joe said, frowning at me. 'That wasn't a good idea.'

The nerve of the man!

'It was for about two minutes,' I said crossly, 'while I ... went inside. The car's locked, it's not hot, there's no one else around. And ... *she's* a girl,' I added, as if it made any difference.

'Well, I'd just pulled in to fill up the Jeep with fuel and I heard her crying. She sounded distressed, so I thought I should check whether anyone was with her. She might have been abandoned, for all I knew.'

'Unlikely, I'd have thought.'

I unlocked the petrol cap and turned my back on him as I started to fill up. I was hoping he'd take the hint and go away, but still he stood there. I could feel his eyes on the back of my head.

'So you're back again?' he said after a few minutes. 'I thought you'd gone back to London.'

'I have.' Damn it, why should I tell him what I was doing, or why? He was so bloody rude to me before, when *I* was the one being nosy!

'I didn't know you had a cat,' he persisted.

'I haven't. Not exactly.' I hung up the petrol pump nozzle with a clunk. I didn't want to say any more, but I couldn't seem to help myself. I turned round to see he was looking through the car window at Ebony again. 'She's a stray,' I said more quietly. 'I'm taking her to my nan. Hoping she might like to keep her.'

He nodded. 'I did notice she looks very thin. And her eye looks infected.' He turned to face me now, and there it was again, just for a moment – the warmth in those deep brown eyes, the gentleness in his expression. I was *not* going to be taken in by it, I told myself sternly. That warmth was for Ebony, not me! I wasn't going to be such an idiot this time. 'Would you like me to check her over for you?' he went on.

'No, thank you,' I replied. It came out even more sharply than I'd intended. 'She's already been under the care of a vet. Her eye's much better than it was. I know how to look after it.'

He shrugged, his expression darkening again.

'Suit yourself,' he said, and walked briskly to fill up his Jeep. I also walked away, wishing the encounter hadn't unsettled me so much, wishing that man didn't always end up putting me in such a bad mood!

But by the time I was parking outside Meadow Croft cottage, I was too busy trying to decide how to introduce Ebony to Nana to waste any more time thinking about Joe Bradley. I got out of the car and nearly jumped out of my skin – someone had crept up behind me and reached out a hand to tap me on the arm.

'Sorry, love,' the person said. 'Didn't mean to make you jump.' It was Irene Parks, Nana's next-door neighbour. 'I've been looking out for you. Peggy said you were coming this evening.'

'Oh, hello, Irene.' I noticed the worried frown on her face. 'Is something wrong? Is Nana OK?'

She sighed. 'Not really, love. I've told her she ought to see the doctor, but you know what she's like, she just tells me to stop fussing, that she's fine. But she's not, to be honest, Sam.'

'What – is she ill?' I felt a rush of alarm.

'No, love, not ill. Depressed, in my opinion.'

'I see.' I swallowed. I wasn't really surprised. After all, I'd been suspecting it myself recently. But hearing someone else say it made it sound more real. And Nana had always been so strong, so resilient, so ...

'*Lonely*, you see,' Mrs Parks was going on. 'That's the trouble. She'd never admit it, but it was bad enough after Bert died. She put on a brave face, but I knew how bad she took it. She was getting over it a bit, though, and at least she had old Rufus, didn't she ...' She tailed off. 'But now it's different. Since you went home, she's gone downhill something dreadful. Spends too long in bed. Can't be bothered to cook for herself properly. I just thought I should let you know. Hope you don't think I'm interfering, love.'

I knew Nana wasn't going to admit to being depressed or lonely to me any more than she did to Irene. But it was obvious the situation now needed to be watched more closely.

Needless to say, she showed no sign of depression when she answered the door to me – grasping me by the shoulders and kissing me firmly as always. 'So what's wrong with that dratted London, all of a sudden, that you've made two trips down here in a matter of weeks?' she said, and then under her breath: 'As if I didn't know ...'

I'd evaded questions about Adam when I told her I was coming. But Nana appeared to have put two and two together and made, if not four, then at least three and a half.

'All in due course, Nana. But first, I hope you don't mind, but I've brought a little friend with me.' I lifted the cat basket from behind my legs, holding my breath. 'Don't worry, I've brought some food along for her.'

'What's all this, then?' She stared at Ebony. 'Looking after her for someone, are you?'

'In a way, yes.'

I carried the basket indoors, explaining Ebony's situation as I went. I pretended I'd offered to have her for the weekend to save the nurses having to look after her.

'They're too busy, I suppose,' Nana said with a sniff. 'Poor little cat. Well, it's a good job you're kind enough to help out, Sam. I suppose *that's* why you've come down here, then, is it?'

'Well, pets aren't allowed in my flat,' I said with a smile. 'But no, of course that's not the *only* reason, Nana! I wanted to see you.'

'Yes, I'm sure,' she said with a note of sarcasm in her voice. 'And you *didn't* want to see that boyfriend of yours.'

'Not my boyfriend any more, actually.' I shrugged. 'Didn't Mum tell you?'

'Your mum? No. She only called to tell me all about her cruise and the friends they've got staying for the weekend. So what happened with your young man?' She shuffled into the kitchen. 'Shall I put the kettle on, or is your extended version of Lent still going on?'

I met her eyes, and quickly looked away again. 'I'd still prefer orange juice, thanks. Look, I'll tell you the whole story in a minute. But is it OK if I let Ebony out of the basket? She's a bit shy, though. She might just run behind the sofa and hide.'

'Ebony? Is that her name?'

'Well, it's what I've called her. What do you think?'

I lifted the little cat out of the basket, and Nana paused in pouring out my drink to give her a quick glance.

'Yes. Nice enough name for a black one, better than Sooty or Blackie, I suppose. Cute little thing, isn't she? A stray, did you say?'

'The vets think so. She was very bedraggled and thin when she came in, poor thing.'

'Still looks a bit scrawny to me. Needs some fattening up.' She gave me a look. 'Much like yourself.'

'Well, I'll be getting fat soon enough, anyway.'

She turned round sharply to face me then, delight barely concealed on her face. 'Oh, my Little Sam, is it true, then? I did wonder. What with no tea and no wine.'

I laughed. 'That's all it takes, is it? How to sum me up: if she's not drinking tea or wine, she must be pregnant.' And then with no warning, I suddenly went from laughing to full-on crying. 'Oh, sorry! It's my hormones!' I blubbed. 'I just keep crying, but I'm not really upset. Don't worry. I'm fine. I ... I came to cheer *you* up.'

'Here.' Nana gently took the little cat out of my arms and put her down, turning back to hug me. 'For God's sake, girl, you're not fine at all. You're pregnant and I don't suppose you have a clue what you're going to do. D'you think I'm so old I can't imagine how that feels? And as for cheering *me* up, what in God's name made you think I needed it?'

I'd been in the house for five minutes and already I'd blown it. Instead of carefully trying to find out how depressed Nana was, I'd not only got *her* comforting *me,* but I'd blabbed about thinking she needed cheering up! At this rate, before the evening was out I'd be admitting I'd brought Ebony with the sole intention of leaving her with Nana, instead of waiting and hoping for her to make the decision for herself.

'Oh, I've just been so worried about you missing Rufus,' I said, blowing my nose noisily. 'I know how upset you were to lose him.'

'I see.' She nodded thoughtfully. 'Look, come and sit down in the lounge, for heaven's sake, and bring that poor little cat with you. We can feed her in a minute. Want a piece of cake to go with that orange juice? Coffee and walnut, your favourite, unless you've gone off that too?'

'No, of course I haven't.' I tried to smile in response. 'Thanks.'

I followed her into the lounge, Ebony trotting behind me, meowing.

'Well, of course I do miss old Rufus,' Nana said once we were both settled on the sofa. 'I'm lonely, Sam, I don't mind admitting it. He gave me a reason to get out of bed in the mornings, and a reason to force these stiff old knees of mine to carry me up and down the road every day. Now, sometimes it hardly seems worth it. Oh, don't worry, I'm not about to swallow a bottle of pills or throw myself under a bus or anything like that – and don't give me that look, I'm well aware that's what you and your mother are probably frightened of. I've got too much respect for the sanctity of life, if you must know. And not only that, your granddad would be livid with me when we met up on the other side. No, I'll soldier on, Sam, don't you worry. It just all feels a bit pointless at times, that's all.'

'Oh, Nana, I hate to hear you say that. You've always had such a zest for life,' I said. 'You've still got your friends, here in the village, haven't you?'

'Well, yes, although they're dropping like flies, of course, that's what happens when you get to my age – more funerals than there are birthdays – and those that are left, half of them are more dead than alive. Unless you count nosy-parker Parks next door, of course. She's in and out of here like a dose of salts these days, wanting to know if I've had my dinner and got my shopping in.'

'It's good of her to keep an eye on you,' I said. 'I only wish you lived closer to the family.'

'Huh! I'm not moving up there with your mum and dad, if that's what you're thinking. I'd be lonelier in their house than I am here, Sam, and that's the truth. They're never there, the pair of them, always gallivanting off on holidays and business conferences and whatnots. Anyway, enough about me. Tell me what happened with that boyfriend of yours, and how long you've known about the baby – if you can talk about it without crying?'

'Yes.' I managed a smile. 'I'm sorry, Nana, I'm just a bit emotional at the moment, but honestly, it's all fine,' I lied. And I gave her an edited version of my break-up with Adam. Trying not to worry her, I made light of my anxieties about the future. 'I do want the baby,' I finished. 'Although I suspect it's going to be hard, on my own.'

'You'll find a way,' she said gently. 'You're a coper, you are. Like me.' She looked down at Ebony, who I was surprised and pleased to see, after a little while of walking around the room mewing anxiously, had now jumped up on to Nana's lap. 'Now, this is all very nice, but we need to sort out a litter tray and things like that, Sam.'

'I've brought everything she needs.' I'd made a trip to a pet shop before I left London, loading my boot with a cat bed, boxes of food, food bowls and a scratching post, as well as a covered tray and a sack of litter. I'd have to make sure I didn't touch any dirty litter myself, though – I knew it was dangerous for pregnant women. And I'd have to donate all this stuff to the shelter if I ended up having to take Ebony back with me. But for now, I wasn't going to think about that. 'I'll go and get it in from the car,' I said. 'Look at her! She's really taken to you, Nana.' Ebony had climbed up to Nana's shoulder, where she was now nuzzling her cheek.

'Yes,' she agreed. 'She seems to have done, doesn't she, bless her.' And as I left the room with my car keys, I thought I heard her add, half under her breath, 'And I suppose that was the whole idea, wasn't it?'

Depressed or not, Nana was always one step ahead of me!

CHAPTER ELEVEN

Nana was determined to make a fuss of me, even bringing me a couple of dry biscuits to eat in bed before I got up, saying it would help with the nausea. It didn't, but I ate them anyway to please her. She fed me so much, I had to gently explain that doctors didn't advise 'eating for two' any more during pregnancy and that I wasn't actually underweight, anorexic or wasting away, just because I was still perfectly slim at only seven weeks pregnant.

Meanwhile, I concentrated my efforts on Ebony, giving her lots of cuddles, grooming her to try to encourage her coat to grow back nice and thick and shiny, and feeding her lots of small meals. It took me a while to get Nana to understand that she mustn't be given too much to eat at one time just yet, because she'd been undernourished and needed little and often for now. Nana was all for buying her some fish or chicken and filling up her food bowl.

'I see.' Nana nodded, watching Ebony eating her food. 'She looks like she's still starving, bless her.'

It was true – she did. The poor thing probably thought each meal might be her last.

'Once she's in a permanent home with someone to love her, she'll settle down,' I said, keeping my fingers crossed behind my back.

Nana glanced at me and smiled. 'You should've been a vet, Sam. Shame you didn't—'

'Yes, well, it's too late to think about that now,' I said brusquely.

'But you're going to be a good mum,' she added, giving me a hug. 'Because that needs all the same things – being patient, caring and loving. You'll be a natural, Little Sam.'

Once again I had to blink back the tears. Was Nana right? Would I be able to care for the baby properly on my own? Would it come naturally to me, as she suggested? I smiled at the thought of holding my own tiny child. I already pictured him, for some reason, as a boy, although of course I didn't mind either way. I tried to imagine feeding him, rocking him, playing with him, and I found I was smiling, despite all my worries. I remembered how I'd been reassured, last time, by talking to Izzie, at the shop, and suddenly wanted desperately to listen to some more of her cheerful, friendly chatter.

'Let's go out for a walk,' I suggested to Nana.

I made sure Ebony was shut safely in the kitchen before we opened the front door and explained to Nana that the chances of her running off again and getting lost would be worryingly high.

It still felt odd walking down the village street with Nana without Rufus. It was a fresh, sunny day, the trees around the duck pond waving their bright new green leaves in the breeze, beds full of tulips in people's front gardens startling the morning with their vibrant reds and yellows. As usual, people stopped to talk to us. This time my visit was too sudden for word to get around about it, so I had to explain a dozen times or more that I was only there for the long weekend.

'That's a shame,' red-haired Maggie Stammers said. 'I bet your nan loves having your company – don't you, Peggy?'

''Course I do,' Nana retorted. 'But Sam's got her own life to live, in that dratted London. She can't keep running down here just to keep me company. I'm perfectly fine on my own.'

It was becoming one of her constant refrains. I just wished I could believe it.

Izzie was sorting out a delivery of groceries at the back of the shop when we arrived. She looked pleased to see me, explaining, as Nana toddled off to look for her favourite magazine, that it was always good to have someone nearer her own age to chat to. The village, she confided, was full of older people – not that they weren't all lovely, she added quickly. Apparently a lot of the young families I'd seen at the Easter service had merely been visiting their parents and grandparents here rather than being permanent residents.

'There's so few of us around here now with kids,' she said sadly. 'I worry about the school.'

She explained that the little village school now consisted only of two very small mixed-age classes.

'My Oliver starts in September,' she went on. 'But there are only two of them going up this year from the preschool. That's getting smaller and smaller too – just as my little Evie is due to start there. I'd be so upset if they have to close down eventually. They look at the population, you see. And, well, it speaks for itself. There have been no new families with kids moving in.' She smiled. 'And don't look at me to have any more! I've done my bit!'

I laughed and said she certainly had.

'Anyway,' Izzie said, rubbing her back before bending over her boxes again. 'You're lucky you don't have to worry about things like that.'

'Actually,' I said, lowering my voice. 'I will have to, before too long.'

'You're expecting?' she said, looking back at me with excitement. 'Oh, congratulations!' She gave me a hug and I felt a rush of warmth for her. 'I *wondered* why you were staring so hard at the baby knitting patterns that day!'

'Oh, I was just terrified that I might have to learn to knit bonnets and shawls,' I joked, and we laughed together again.

When I looked around for Nana, I found her at the pet shelves, picking out some treats for Ebony, together with a couple of jingly plastic balls. She looked a little bit abashed to be caught in the act.

'Well, if she's here for the weekend, she's going to need a few extras,' she excused herself, trying to sound nonchalant about it.

Ebony already seemed to be making herself at home in the cottage. I'd put her little bed near the radiator, and whenever she wasn't curled up in there, with her chin resting on the edge of the bed, watching us, she was on Nana's lap. Nana pretended not to be pleased. ('It's just this chair, I reckon – it must have a nice smell to it.') But I saw the way she smiled at the little cat as she stroked her, the way she whispered to her: 'There now, get yourself nice and comfy, that's right. Poor little soul, are you feeling better now?' And when Ebony started chasing one of her new jingly balls across the floor, batting it with her paw and pouncing after it with her tail twitching, Nana positively shrieked with delight. 'Ah, Sam! She *must* be feeling happier, mustn't she?'

I had to agree. Up till then she'd been too poorly, and far too timid, to indulge in that sort of spontaneous play. It was lovely to see. Becoming ever more hopeful of a positive outcome for Project Ebony, I showed Nana how to bathe her bad eye, how to brush her poor thin coat and check that her mouth wasn't sore from where Mr Fulcher had removed a couple of bad teeth. Ebony seemed to relax when Nana held her and didn't struggle so much while these ministrations were carried out. When I woke up on the Sunday morning, I could hear Nana talking to Ebony in the kitchen, to which the little cat answered with squeaky-voiced meows. The two of them definitely seemed to be developing a rapport.

I decided to make myself useful by cleaning the windows upstairs and, when I came back down, it was to find her sitting in the lounge, stroking Ebony with one hand and holding her framed photo of Granddad in the other.

'He was a good man, was my Bert,' she was telling the little cat, who was looking back at her with big eyes as if she understood every word. 'If he was here now, d'you know what he'd be saying? "Pull yourself together, you daft old bat!" But ...' And at this point she put down the picture and wiped her eyes with her apron. 'But it's really hard, you see, when you lose someone you love so much, and then when my poor old Rufus went too, well – Oh! Sam!' She jumped, and Ebony flew off her lap in fright. 'I didn't see you there. I was just chatting to the little cat, trying to cheer her up a bit, you know ...'

'I know.' I ran to put my arms round her. I felt so bad for trying to convince myself Nana wasn't really too sad or lonely. Of course she was. I couldn't bring back my granddad, or Rufus, but I'd do anything I could to make her feel better. I picked up the framed photo and gazed at it with her. 'Granddad was such a lovely man, wasn't he? You must miss him so much.'

'But he wouldn't want me being like this, Sam. Silly and emotional. It doesn't help,' she said crossly. 'You know what he used to say, if ever I was feeling sad about anything?'

'No?'

'Get your hat on, woman, we're going to the Horse!'

I smiled at her. 'So maybe we should do that right now. It's nearly lunchtime. Come on: get your hat on, then!' I knew she'd feel better for chatting to some of her friends at the pub. But I was all too aware that, if I hadn't been there to encourage her, she wouldn't have bothered.

The pub was packed with people, but luckily, thanks to Nana's ways, we had managed to secure our favourite spot by the window. While I was at the bar getting our drinks, I felt a blast of cold air behind me as the door flew open and I turned to see an excited Jack Russell terrier and a beagle rushing in, pulling David the dog-walker behind them.

'Apollo! Brian!' he yelled.

A couple of people sniggered.

'He doesn't have any control over them dogs whatsoever,' Suzie the barmaid muttered.

I felt a flash of sympathy for poor David, who had now joined me at the bar, red-faced, and was asking for a bowl of water for the panting dogs.

'Not Tess and Mabel today, then?' I asked him, and he told me that these two were his *weekend* dogs, and that they were usually better behaved than his other two charges.

He'd looked surprised and pleased to see me, and I had to explain again that I was only there for the bank holiday. While he waited for Suzie to pour him a beer, he told me he had a bit of gossip for me.

'Daisy-May, at the vets, has decided to retire.' He gave me a meaningful look. 'I reckon she's had enough of our *mutual friend.*'

'I don't blame her,' I said with feeling, remembering Joe Bradley's attitude when I met him at the petrol station. 'He must be the most difficult person I could imagine to work for. Good for Daisy-May, I could tell she was getting stressed out by the job.'

'Yes.' He nodded. 'Everybody around here is saying the same thing. He seems to upset everyone he talks to.'

I wanted to agree with him, although when I looked back at Nana, I couldn't help remembering how kind and gentle Joe had been to her when Rufus died. But no, I wasn't going to allow myself those sorts of thoughts about him. Look where they'd led me before – feeling like a complete idiot!

'I'd better get back to Nana,' I told David. 'She's been feeling a bit down.'

'Of course. Sorry you're not staying for longer, Sam,' he added.

'I daresay I'll be back again soon,' I said as I turned away. I'd be wanting to come back and check on Nana again before too long. Whether she kept Ebony or not.

And in fact, when we came home from the pub, Ebony helped to make the decision for her.

'She's not in her bed,' Nana said, looking around the kitchen. 'Oh, Sam! I forgot to shut her in the kitchen this time, when we went out.'

'She'll just be in the lounge, asleep in your chair,' I said.

But she wasn't. She wasn't lying in the sunshine on the windowsill, or chasing her ball under the table. The cottage was very quiet.

'Ebony!' Nana called in a quavering voice. 'Where are you? Oh God, Sam, please don't tell me she ran out of the front door when we opened it – you know how long I take getting up the dratted steps.'

'No, we'd have seen her,' I tried to soothe her. 'She's probably upstairs.'

'She doesn't *go* upstairs!'

'There's a first time for everything. Ssh, stop talking for a minute and just listen,' I said, trying to sound calmer than I felt. 'Ebony!' I called.

Sure enough, there was a squeaky little answering cry.

'Yep, she's hiding upstairs somewhere,' I said. 'She was probably scared when she heard us open the door, so she scarpered. I'll go and bring her down.'

'Oh, Sam, thank goodness she's safe,' Nana said when I'd retrieved Ebony from where she'd been hiding behind the bedroom door and put her in her arms. Her voice was shaking. 'I'd never forgive myself if she ran off and got lost again. I've got quite fond of the poor little thing.'

I smiled. 'If we were to get her microchipped, you'd be able to let her out after a while – for a few minutes at a time, till she got used to the area. I mean, you could, if she lived here permanently,' I added quickly.

'If she lived here permanently?' She gave me a funny look. 'I thought you were taking her back with you tomorrow.'

'I don't *have* to. I told you, didn't I – she's going to the shelter. For re-homing.' I paused, watching the expression change on Nana's face. 'But if someone were to offer her a home right now, she wouldn't have to go ...'

'"Someone"?' Nana said, trying to sound indignant. Then she laughed. 'You know damn well I'd miss her now if you took her away to the dratted shelter. Poor little thing needs a proper home,' she said, as the cat began to purr in her arms. 'Of course I'll keep her. You knew I would! Crafty little moo – I knew you had this planned all along.'

'Well, I couldn't plan for you to fall in love with her. That bit was up to you. But I must admit I *was* hoping. I love her myself, but I can't take her. I know you'll give her the best home she could wish for.' I hugged her. 'I'm so pleased you want to keep her.'

'She needs someone, that's for sure, poor little mite.'

And so do you, I thought. But of course, I knew better than to say that. I didn't want to push my luck!

That evening, as Ebony dozed on Nana's lap as usual, her ears twitching as she snored with gentle little grunts, we talked some more about my life in London and how I imagined things might work out for me. I think Nana was trying to reassure me, but the more we talked, the more depressed I felt about going back.

'To be honest,' I said eventually, with a sigh, 'I just wish I could give it all up – my flat, my job, my whole life in London, and move ... somewhere like this. Somewhere quiet and friendly, to bring up my baby. But I know that's just make-believe. Escapism.' I remembered what Adam had called it, and I added sadly, 'A silly roses-round-the-door fantasy.'

'Why?'

I laughed. 'Well, for a start I'd have to find somewhere to live. And just as important, I'd need to *work*.'

'Don't be daft. My spare room's big enough to put a cot in, isn't it? What more do you need? And I thought you said your mum and dad were going to help you financially?'

I looked up in surprise. 'You're suggesting I move in with you?'

'Not if you don't want to, of course,' she replied slightly grumpily. 'I'm only your grandmother; it's nothing to do with me. I suppose you're too independent, what with your London flat-share and all—'

'No! I don't even *like* the flat any more, and London, well, it was great when I first moved there, but now, it's just not really what I want. It's one of the things Adam and I argued about.'

'So what's stopping you? You love your job, I suppose.'

'I'd miss my favourite clients and their pets, of course, and I'd miss Claire, but other than that, well, I've been feeling for a while that I needed a change. But Nana, I know I'm going to need Mum and Dad's help and I'm grateful for it, but I don't want to be dependent on them any more than I can help.'

'Course you don't. But you'll get a job sooner or later won't you, and meanwhile you'll be saving on your rent, and your fares on the dratted Tube trains, and your mum and dad can afford to help out, so let them! It'll be their grandchild!'

'That's what Mum said too. I think she was just relieved I didn't want to move back in with them.'

Nana laughed. 'I can imagine! Well, I'm not going to try to talk you into anything. I'm saying nothing, I'm only your—'

'—grandmother!' I finished for her, laughing.

'Exactly, and you're not to worry about me, if that's what you're thinking. I've loved having you here, but I've got company now, thanks to you.' She nodded at the sleeping cat on her lap. 'But think about it. That room upstairs is yours, whenever you want it. I wouldn't want any rent from you or any nonsense like that. Just some help with the shopping, perhaps. And Hope Green is a lovely place to bring up children.'

I knew that. And Nana's offer was a complete surprise, but I had to admit I was very tempted. I thanked her and said I'd think about it and went to bed with my head buzzing. I tossed and turned all night, trying not to imagine a cot next to the bed, baby clothes in the chest of drawers, a chair by the window where I could sit, for the endless night feeds I'd heard all about from Claire. Could I *really* move in here? Make a life here for myself and my baby in Hope Green? If I was honest … I couldn't actually remember the last time I'd felt so excited by anything.

CHAPTER TWELVE

Claire thought I was being too impulsive. She was so shocked by my decision, she was nearly in tears. It was hard, knowing I wouldn't be working with her any more, and I knew she was worried about me. But I couldn't let myself waver. If I started thinking about the people I'd miss, I might change my mind – and I didn't want to. Claire and I would keep in touch, and when I reminded her how long I'd been feeling unsettled and explained that Nana needed help and company now, she could see where I was coming from.

Mum was equally gobsmacked. But without either of us actually saying so, we both understood that it would be a huge weight off her mind to know I was keeping Nana company and looking after her. She was obviously concerned that I was giving up my job without having a new one. But as the holiday season was approaching, I'd look for a hotel receptionist post in one of the nearby seaside resorts. And if I didn't find anything else there was always the Old Black Horse or the village shop which would both need temporary summer staff.

I handed in my notice straight away. Now it was all settled, I didn't want to waste any time. The time spent in London just seemed to intensify my longing for a new life in Hope Green. It seemed to be calling me back, and Nana was bubbling with excitement, telling me how pleased all her friends in the village were about me moving in, and how much she and Ebony were looking forward to it.

'I keep telling her: "Little Sam's coming back!"' she said happily. 'And she puts her head on one side and purrs at me, Sam! It's like she knows exactly what I'm saying.'

I couldn't wait to see the little cat again. I was missing her almost as much as I missed Nana. Everything seemed to be falling into place. My landlord happened to have a niece who wanted a room, so he was happy to take a fairly short notice from me. And the practice manager at the vet clinic had deducted some notice in lieu of holiday I hadn't used, so it looked like I'd be able to make the move quite quickly. The only person who'd been really negative, not to say sarcastic, about my news was Adam. But his (so predictable) comment that I was finally getting my little country cottage fantasy out of my system just made me laugh.

'Well, good luck, then, let me know how it goes,' he'd said, not sounding particularly sincere. I was sad to think that he wasn't even a little bit interested in the baby. I wondered if he'd change his mind and regret it later. I decided I'd make a point of emailing him updates and pictures of the scans, but other than that I thought it was unlikely we'd be in touch again until I had the baby. The thought didn't bother me. I had too much else on my mind.

During my remaining time at James Street, I spent my lunch breaks on job websites. Looking back, I can't imagine how I failed to realise what later became blindingly obvious. I was so focused on the presumption that I'd have to settle – at least in the short term – for hotel work or something similar, it didn't even cross my mind to look for anything else. And then, one day as I scrolled down the lists of temporary vacancies being offered by yet another Dorset-based employment agency, Mr Fulcher paused as he passed me.

'No luck yet?' he asked.

I shook my head. 'There seem to be at least fifty people going after every vacancy – even for temporary summer jobs.'

'You don't want to stay in this same line of work, then?'

'I didn't think there'd be much chance of that, at such short notice. These jobs are so popular, aren't they – they get snapped up ...'

'Well, have a look at one of the vet staff job sites, if you haven't already,' Mr Fulcher suggested. 'I'll obviously write you a good reference.'

And then it suddenly came back to me. Daisy-May was retiring. Had I deliberately blanked that out of my mind? Well, let's face it, I'd rather work for the rest of my life in a dead-end, low-paid, no-prospects job than put up with *that* particular person as a boss! But to stay working in a vets was too big an opportunity to pass up …

If I'm honest, I was kind of hoping that, when I looked at the website, the Hope Green vacancy might have already been filled. But no, there it was, glaring back at me, the proposed salary naturally lower than mine in London, but higher than the hotel jobs I'd been applying for. I knew that anyone in my position with an ounce of sense would be rushing off their application and praying with all their might that they'd get the job. Anyone who didn't know Joe Bradley, that is.

I sat for several minutes thinking about it. OK, I had to go for it, didn't I? The timing was perfect and I was ideally qualified for it. It would be immature of me to ignore the opportunity because of what amounted to … a personality clash. *Stop being such a wimp, Sam*, I thought to myself. *What's the worst that could happen?* I might not even get an interview – Joe Bradley didn't seem to like me any more than I liked him. He'd probably be horrified to see my name on the application. Well, I'd email it off now, and then put it out of my mind. And keep hoping something else would turn up.

Of course, nothing else did. And on my very last day in London, there was an email from the recruitment company, offering me an interview the following week. Nana was full of excitement when I told her.

'What a stroke of luck! Just when you needed it! Silly me, I forgot Daisy-May was retiring, or I'd have put you forward for the job myself.'

'I'm not even sure I want it,' I said. But she didn't hear me.

When I arrived at Meadow Croft cottage, the car full to the brim with my belongings and a bright smile on my face, I was greeted with a gratifying display of purring and tail waving from Ebony and the aroma of Nana's usual freshly baked cake emanating from the kitchen. I could see straight away that the little cat was already looking more healthy and energetic. And after lots of hugs and cuddles with both her and Nana, I started carrying my stuff in from the car. I was just struggling to get through the door with a box full of extra kitchenware that I knew Nana would never use, when David passed by with Mabel and Tess.

'Good to hear you're back to stay this time,' he called out cheerfully, adding, 'That looks heavy. Can I help?'

'No, you've got your hands full with the dogs. I'm OK, honestly – that's the last one.' I put the box down just inside the front door and pulled the door closed behind me. 'Got to keep the door shut – can't let Ebony escape.'

'Oh, yes, your nan's little cat. Is she still not allowed out?'

'I'm taking her to be microchipped tomorrow, then we're going to start letting her out. I wanted Nana to wait till I was here. She's panicking a bit about the thought of losing her.'

'Of course. Understandable, in the circumstances, her having been a stray, I mean.' He smiled. 'I've got a cat myself, did I tell you? So I know how worrying it is if they disappear. Good idea to get her microchipped, just in case.' He pulled a face. 'Pity it means you have to face our miserable vet, though.'

'Yes.' I hesitated. 'Although, as it happens ...' And I explained about the job interview, wondering if he'd tell me I must be raving mad to consider it. But he was apparently far too tactful.

'Well, good luck, then. It'd be really convenient, wouldn't it? If you get the job. I'd see you when I have to bring KitKat in for his vaccinations—'

'KitKat?' I asked, laughing.

He shrugged, looking a little embarrassed. 'I couldn't think of a name when I first got him, so I started calling him that as a kind of nickname, and, well, it stuck. He seems to like it,' he added.

'That's a good enough reason to call him it,' I agreed.

The dogs were straining on their leads by now and I needed to go in and get on with my unpacking.

'See you soon, Sam,' he said, and then stopped suddenly and added, 'Look, if you ever fancied joining me on a dog walk, you'd be very welcome. I do a couple of evening walks for the Crowthers – they're always working late – and I walk the beagle and the Jack Russell every weekend.'

'Oh, thanks. Yes, I'd like that,' I said.

We arranged that he'd call for me on the Saturday morning, and I was smiling to myself as I went back indoors. I'd been resident at Hope Green for less than an hour and already I'd got a play date with a friend and two dogs! It was so nice to have met somebody I could have a laugh with, someone fun and uncomplicated who seemed to enjoy the same things as I did – walking, and animals, and generally not taking life too seriously. I was already looking forward to seeing him again on Saturday.

The following day, with Ebony in her new carrying basket, I walked down the road to the vets. It was a beautiful morning, with apple trees laden with blossom in people's gardens, the clematis in full bloom climbing up the wall of the pub. I breathed in the fragrant air as I passed the lilac bushes bordering the teashop's little patio and felt glad to be alive, glad to be out of London, away from the traffic fumes and, yes, the dratted Tube trains! But then I pushed open the door of the vets, and my good mood evaporated as I remembered just how unpleasant and arrogant Joe Bradley could be, and how embarrassing it had been to bump into him at the petrol station.

Daisy-May was busy on the phone, looking stressed out as usual, so I just waved at her to let her know I'd arrived, and didn't even have the time to sit down before Joe called me in. I was uncomfortably aware of the fact that he knew I'd be coming back for a job interview with him a few days later. I wondered if he would mention it, and couldn't help getting the feeling that he'd be assessing me even while I was here as a client, and finding me lacking in some way.

'I've brought Ebony in for microchipping,' I told him, doing my best to sound assertive.

'Ah, yes.' He raised his eyebrows at me. 'The little cat you left in your car at the petrol station.'

'It was only for a—'

'Few minutes, yes I know. And the car was locked. So no harm done,' he finished for me. *So why bring it up?* 'OK. Pop her up on the table for me, would you? She's a cute little thing, isn't she?' he added in his gentler voice that I had come to recognise.

He stroked the little cat's head as she tried to shrink away from his touch. I watched, suddenly aware of how strong and brown his hands were. Then he looked up at me and I flushed and looked away. The young nurse Natalie was handing him the microchip implanter and I concentrated on giving her the details for the register.

When it was time, I held Ebony still for Joe as he pinched the skin between her shoulder blades and swiftly inserted the microchip. 'It's all right,' I soothed her.

'Good girl, that's it, all done,' he said, stroking her again. 'You'd better not start letting her out yet, though,' he added. 'She hasn't been spayed. Would you like to book her in for that?'

'Oh – yes, I'd better. I don't want Nana to have the worry of a litter of kittens!'

'Good. She looks like she's already in better health. Your grandmother must have been looking after her well – and you, I suppose, now you're here,' he added grudgingly. He turned back to me, looking as if he was trying to force a smile. 'It's good that your grandmother's got a new companion, after losing her dog.'

'Oh, well,' I said, flustered. 'I'm just pleased to be here, to look after her and help her a bit.'

The smile disappeared.

'I meant the cat,' he said flatly, and turned away to update his computer.

I paid Daisy-May, booked an appointment for the operation and left feeling stupid, wondering why I let him get to me, wishing I didn't. Feeling in need of a friendly chat, I went over to the shop to see Izzie. She waved to me from the till as I headed in her direction.

'Fantastic news that you're here to stay!' she exclaimed. 'It's so nice to have someone new here. Most of the villagers – including my family – have been here since the year dot.'

'Well, my nan's been here since she and my granddad retired. And I've been coming for holidays every year. I just never seemed to meet you before.'

'So we've got lots to catch up on,' she laughed. 'And especially as you're going to be having a baby. When's it due?'

'December. I'm pretty nervous about it all,' I admitted. 'I'm not with the father any more.'

'Ah, who needs them, anyway? We can manage fine on our own, us girls.' She smiled at me. 'Seriously, you'll be all right. Everyone around here's so friendly and helpful, and I can give you loads of advice. If you want it, that is!'

Just as I was assuring her I needed every bit of advice I could get, we both turned to the sound of loud voices at the other end of the shop. Izzie raised her eyebrows at me.

'Someone else having a moan about Nora,' she whispered. 'Everyone's furious with her. She still hasn't done the hanging baskets. They should have been up long before now.'

'Oh no. For the Best-Kept Village competition? When's it being judged?'

'The judges start touring this month. In fact they might already have been round. Nobody knows: it's anonymous. But the final judging is during July and August.' She sighed and shook her head. 'It's mainly the older people who get so het up about it. But it's good in some ways, you know. It makes people think about litter, and keeping things trim and tidy. And the judging includes the school playground, the playing field, facilities for kids, all that kind of thing. It's not all about pretty flowers and stuff, but that's what some people focus on. Trouble is, Nora's always insisted on doing everyone's baskets, making them all the same. They do look good, I'll give her that. But this year, she's really let us down.'

I thought about this on the way home. Hanging baskets seemed such a funny thing for people to get worked up about. But on the other hand, if it she knew it was important to her friends and neighbours, why wasn't 'Miserable' Nora getting on with it? I could see already that life in a small village was going to be a lot more full of interest and intrigue than I'd imagined. And with Izzie as a friend, hopefully a lot of fun, too.

Things were looking up, and I couldn't wait to get more settled into my new life here.

CHAPTER THIRTEEN

I felt ridiculously nervous on the day of my interview at the vets – whether about the interview itself, or about facing Joe again, I wouldn't have liked to say. Daisy-May, at least, was pleased to see me.

'It's my last day today,' she said, sounding overwhelmingly relieved about it. 'I did warn Mr Bradley he needed to hurry up and hire a replacement, but he obviously won't have anyone in place in time now.' She gave me a smile that I think was meant to be encouraging and added, 'I hope you get the job, Sam. You'll be just what he needs – someone who can stand up to him.'

I wasn't at all sure about that, and it certainly didn't help to make me feel less nervous. When I sat down opposite him for the interview, he was already giving me one of his most disconcerting glares.

'You need to understand,' he began, 'that this is a very busy job.'

'I do. I do understand that, obviously,' I said, trying to swallow my annoyance. 'As you can see from my CV, I've been working in a very similar position for the past four years—'

'With respect, you haven't,' he interrupted. 'You've been working in what I gather is a posh clinic in a posh part of London where posh people bring their pampered pets.'

I resisted the temptation to congratulate him on his alliteration. He'd been practically spitting all the Ps at me across the desk.

'A very *busy* posh clinic,' I said. 'It was a very busy job.'

He leant back in his chair, still staring at me. I stared back. I was beginning to wonder why I'd bothered to turn up for the interview. I'd suspected all along that this would be a waste of time. Even in the unlikely event that I ended up being offered the job, I'd hate working for Joe Bradley as much as Daisy-May seemed to have done.

'Look, I'll be honest with you, Sam,' he said. 'It appears you do have *some* of the relevant experience for this position, which is more than I can say for any of the other applicants who've wasted my time. But what concerns me is that you've probably moved here from London expecting an easy life.'

'What?' I gasped. 'How could I possibly have given you that impression?'

'Common scenario. People want a break from city life; they think moving to a country village is going to be stress-free, that life here is slow and peaceful, an easy ride—'

'I certainly don't expect an easy ride,' I retorted. 'I'm prepared to work hard at *whatever* job I take on.'

'If you say so. But I have to warn you: this role isn't straightforward. It's evolving. There will be far more difficult duties than you've been used to, and frankly I'm not sure you'd be up to it.'

I'd started to think by now that nothing on earth could persuade me to work with him. But the condescending tone of his voice and the implication that I wasn't capable suddenly offended me so much, that against my better instincts I replied: 'Well I am *absolutely sure* I'd be up to it. And I presume you'd be able to give me a list of the duties that are so much more difficult than I've been used to? In case I need to study for extra qualifications?'

I was being sarcastic, of course, but he responded in a similar tone.

'Certainly, if you really need it. The list will be a short one, but I'm still not convinced you'd cope with it. The extra duties will involve a certain amount of contact with the animals.'

'Oh!' I didn't see *that* coming.

'I only have two nurses here. They work shifts, usually one on and one off. But there are occasions, unfortunately, when they can't seem to organise themselves much better than my current brain-cell-challenged receptionist can and I end up with neither of them here. So I want the new receptionist to be able and willing to lend an extra pair of hands from time to time.' He looked me up and down. 'I doubt you'd be prepared to do that, so—'

'Yes, I would! I'd love it!' I said quickly.

But instead of seeming pleased, he just raised his eyes and sighed. 'It's not just pampered pets around here. It won't be all about stroking cute kittens.'

'I wasn't expecting—'

'This is a country practice. We treat farm animals too. And I might need help in an emergency: assisting at surgery; passing me instruments; helping me hold an animal that's in pain, distressed, bleeding, dying; dealing with bloody swabs and bandages; clearing up vomit and faeces.' It was almost as if he was trying his hardest to put me off. Or was it a test? He was watching me for a reaction, but I didn't flinch. 'So to be honest, I should probably just hire another nurse instead,' he went on, picking up my application form, looking like he was going to put it to one side.

'But that'll be more expensive. And you don't really need three nurses. And you still won't have a receptionist,' I pointed out. 'Whereas I can do exactly what you need.'

What was *wrong* with me? I'd already decided I didn't want to work for him – hadn't I? But ... if I could only manage to ignore *him*, wouldn't it be just the sort of job I'd always wanted?

'That's what you think, is it?' he said, looking up at me now and meeting my eyes, the challenge in his own quite clear. 'You think you're capable? You wouldn't start crying over dead calves or squealing about a bit of blood?'

'I'm not squeamish, if that's what you're suggesting. To be honest I doubt you'd find anyone else more suitable.

As you'll see from my CV, I've got a City & Guilds certificate in animal care too.'

'Oh have you. Well, I'd better let the animals know about that.'

I couldn't tell any more whether he was being nasty or just trying to be funny. It didn't matter, though, because I was suddenly completely certain that I wanted the job. Daisy-May was right. I could learn to cope with his attitude, his rudeness. I would. I could do it.

'So when could you start – if I were to offer you the job?' he went on, looking down at his desk again.

'As soon as you like. Monday?'

'I'd better see you on Monday, then, as you seem to have appointed yourself, and I'll just hope you're not totally useless. You'll have a three-month probation period to start with,' he said, dismissing me. 'Start at eight-thirty sharp.'

It seemed I had a new job. I was just hoping I wasn't going to regret it!

I told David about the job when I had my first walk with him on Saturday morning, accompanied by Brian the beagle and Apollo the Jack Russell. And despite his apparent dislike of Joe Bradley, he was nice enough to congratulate me and wish me well.

It was another fine day, sunny but breezy, and we kept up a brisk pace through the meadow and along the path that led to the coast where, because the tide was out and there were no picnickers to disturb, we let the dogs have an ecstatic gambol on the beach before heading back to the village again.

'Poor Brian will be shattered. He's only got little legs,' I pointed out, making David laugh.

We'd done a lot of laughing during the walk, and a lot of chatting. I'd told him about my situation, and it turned out that he, too, was single following the break-up of a serious relationship, although in his case it had ended more than a year before. And of course, we talked about our cats.

'You must come and meet Ebony,' I told him. 'She's so sweet. She was very neglected and nervous, but she's settled down really well.'

'I'd love to,' he responded warmly.

And to prove he meant it, he came round the very next day and made such a fuss of Ebony, she not only sat purring on his lap but climbed up his chest and draped herself around his neck. He made a fuss of Nana, too, complimenting her on her ginger cake and offering to help her with shopping if ever she needed anything while I was working.

'I'll tidy up the garden for you, too, if you like,' he suggested, looking out at the little rough overgrown plot at the back of the cottage. 'I don't think Sam ought to be doing any heavy work – well, not just now,' he added quickly as I started to protest. 'I like gardening, as it happens, and I've only got a tiny little backyard in the place I'm renting at the moment.'

'I wouldn't put it about too much that you like gardening, or you might find yourself in demand right now,' Nana said. 'Have you heard about Nora?'

David shook his head, so I explained that everyone was annoyed that she hadn't done the hanging baskets.

'Oh, but you haven't heard the latest, Sam,' Nana said, looking serious now. 'Irene next door knocked earlier and told me. Nora hasn't done the baskets because she's ill.'

'She's had long enough, though, hasn't she? And apparently she's taken people's money.'

'She was waiting for test results, Sam.' Nana sighed. 'I know she's not everyone's favourite person, but the fact is, the poor woman's got cancer.'

'Oh no! Poor thing, that's awful.' I immediately felt terrible for being so heartless.

'Yes. She kept it quiet until she knew for sure. She's got to have chemotherapy, and what with all the worry about it … well, the baskets haven't been uppermost in her mind. She'll be paying back everyone's money. But we won't have hanging baskets this year now. It's too late, unless people just do their own.'

'I'll do one for you, Peggy,' David said at once. 'And your neighbour, if she likes. I could do them to match. I'd enjoy it.'

'I'll help you, then,' I offered. I'd never planted anything in a basket in my entire life, but how hard could it be?

Needless to say, Nana was smitten by David, making several comments after he'd left about how charming he was, how helpful and what lovely manners he had. 'Nice-looking, too, wouldn't you say?' she added with a twinkle in her eyes.

'Yes. He's nice,' I agreed without thinking too much about it.

At least – unlike a certain other person – he didn't make me feel cross, embarrassed or just downright confused.

However, despite my misgivings about working with Joe Bradley, my new job started well. Joe was his usual brusque and impatient self, apart from when he was dealing with the animals. By the end of the first day, I was fairly sure it wasn't just me who thought he had some kind of split personality. The young nurse Natalie admitted to me quietly, after he'd snapped at her for no apparent reason, that he used to make her cry when she first started working for him.

'But actually, you know, he's really lovely when he's not in a bad mood,' she added, giving me a secret little smile. The poor girl had it bad. I wondered if she knew he was married.

My first opportunity to help him with a patient came sooner than I expected – during that first week, when Natalie had to leave early for a dentist's appointment.

'I shouldn't have let her go,' Joe said crossly. 'She should have made the appointment half an hour later, then Val would be here to take over.' Val was the other nurse, an older, no-nonsense woman who merely raised her eyes and shook her head when Joe had one of his snaps.

'But it was an emergency,' I reminded him quietly. 'She's had a terrible toothache. This was the only time the dentist could fit her in.'

'We all have our problems,' he retorted, and I wondered how on earth he could be so unsympathetic to human ailments at the same time as being so kind with animal ones.

He'd told me the patient he needed my help with was a cat being brought in for vaccination.

'I've only treated this cat once before,' he explained. 'He needed an antibiotic shot and he fought me like a thing possessed. His owner couldn't help because he has needle phobia.' He shook his head as if the phobia was blatant stupidity on the part of the owner.

'Oh dear,' I said. 'That's unfortunate.'

'Yes. Luckily Val was here on that occasion to hold the cat still. You'll have to do it today. We'll wear gloves.'

I found it hard to believe a little cat was really going to be such a problem, and when I looked at the appointment details on the computer, I nearly gasped out loud in surprise. It couldn't be a coincidence. Surely there couldn't be more than one cat in the village called KitKat!

'Hello again!' David said cheerfully when he arrived in the waiting room. 'How are you settling in?'

'Well, thank you.' I smiled at him. 'And I see you've brought KitKat for his vaccinations.'

'Yes. Um – the only trouble is, I know it sounds daft, but I can't go into the room with him.'

'I know. Mr Bradley's just explained about your … difficulty.' I tried to suppress my smile.

'It's a real nuisance, but, well, I'd be no use to anyone if I passed out in a heap on the floor.'

'Don't worry. The nurse isn't here, so I'm going to help Mr Bradley myself. Hello, KitKat.' I crooned at the cat through the bars of his carrying cage. He was a large, long-haired black and white moggy and he was growling loudly in fear.

'He's normally a big lovable softie,' David said. 'But when I bring him through the door of this place, he undergoes a personality change.'

'That's perfectly understandable,' I said. 'Most animals are nervous at the vets.'

But even so, I had to admit KitKat was in a league of his own. As soon as I opened the cage to take him out, he backed into the corner of it, his back arched, hissing and spitting at me.

'Come on, sweetie,' I said, 'we're not going to hurt you.'

'You're going to need to be firmer,' Joe said. 'Look.' And he reached into the cage himself, grasping the cat quickly and efficiently and putting him on to the table. KitKat was yowling loudly in protest, tossing his head from side to side trying to bite Joe's arms. 'OK, hold his head very firmly with one hand and hold his back down with the other,' he told me. 'Got him?'

'Yes.' It was a struggle, but I was determined not to annoy Joe by letting the first animal I'd helped him with get the better of me.

'OK. Here goes. Don't let him wriggle.' He administered the vaccine smoothly and quickly and KitKat gave a further snarl of anger before I carefully lifted him back into the cage. 'Thank you,' Joe said. 'Well done – easy with two of us. Not so much fun trying to jab an angry cat like this on my own.'

'I can imagine. And his owner says he's docile and lovable at home!'

'Is that right?' Joe looked at KitKat through the bars of the cage. 'It's just us that you show your nasty side to, is it, boy?' he said gently. 'Well, maybe you're needle-phobic like your owner!'

He smirked as he said this, and I reacted a little sharply in David's defence: 'Needle phobia must be quite horrible, don't you think?'

'I suppose so. It's understandable in children, I guess, but in adults? Really?'

'David might have had a nasty experience that left him nervous of it happening again,' I said.

'Oh, *David*, is it?' Joe raised his eyebrows at me. 'Friend of yours, is he?'

'As it happens, yes.' I didn't bother to explain that actually I was only just getting to know him. 'He's a nice guy. Walks dogs for people in the village.'

'Yes, I know. Pity he can't seem to keep them under control. Well, go on, then, take *David* his cat back, then, and sort out his payment. I don't think I'll need you for the next patient, and hopefully Val will be here soon.'

I was dismissed, and the mood seemed to have changed between us again.

'All done – he's fine,' I told David.

'Thanks, Sam. I hope he wasn't too much trouble?'

'Not at all.' I smiled.

Just as I was taking his payment, Joe came back out into the waiting room to see whether the next patient was here. David gave me a friendly nod and said, 'See you later, then, Sam. I'll pick you up after work.' We'd arranged to go out together to buy plants for the hanging baskets. 'And you must come and see KitKat at home some time. I want to prove to you that he's actually a nice, friendly cat most of the time!'

'I'll take you up on that,' I said, laughing.

With a glare at us both, Joe turned and strode back into the consulting room, shutting the door with a bang.

David raised his eyebrows at me and shrugged. 'He doesn't like me,' he said. 'And the feeling's mutual.'

I'd already gathered that. I was too busy to ask him about it right then, but frankly I couldn't understand why anyone would take a dislike to David; he was so friendly and easy-going. Which was certainly more than I could say for Joe Bradley.

CHAPTER FOURTEEN

The following Saturday morning, as David and I walked the dogs again, we bumped into Izzie, who was pushing the baby in her buggy and shepherding the other two children along beside her. The toddler was crying about some imagined insult and I bent down to chat to her, smiling when she rewarded me by stopping her fussing with a hiccup of surprise. Izzie told us she had the day off and was on her way to a children's fun day at the church hall.

'It's a fundraising event for the preschool,' she told us, going on to explain that the preschool was a privately run business, with a committee of parent volunteers helping to support it. 'There are so few of us parents now that we're nearly all on the committee,' she said. 'It's running on a shoestring at the moment. They're starting a playgroup for mums with babies and toddlers now, to run alongside the preschool, although there aren't too many of those in the village either.'

'I hope it goes well today, then,' I said, adding that I'd be one extra mum for the playgroup after December. She laughed and said she certainly hoped so. I realised I was looking forward to it – to getting more involved with Izzie and the other young parents in the village. Even if there weren't enough of them!

There was some real warmth in the sunshine now, and the village was slowly beginning to resemble the one I was used to from coming here for my summer holidays every year. People were out in their front gardens, calling out hello to us as we passed. The first few holidaymakers were making the trek along the coast from the nearby resorts, and the pub and tearooms both had their tables outside, ready for al fresco lunches and snacks. It was definitely time we started letting Ebony out into the garden. She'd recovered well from her operation, but Nana was nervous about the little cat getting lost, or being picked on by some of the bigger cats in the village.

I tried to persuade her when David and I arrived back in the cottage to find her watching Ebony walking back and forth on the kitchen windowsill, meowing at birds in the garden. 'She's getting restless, Nana. If we don't let her out, she'll just make a break for it out of a window one day. And she's got her microchip in now. Let's do it today while I'm home and we can both watch her. I bet she doesn't go far the first time.'

David and I had already planned to be in the garden anyway, planting the baskets for Nana and Irene next door. So I carried Ebony outside with us, put her down on the grass and we both stood back, Nana right behind us, watching anxiously as the little cat looked hesitantly around. She lifted her head up as if to sniff the air, flicked her tail back and forth a few times and then bounded off into a flowerbed where she crouched under a shrub, peering out through the branches. We all laughed.

'What did I tell you?' I said to Nana. 'She's too nervous to run straight off. She's got to get her bearings, check out the territory and make sure she's safe.'

'She'll want to go further afield and explore the area before long, though,' David warned. He smiled at Nana. 'I could put a cat flap in the kitchen door for you, if you like. You can lock it at night, or whenever you want to keep her in.'

While David and I worked on the baskets, Nana sat on her garden bench in the sun, watching Ebony creeping from one shrub to the next, looking around her, lifting her head to check out the sounds and scents of the garden. As soon as we'd finished the planting, David helped me clean the garden chairs ready for the summer. Nothing seemed too much trouble for him. He'd already mowed the lawn and put up shelves in Nana's little garden shed, and she'd repaid him with countless cups of coffee and home-made cakes. I wondered again what on earth Joe Bradley could have against him. While we worked on the chairs, I asked him to tell me what had happened between them.

'Oh, it all started when we had an argument about Tess and Mabel.'

'The Crowthers' dogs? Why? What happened?'

'He bumped into me one day when I was walking them along the road here. Much the same way as you did,' he added with a grin, 'but, well, he was in a hurry, he wasn't looking where he was going and he tripped over one of their leads.'

I stifled a giggle. It wasn't altogether surprising, the way Tess and Mabel dragged David along.

'Did he hurt himself?' I asked.

'No. He stumbled and nearly fell, but he just brushed himself down, swore out loud and scowled like this.' He did such a superb imitation of Joe's scowl that I burst out laughing. 'And he proceeded to tell me that if I couldn't keep the dogs under control I shouldn't be allowed out with them. I didn't even know who he was at that point – he'd only just moved here, apparently. I said it was his own fault he'd tripped over – he should've been looking where he was going – and he came back at me with a load of abuse about me not being fit to own dogs. So I explained they weren't even mine, but that just seemed to make things worse. Anyway, when he finally shut up, I told him he ought to have anger-management therapy.'

'Oh my God! I can imagine how that went down!'

'Quite. And then, of course, I heard people in the village talking about the new vet, saying he seemed a bit grumpy and impatient. And I had to take poor KitKat to see him because he had an infected scratch from a cat fight – and it turned out he needed an antibiotic shot. So Joe got his own back by being obnoxiously scathing about my needle phobia. He's just a thoroughly unpleasant man, if you want my opinion.'

'I agree.' I sympathised. 'And if it's any comfort, it's not just you. It seems he's horrible to everyone. I feel sorry for his poor wife and daughter.'

David raised his eyebrows. 'Didn't know he was married.'

'Me neither, till he snapped at me for daring to ask. Maybe it's a really unhappy marriage.'

This hadn't actually occurred to me until I voiced it, but now, the more I thought about it, the more sense it made. Perhaps it was his wife making him so bloody miserable and bad-tempered. Maybe she'd gone off him – you couldn't blame her! – and they were only staying together because of the child. Perhaps he wasn't getting any action in the bedroom department. *Stop it, Sam*! I chuckled to myself, and then felt silly and flustered when David asked me what was funny. Then, to make things worse, I had a sudden memory of Joe's hands when he was holding Ebony – how strong they looked, how gentle they were – and I had to give myself a little shake. I turned away, looking for Ebony, and changed the subject.

By now she had become far more confident, darting in and out of the flowerbeds, chasing the odd beetle and leaping up into the air after passing flies. She was certainly enjoying her first taste of freedom. She was a healthy-looking cat now, with a sleek glossy coat and bright eyes. It was hard to remember how poorly she'd been just a short while ago. She suddenly came running back towards us and scurried around, chasing a piece of greenery that

I'd dropped while I was planting the flowers, batting it across the patio and pouncing on it, her eyes wide with excitement. I sat back on my heels, laughing out loud with pleasure. It was just so lovely to see her enjoying life at last – more than I could ever have wished for when I'd taken such a chance in bringing her here from James Street vets. I wasn't the only one who was benefiting hugely from a move to the countryside! All my fervent hopes for her had been realised: she'd turned out to be the lucky black cat, the one who found a perfect forever home, and I couldn't have been happier.

I hoped the same would work out for me, and that when the baby came in December, it would be equally happy.

After lunch, David and I went out to the front of the cottage to hang the baskets up for Nana and her neighbour. Irene Parks was just thanking us and saying how pretty they looked when Maggie Stammers walked past on her way to the shop. She stopped and stared in surprise. 'Nora hasn't managed to do them after all, has she?'

'No. Sam and David have. Don't they look lovely?' Irene said.

'They certainly do.' Maggie glanced at us hesitantly. 'I don't suppose you'd be up for doing a couple more, would you? I'd pay you,' she added quickly. 'I've got my money back from poor old Nora, so I'd give you the same. And I bet other people will ask you, too, when they see these. Especially if you can get them done before the competition judging.'

David hesitated. 'Well, Sam's at work all week, but I suppose I've got enough time,' he said.

I nodded. 'Go for it, David. I wasn't much use anyway, but I'll help out at weekends if you do get other people asking.'

And so the deal was struck, and sure enough, within a few days David had a list of orders from around the village. I was pleased for him: he admitted it was helping to fill his days between the dog-walking and the bits of work he had from his few copywriting clients. Hope Green began to look prettier than ever with cascading bright blooms of geraniums, petunias, salvia and lobelia decorating the outside walls of the pastel-coloured cottage. I knew he wasn't charging the villagers much for his time and that endeared him to them even more. 'Such a nice chap, that David', was the general theme among the older ladies as they chatted on the street corners and outside the shop.

We walked the dogs together regularly, and I was loving spending time outdoors in the countryside after so long with only the London parks to walk in. One evening, David came to meet me from work with a collie in tow, and Joe, who'd been talking to me quite civilly about a pet rabbit he'd be treating the next morning for a dental abscess, afforded him only a muttered and scowling 'Hi' before retreating rudely to his consulting room.

'Take no notice of Jekyll and Hyde,' I said, aware of David stiffening with annoyance beside me. 'He's not worth getting upset about. I should know, I have to work with him all day—'

'God knows how!'

He was right, of course. To be honest, I wasn't sure myself how I was managing it – sometimes Joe's rudeness and abruptness made me want to walk out. Occasionally, though, when I was actually driven to answer him back, it seemed to stop him in his tracks, as if he hadn't even realised how unpleasant he was being. Not that he ever apologised. But it was on those occasions that I noticed the sadness in his eyes, and my theory about his unhappy marriage was gaining ground in my mind.

'Professionally, though, I've got a lot of admiration for him,' I told David as we set off on our walk that evening. 'He's got an amazing way with the animals he treats. They all seem to trust him instinctively—'

'Apart from KitKat,' he reminded me.

'Well, yes, there's always an exception!' I laughed. I didn't tell him that there was also, despite his moods, something about Joe that I still, annoyingly, found very attractive. Anyway, since I'd found out he was married, I was ignoring that.

And blaming my hormones.

As my first few weeks as a resident of Hope Green passed, Nana seemed to be positively blooming with happiness, the shadow of her loss and sadness fading now that she had me to chat to, and cute little Ebony for company while I was at work. I was finding my new job interesting and stimulating; I loved seeing all the familiar folk from the village coming in with their pets, as well as local farmers calling about problems with their livestock. It was a huge bonus, too, being only a stone's throw from home. My early pregnancy nausea had finally eased off, and with all the walking and fresh air, I was feeling fit and healthy. The break-up with Adam was already losing its sting, and I'd found a lively and entertaining new friend in Izzie, who never failed to share the latest village gossip with me, as well as reassuring me, in her down-to-earth way, about being a single mum. However, one day our conversation took a completely unexpected turn.

'How's it going with the new man, then?' she asked with a cheeky grin.

'New man?' I repeated. 'What new man?'

'Come on, everyone's seen you out and about together! Walking the dogs, making hanging baskets for everyone, cuddling each other's cats and all that ...' She stopped, clocking my astonished expression. 'You and David,' she added, sounding less sure of herself. 'No?'

'No!' I said, horrified. 'God, Izzie, you mean to say everyone's *gossiping* about us?'

'Well, don't sound so surprised about it. You know what it's like around here. People put two and two together—'

'And make a dozen, by the sound of it! No, we are *not* an item, it's nothing like that! We're just friends, we just – you know, we like each other's company, and ...' I tailed off again. 'I don't feel that way about him, at all. He's ... well, I think of him like I do my older brothers.'

'And are you sure he's on the same page as you with that, then?' she said. 'Only I've seen him looking at you a couple of times and I have to say, it's not exactly the look of an older brother.'

'What? No, you're imagining it, you must be.'

'OK. Maybe I am,' she said lightly and quickly changed the subject.

I tried to put the conversation out of my mind, but that Sunday afternoon after David had been round, as promised, to fit a cat flap for Ebony and help to tidy the garden, Nana only had to comment, as usual, that he was 'such a nice young man' for me to demand what she meant by it.

'You do know that David and I are just friends, don't you,' I said a little sharply.

'Right. If you say so.'

'I *do* say so,' I retorted. 'Have I said anything to make you think otherwise?'

'It's not so much what *I* think. It's ... well, perhaps you should ask yourself what *he* thinks.'

I stared at her. 'Izzie said much the same thing the other day. Have people been gossiping about us?'

Nana looked away, coughing slightly, smoothing her hair, muttering about making a cup of tea.

'You've all got it wrong!' I said, heatedly. 'Apart from anything else, I can't believe you think I'd be interested in another relationship already, Nana! It's far too soon after Adam. I'm not sure if I'll ever want one, and certainly not until after I've had the baby.'

'All right, all right, keep your hair on. Sorry I spoke. I know I'm only your grandmother, it's nothing to do with me, I'm saying nothing. But I can't help noticing how much time you spend together. And how that young man looks at you.'

Had I really been so blind? Well, it wouldn't be fair to let him think I felt the same. I'd have to make it clear to him, and hope that it didn't ruin a lovely friendship. But as it happened, I didn't quite get that far before I had something far more serious to worry about. David had asked me round to his place one evening after I finished work to look at the latest flower baskets. When I'd finished admiring his work, he suggested we might have a quick drink together at the Horse. I decided that might give me a good opportunity to try to tackle the awkward talk we needed to have.

'Hang on, I'll just give KitKat his dinner, or he'll sulk all the time we're out,' he said cheerfully. I laughed. KitKat was, as David had said, a big softie when he wasn't at the vets. I went to the bathroom while David dished up his food.

But all thoughts of dinner left my mind by the time I returned to the kitchen. I called out to David with a trembling voice, and he spun round in surprise. 'What's wrong?' he asked, his voice full of concern.

I felt weak and had to sit down abruptly. Something wasn't right at all. 'I think I need to go to the hospital,' I said, suddenly feeling faint from the shock. 'I'm bleeding, David. I ... think I might be going to miscarry.'

'Oh my God. What – it's just happened, just like that?' he said, looking horrified.

'Yes! I ... don't know why – I've been feeling fine, I don't think anything's changed, but – oh, David, I'm sorry to ask you, but please can you get me to the hospital?'

And at that moment, I realised nothing else really mattered to me. Not whether David did, or didn't, like me as more than a friend. Not whether Adam would ever forgive me for finishing with him, or whether Joe was ever going to become less of an enigma and more easy to work with. None of them were as important to me as this baby. It hadn't even crossed my mind for a minute that anything could go wrong with the pregnancy and now that I was afraid it might, I was desperately, acutely aware that it would break my heart. I couldn't lose this baby. Anything but that. And as David helped me into his battered old car, frowning with anxiety and trying his best to soothe me, I found myself praying like mad – to a God I wasn't too sure about these days but who desperately hoped might listen anyway.

'Please, God!' I whispered, and David squeezed my hand before starting the car for the journey into town. 'Please, please don't let me lose this baby.'

Not when I'd only just realised how terribly much I wanted it.

PART 3

TOO CLOSE TO HOME

CHAPTER FIFTEEN

In the crowded waiting area at the hospital, sitting anxiously for what seemed like hours, I was rigid with tension, wondering if this was going to be the end of my pregnancy, the end of my dreams of motherhood. David kept a constant flow of gentle chat, hoping to stop me from getting stressed, but I couldn't pay attention to what he was saying and in the end he gave up and simply held my hand. It was the first time he'd done so, and because it was exactly the comfort I needed at that moment I forgot to worry about whether he might think of me as more than a friend.

Eventually I was called through to see a doctor, who took my history and symptoms.

'There are lots of reasons for bleeding in early pregnancy,' said the doctor, trying to reassure me. 'And very often, everything continues perfectly normally.'

'So you think it might be OK?' I said, hardly daring to believe what I was hearing.

'I think it will depend on how things go overnight,' he said. 'If the bleeding starts again and gets worse, with cramping pain, you'll need to come straight back. But in any case I'll arrange an appointment in the early pregnancy unit for you tomorrow morning. They'll give you a scan and all being well, that'll set your mind at rest.'

'Thank you.' I sighed. 'I'll just have to wait till tomorrow, then.'

'Yes. But try not to worry. I know it's hard, but you need to get some sleep if you can. Have you got someone with you to take you home?'

'Yes. My friend's waiting for me.'

David was still sitting where I'd left him in the waiting room, looking worried.

'I've got to come back tomorrow for a scan,' I said, swallowing back tears. 'But the doctor thinks it could still be OK.'

'Well, that's something. And it's good that they can do the scan so soon, isn't it?' He looked at me anxiously. 'You look exhausted. Come on, let's get you home.'

By the time we'd arrived back at the cottage and explained what had happened to Nana, I was feeling shattered and weak, and when David insisted that he'd pick me up to take me back to the hospital the next morning for my scan, I was too tired to argue.

I stumbled upstairs to bed, and the next thing I knew, the sun was streaming through the curtains and I was surprised to see it was already nearly nine o'clock.

Physically, I was feeling a lot better and even managed some breakfast, but by the time I was shown in for my scan, I was almost shaking with nerves.

'You are allowed to breathe,' the sonographer joked with me. 'In fact, we tend to prefer it.'

'Sorry.' I tried to smile. 'I'm a bit tense.'

'Well, you'll be pleased to know your baby appears to be absolutely fine,' he said. 'Look! He's turning somersaults in there!'

I stared at the screen. 'He?' I repeated. I felt my pulse quicken. The baby was a *he*?

'He or she.' The doctor chuckled. 'Sorry, it's too early to determine the sex yet. But *he or she* looks a lively little one. Ah, don't cry!'

I couldn't help myself. He passed me a box of tissues sympathetically.

'Sorry! It's just been such a worry, thinking I was going to lose him – *or her*,' I said, now laughing and crying at the same time.

'Well, you did the right thing, coming to have it checked out, but as you can see for yourself, your baby seems to be perfectly OK.'

I rushed back to where David was sitting outside. 'The baby's all right!' I said, and promptly started to cry again.

'Oh, what a relief.' He gave me a hug. 'I'm so glad.' He wiped the tears from my cheeks with his thumbs. 'Shall we celebrate with a cup of tea in the hospital café? No, sorry, I forgot. A glass of orange juice?'

'Actually,' I said, thoughtfully, trying the idea out in my head. 'You know what? I think I do fancy a cup of tea, for the first time in eleven-and-a-half weeks!'

'That's good news too, then!'

I laughed, feeling almost drunk with the relief of seeing that precious image of my baby alive and swimming around inside me – and without thinking, I took David's arm as we walked off to the cafe.

'I meant to ask you what Joe said when you called him?' I asked. I was starting to fret about having taken the day off. David, ever helpful, had phoned the office to tell them I wouldn't be coming in for work.

'Oh, not a lot,' he said, shrugging, not meeting my eyes.

'Come on, tell me. I need to know before I face him tomorrow. Did he ask what was wrong?'

'No.' David turned to me, looking angry. 'To be honest, I was pretty upset by his attitude. He didn't seem to have any interest in what might be wrong with you at all – just said it was a damned nuisance, and he didn't even wish you better.'

'Oh, well. That's typical.'

'Is it? I don't know how you can stand to work for him! What a selfish, charmless, arrogant—'

'Yes, he is. I agree.'

'If I were you, I'd be looking around for another job. Seriously, Sam, it's not exactly a very good atmosphere for you to be working in, in your condition, is it? I don't think you should put up with it.'

'I mostly just ignore him,' I said with a sigh.

'Well, if you want my opinion—'

'I don't!' I snapped. And then, feeling bad, I apologised: 'I'm sorry, David. You've been brilliant, but please don't ...' I hesitated. I'd been about to say *please don't worry about me*, but sounding hurt, David finished for me: 'Please don't interfere? I suppose that's what I'm doing. Sorry. It's just that I care about you. I'm sure you must have realised that. I care a lot.'

I closed my eyes. So Nana was right. I needed to be straight with him and I needed to do it quickly, before he got any more ideas about where our friendship was heading.

'I'm so sorry if I've given you the wrong impression, David,' I said quietly. 'I really like you. I enjoy your company so much; you've got no idea how glad I am to have you as a friend.' I put a heavy emphasis on the word 'friend' and waited, watching his face.

'I see,' he said. And then his expression suddenly softened. 'God, you must think me such an idiot. Of course you aren't interested in me. Why would you be?'

'But only because it's too soon! You must see that? I've only just split up with my ex and I'm expecting his baby. That's all I can think about, right now. I can't even consider the possibility of another relationship until after the baby's born.'

'I understand. I didn't mean to come on too strong. I just can't help feeling a bit protective about you.' His face betrayed what he was saying and I felt terrible.

'I don't need protecting, honestly,' I said, smiling. 'I'm quite a tough cookie. Apart from last night, of course. And this morning.'

'Well, I'm glad I was there for you then, anyway.' He hesitated. 'Can we still be friends?'

'Of course, don't you dare stop coming round! Ebony would miss you now! And so would I,' I added quickly, and I meant it.

'Thank God for that. I wasn't looking forward to managing those dogs on my own again.'

I laughed, relieved that our friendship seemed to be back on its easy-going track. I would have hated for David to suddenly become awkward around me or to lose out on our weekly dog-walking sessions.

But after he'd dropped my back at home, I found myself having doubts again. I hadn't liked the way he'd tried to tell me what to do about my job, the fact that he wanted to 'protect' me, and had started getting all macho and cross with Joe on my behalf. I appreciated his help and concern about the threatened miscarriage, of course, but I did not need to be told what to do by a man. I just hoped that now I'd spelled out my position to him things would settle down again. Although he could be a fussy old thing, I'd really miss his friendship if it had to come to an end.

I was glad I had Izzie to talk to, though. She, at least, understood why I was prepared to tolerate Joe's moods.

'You need your job, love, don't you?' she said, as we sat outside the little teashop in the village, having a quick lunch. 'Sometimes we just have to put up with a grumpy boss, unfortunately – it's all about the pay at the end of the month.'

I'd already told her what a foul mood Joe had been in when I returned to work. 'I presume you're feeling better?' he'd said with heavy sarcasm.

'Yes, thank you. And incidentally, I don't make a habit of taking time off sick.'

'Good. It's very inconvenient when I have to get cover at such short notice.'

I looked at Izzie's resolute face now. Yes, I would just have to put up with Joe and focus on the satisfaction of the job itself. 'Exactly,' I said, trying to ignore the fact that I had seemed to have a bizarre, possibly masochistic feeling of attraction towards the grumpy boss in question.

I'd just have to continue to behave as coolly with him as he did with me. And ignore those strange and complex feelings that came over me whenever I saw him picking up a kitten tenderly or stroking a sick dog, his manner going from surly to gentle in five seconds flat. It was quite strange, and I wished it didn't affect me the way it did.

He still hadn't even asked what was wrong with me. And I certainly wasn't going to tell him about my pregnancy until I absolutely had to. I could just imagine how unsympathetic he'd be if he knew. He'd probably even consider me incapable of doing the job.

Izzie had been really sympathetic, too, about my fright with the pregnancy. Apparently she'd had something similar herself with her first one, and it was a relief to know everything had turned out perfectly fine for her.

I asked her how the fundraising was going for the preschool, and she pulled a face. 'Slow. There's just not enough of us.'

'I've been thinking. Couldn't you advertise for new children from some of the nearby towns?'

'No, they're bound to have their own facilities.'

'But they'll probably have waiting lists,' I pointed out.

'Really?' She frowned, and I realised she'd never lived in a town or city.

'That's how it is in London, anyway,' I went on. The thought had occurred to me earlier after the panic of the pregnancy had subsided and I'd allowed myself to think again of my own child's future. Plus, having a distraction from grumpy Joe was always a good thing. 'Parents seem to have a terrible fight to get their kids into good schools and preschools. They're always oversubscribed.'

'Oh. Right. I hadn't thought of that,' she said. 'I'll mention it to the rest of the committee. Worth a try, I suppose. We'd need to tart the place up a bit, though, to make it attractive to people from outside the village.'

The preschool was held in an old demountable classroom in the school grounds.

'It could do with a lick of paint,' I agreed. 'But in the short term, wouldn't a few tubs of plants outside brighten it up?'

'Brilliant idea!' She smiled at me in surprise. 'The kids could water the plants too, and learn a little about nature at the same time. Are you thinking about asking David, by any chance?'

'It had crossed my mind!' I admitted.

I just hoped he wasn't mad at me about what happened at the hospital. I decided to ask him when I next saw him. After all, it might be a project for the both of us, to make sure our friendship was still as well as he promised it was.

CHAPTER SIXTEEN

Joe had told me that he needed me to go with him to the local riding stables in the morning to check on a pony who was recovering from colic. Natalie had booked a day off and, to Joe's annoyance, Val was only able to cover from ten o'clock. Because he needed to be back from the stables in time for his first appointment, he needed to set off at eight o'clock – so I'd agreed to go in early. He'd said he only needed me there just in case another pair of hands was necessary and I was desperate not to let Joe see that, in fact, I was feeling very shaky about the whole thing. The truth was that I'd had nothing to do with horses or ponies at my previous job – or for a long time before that. And if I was honest, I wasn't too sure how I was going to cope.

The stables were only a few minutes' drive out of the village. Joe drove in silence, a constant frown on his face. I looked out of the window at the fresh green of the countryside and tried to calm my nerves by thinking about what

I'd have been doing now if I were still in London. Probably rushing out to catch the 'dratted Tube train' as Nana called it, I supposed.

We'd pulled up in the stable yard and had walked past the first few stables when Joe stopped, leant into the next stable and began to pat the head of the pony inside.

'Hello, Hugo! How are you today? Yes, good boy, good boy, that's right, hello!'

'I thought we were coming to see a pony called Bandit?' I said, my surprise overcoming my anxiety for a moment.

'We are,' he said distractedly, still stroking Hugo's head. 'This one's mine.'

'Oh!' He'd never mentioned owning a pony.

'Well, he's my daughter's. She's learning to ride, so we stable him here. She spends half her life down here,' he added with a smile to himself. 'Comes up here on her bike after school with another older girl. They have their riding lessons, then groom and muck out to their hearts' content.'

It was the most he'd ever said about his daughter.

Hugo was a beautiful chestnut-and-white skewbald with big kind-looking eyes. I imagined the little girl Ruby enjoying this gentle companion and my heart gave a lurch.

'Right, well, come on, we haven't got all day,' Joe said suddenly, looking at his watch and walking on abruptly.

A middle-aged woman dressed in jodhpurs and boots approached us.

'Hello, Mandy,' Joe said. 'How's Bandit getting on?'

'Much better, thanks,' she said, joining us as we approached another stable where a bigger black pony was watching us over the top of his door. 'I think the medication has done the trick.'

'Ah, yes.' Joe watched as Mandy opened the stable door and led Bandit out. 'He certainly looks a lot calmer than when I saw him the other day. You're feeling better now, aren't you, boy?' he said gently to the pony, patting his neck. 'Well, that's a relief.' He checked Bandit over while he spoke. 'I'm glad it wasn't more serious.'

'I'd have called you back if he hadn't started to improve straight away,' Mandy said. 'Are you OK there for a minute, Joe? I've got someone waiting to talk to me in the office.'

'Yep, Sam can hold the reins for me,' he replied without even looking at me or bothering to introduce me.

Undeterred, I took Bandit's reins from Mandy and began to speak gently to the pony while Joe continued his examination. In spite of my worries about how the interaction with it would affect me, I actually found that stroking him, feeling his mane, his coat, the firm muscles beneath his flesh, calmed me as much as it did him. The years fell away, and I was back at the stables in my home town in Norfolk, where I'd spent half my childhood and teenage years. I felt a tear roll down my check and quickly wiped it away.

As Joe finished checking Bandit over, I was struggling to keep at bay the treacherous tears that were now starting to trickle down my cheeks. I hoped Joe hadn't noticed.

It wasn't until we were on our way back to the surgery that he said to me, 'So you treated horses and ponies in your last job, did you?'

'No,' I said. 'Not at all. We didn't tend to see many of them trotting around the streets of central London.'

I regretted the sarcasm the minute the words were out of my mouth, but to my surprise Joe smothered a laugh. I glanced at him, but he was looking ahead at the road and merely nodded to himself a couple of times before saying: 'Well, in that case you did well today. I half expected you to shy away from Bandit's teeth and hooves the way most city people do.'

'I'm not actually a *city person*,' I retorted before I could stop myself. 'I'm from Norfolk. A small town. I'd only been in London for a few years.'

'I see,' he said, and I thought I saw the muscle at the side of his mouth twitch slightly. 'I did wonder about your accent. So where did you get your experience with horses? Do you ride?'

'Well ...' I swallowed. 'I used to, when I was younger.'

'Will you get yourself a horse now you're living in the country again?'

My heart was beating too fast, the threat of tears too close again, for me to appreciate how civilly he was conversing with me for a change. If I had, I might have managed not to snap the 'No!' quite as abruptly as I did.

There was a silence, and I realised too late that I'd spoilt what could have been an unusually good moment between us.

'The thing is,' I began, 'Something happened—'

'None of my business,' he cut me off. 'Anyway, as I said, you did OK today. You seem to have fitted in all right here.'

173

We pulled up outside the surgery and the conversation was over. We were back to the normal routine of barely speaking to each other. I wasn't sure whether to be relieved or sorry that I hadn't managed to explain further why I'd stayed away from stables, from horses and anything to do with them, for so long. It wasn't something I talked about to anyone and it probably wouldn't exactly do anything to help my new career. But I had wondered, just fleetingly back there in the Jeep, whether Joe might actually have understood. *What a silly idea*, I thought ruefully to myself as I settled down at my desk. *He'd never understand in a million years.* Nevertheless, I was pleased he'd seemed to think I'd been helpful that morning. And that I hadn't, at least, made a complete fool of myself by going to pieces at the stables.

When I next saw Izzie she had exciting news for me. 'Guess what, Sam?' she said. 'We've got two families booked in to come and visit the preschool next week, already. You were quite right. One of the mums said she'd been waiting since Christmas to get her little boy a preschool place near where she lives. She seemed quite sold on the idea of him coming here – despite the drive.'

She sounded surprised, but I pointed out that lots of parents elsewhere have to drive their kids a distance to their schools, and that they'd probably think it was worth it for the children to be taught in a friendly little country environment. Thanking me effusively for my help, she pointed out that the final judging for the Best-Kept Village competition might be happening over the next few weeks.

'Watch out for strangers wandering around with clip-boards,' she joked. I told her that with luck, if they didn't come until halfway through the school holidays, David and I should have managed to get the outside of the classroom painted as well as finishing planting the tubs.

'Well, the tubs will help anyway,' she said, 'especially as facilities at schools are taken into account.' She turned to me, smiling. 'You've fitted in so well in the village, Sam, in such a short time.'

'I always wanted to play an active part,' I said, pleased that she thought so. 'And after all, my little one will be coming here one day so all this will benefit me too.'

David and I had been busy planting the new flower tubs outside the preschool building, chatting and joking together as we worked, as if the uncomfortable recent conversation about our relationship had never happened. I was glad we'd been able to move on and that he'd agreed that planting the tubs together was a great idea. But still I was very aware that a line had now been drawn, which I mustn't cross if I didn't want to hurt him.

I enjoyed the sight of the brightly painted plant tubs as I walked to work the next morning. It was a hot day, and I was happy to be wearing short-sleeved tops at last, savouring the feel of the sun on my skin. I hadn't given any more thought to the conversation with Joe on the way back from the stables the previous week, but when I arrived at the surgery to find him on his own in the little staff kitchen, making himself a coffee, I suddenly made a decision. There was something I'd wanted to talk to him about

– ever since he'd surprised me, on the day Rufus died, by asking me why I hadn't achieved my ambition of becoming a vet. Joe was normally so unapproachable, not to say unpleasant, I'd kept putting it off, but as he'd seemed pleased with me the previous day, I thought perhaps the time might be right.

'Joe,' I began, passing him the milk out of the fridge for his coffee. 'I wondered if I could ask you something.'

'If you want another day off, it'll have to wait,' he said without looking at me. 'Natalie's off this week. *Again.*'

'No, that's not it,' I said, immediately rattled. 'And I haven't even had any time off yet, actually, apart from one day sick—'

'Good. Well, what is it?'

I sighed. Now I'd started I'd better plough on or I'd never get the courage again. 'You asked me once about why I didn't become a vet.'

'Yes.' He finally turned to look at me, his eyebrows raised. 'You said you didn't work hard enough at school.'

'No, that's not—' I felt myself going red. Why did I have to explain myself to him? 'That isn't what I said. I did work hard, but I didn't get the grades I needed to be accepted for the course. I'd had a bit of a setback just before my A-levels ...'

'A setback? Broke up with a boyfriend, I suppose?' Joe said scathingly.

'Actually, I'd been in hospital with a burst appendix!' I snapped. I was angry now. What was the point of trying to talk to him? He never listened. But despite myself, I wanted to make him understand. 'I insisted on sitting my exams, against everyone's advice, even though I'd only just been discharged from hospital.'

I sighed, remembering how hard I'd cried when the A-level results came out. I'd recovered from a serious illness and emergency surgery, but the disappointment when I didn't get accepted at any of the veterinary colleges was ten times worse than all of that.

'So you didn't think it was worth trying again? You just gave up and became a receptionist,' Joe said.

'No, I didn't *give up*. I got a job in an estate agent's in King's Lynn, and kept up my studies part-time until I could re-sit the exams.'

'And then – what? You failed them again?'

I took a deep breath. He was sipping his coffee, staring at me over the mug. I had to try to calm down and remember he was my boss. However rude he was to me, I shouldn't retaliate if I wanted to keep my job.

'No,' I said quietly. 'I …' I closed my eyes and swallowed. It was no good; I couldn't do it, couldn't tell him. I'd only end up getting upset, and for what? Just so he could mock me with those brown eyes and that haughty stare? 'I didn't end up re-taking them,' I finished lamely.

'I see.' He gave a nod of satisfaction, as if I'd proved him right. I wanted to kick myself.

I went on quickly, 'But recently I've been wondering if I could do anything about it. That's what I wanted to ask you. Do you think there's any chance, at some point in the future, that I might be able to apply as a mature student?'

'A mature student?' he said, still staring at me over the mug. 'I suppose you do realise how challenging that would be?'

'Of course I do.'

'I doubt many colleges accept mature students.'

'Well, I've been looking on the Internet, actually, and it seems they do, depending on qualifications and experience—'

'And you've got those, have you?'

'I have A-levels in biology, chemistry and maths, so yes, even though I didn't get the grades I needed at the time, and as for experience—'

'You've been a receptionist,' he said bluntly.

'Yes, but I've got the City & Guilds certificate in animal care,' I retorted. I knew I was beginning to sound desperate. I should just forget it, walk away. He seemed determined to make me feel stupid.

'Well done.' He was just being sarcastic now. 'But even if you *were* to be accepted by one of the colleges, I don't think you realise how hard you'd have to work. Lots of kids dream of being vets but they have no idea what it actually entails. It's a tough life. It wouldn't sit well with –' he hesitated, staring at me even more intently '– any kind of frivolous lifestyle, for instance. Or if you've got plans to settle down. You know, do all the wife-and-mother stuff.'

'Wife-and-mother stuff?' I repeated, incredulous. 'Do you realise how sexist and ... well, *archaic* that sounds?'

'Yes, I do. But it's also true, unfortunately, so I'm just being realistic, and suggesting you do the same. Now, I imagine the first few patients are probably already sitting anxiously in the waiting room, so do you think you might turn your attention to doing your actual job and letting me get on with mine?'

I turned away from him quickly, desperate not to let him see how stung I was by his dismissive and insulting attitude. It was my own fault, I told myself crossly, as I booked in a woman whose cat had suffered a torn ear in a fight. I should have known better than to think, just because Joe had mentioned that I'd settled in OK – in other words, I was serving his purposes as a humble downtrodden servant – that he'd suddenly undergone enough of a personality change to be able to discuss my thwarted ambitions with any kind of sensitivity. He clearly thought I was just a moronic, frivolous girl who wanted nothing out of life other than to become some bloke's wife. *Frivolous*! As if I was always flitting off to parties and nightclubs. How dare he categorise me in that way when he hardly ever even bothered to talk to me?

But of course I had to calm down while I discussed people's dogs and gerbils with them, and took messages from farmers about their sheep and their cows. And, gradually, I realised that in one infuriating way, Joe was right. Not about the frivolity – my frivolous days were over – nor about becoming a wife. But I *was* going to be a mother, although he didn't know that yet. And it was one thing to dream of trotting off to become a mature veterinary science student, putting my child in a nursery perhaps, and rushing home every day to work on my studies at night after feeding him and putting him to bed – but the reality of such a situation was probably far more daunting than I imagined.

Nevertheless, I felt dejected and upset as I walked home at the end of the day. I didn't want to discuss it with Nana, or even with David. For such an even-tempered man, the subject of Joe Bradley and his rudeness was, for David, like a red rag to a bull. But there was someone I could look forward to talking to – Claire had arranged to come and stay with me at Nana's for the following weekend while her other half looked after her son. I knew she wouldn't mind me offloading all my moans and frustrations on her. Sitting around chatting to my friend for hours on end was exactly what I needed. So maybe Joe was right, and I was just a frivolous female after all.

CHAPTER SEVENTEEN

'Oh my God, he's *seriously* cute!' Claire was sitting with me on the bench seat in Nana's little garden. We'd just got back from walking the dogs with David. 'I can see now why you've got over Adam so easily.'

'Stop it, Claire,' I protested. 'I've just spent the last few weeks convincing him that I'm not interested in him in that way.'

'Well, if I wasn't happily married, I'd definitely be interested! Oh well.' She shook her head, looking disappointed. 'I suppose you're waiting till after you've had the baby, fair enough.'

'Yes, I am. And even then, as far as I'm concerned he'll still be just a friend.'

'So maybe you're not completely over Adam, then?'

'It's nothing to do with Adam. I'm not looking for a man at all, OK? I've got other things on my mind.' I sighed, and went on to tell her how I'd started indulging in my old fantasy about trying to get into college as a mature student. 'But it's just a stupid fantasy, really.'

'Why? It's a great ambition, Sam, and if you don't go for it you'll never know.'

'It's *too* ambitious, that's the trouble. I probably wouldn't be accepted, and even if I was, it'd be taking on too much, in the circumstances.' I hesitated. 'I've been told.'

'By who?'

'Joe. He's kind of talked me out of it.'

'Your nasty boss? You're surely not going to be dissuaded by him, are you?' she said, raising her eyebrows at me.

'Yes, I am, actually, because although he made me really angry and upset, I've since realised he's probably right. To be honest, I'm embarrassed, now that I even raised the subject with him. I should've known better. As far as he's concerned I'm just a silly little receptionist.'

'How dare he! He sounds like a total pig.'

'Yes, he is.' I hesitated. 'Well, most of the time he is, anyway. But I have to admit, although he's a bad-tempered, stroppy pain-in-the-neck, I do … well, admire him, in a funny kind of way.' I hadn't realised I was going to say this until the words were out of my mouth, and I added quickly: 'Professionally, I mean.'

'OK.' She gave me a puzzled look. 'If you say so. But about Adam, though—'

She'd already talked to me quite a lot about Adam since she'd arrived the previous evening. How she'd bumped into him a couple of times since I'd left, and that he seemed sad and lost and lonely without me. I was beginning to wish she'd shut up about him; it was making me feel guilty, even though I knew it wasn't my fault if he was unhappy.

'I'm sorry,' I interrupted her now, 'but our break-up was mutual, Claire. I haven't found it easy either, but we both agreed our relationship had run its course.'

'You haven't kept in touch with him at all?'

'I've kept him up to date via email,' I said. 'Talking on the phone isn't going to help either of us. I do want him to know what's happening – it's his baby, after all – but I don't think that's quite sunk in yet for him. Anyway, it's been a fairly straightforward pregnancy, so there hasn't been that much to say.'

I patted my stomach, and Claire looked down at it.

'You're really starting to show, now.'

'It's just this dress. It's a bit tight.'

'Don't wear it for work, then, if you don't want that miserable boss of yours to know about it yet.'

'Don't worry, I won't.' But I felt a little knot of anxiety as I realised it might not be too long before I wouldn't be able to keep my pregnancy a secret any more. I didn't mind anyone else knowing. Just not Joe Bradley.

A little later Nana and I took Claire to the Horse for lunch, and that was when everything started to go wrong. She seemed astonished to learn that there was nowhere else in the village where we could get a meal out.

'No restaurants? Not even a wine bar?' she asked, sounding incredulous. 'What the hell does everyone *do* all the time?'

Nana gave a derisive snort, and I answered Claire quickly before Nana could start sounding off about dratted wine bars in dratted London.

'Well, we have some lovely walks around here,' I said. 'And there are a lot of clubs that meet in the church hall. And there's always something different going on in the village. There was a maypole-dancing display at the school last week, for example – the children were brilliant! – and the village fete is next week …'

'Oh, goody, I bet you can't wait,' she said sarcastically.

'And Sam's been helping David with all these lovely flower baskets, and planting tubs outside the kiddies' classroom, haven't you, Sam?' Nana said. She sounded so proud of me, I suddenly wanted to shake Claire for her condescending look. 'It all helps with the Best-Kept Village competition, you see. We usually win it, unless East Pentleford pips us to the post.'

'Well, it all sounds riveting, I must say.'

I gave Claire a nudge and a glare. Perhaps she thought she was being funny, but it seemed quite rude of her to patronise Nana like that. We walked the rest of the way to the pub in silence, but began to chat about other things over our drinks while we waited for our food orders. And then I looked up at the next table and sighed.

'That's Joe over there,' I muttered to Claire. He was sitting on his own with what looked like a Coke in front of him. I'd caught him watching us and, as usual, he was scowling to himself.

'Oh, *that's* Mr Charming Personality, is it?' she said, and scowled back in his direction.

I gave him a nod, and cheerily called out 'Hi! Lovely day, isn't it!' half expecting him to ignore me.

'Is it? Too bloody hot, if you ask me,' Joe said with a straight face. He finished his drink, banged down his glass and got to his feet. 'Well, I'd better get on, we can't all be wasting our time lazing around in the sunshine.'

'See you Monday, then,' I said faintly.

'Honestly, I don't know how you put up with that,' Claire said. And to my horror, as he went to pass our table, she got up and blocked his path, holding out her hand. 'I'm Claire, Sam's friend from London,' she said. 'And I have to say, you're very lucky to have her working for you.'

I groaned and tried to will my cheeks to not go red from embarrassment. *What was she doing?* I thought to myself.

Joe looked down at Claire's proffered hand and back up again, without shaking it.

'Well, "Sam's Friend from London",' he replied, staring her straight in the face, 'I think that's for me to decide, don't you? This isn't London, and thank God for that, if everyone there is so bloody full of their own importance they have to interfere in what doesn't concern them.'

Claire gasped. 'It seems Sam's quite right about you – you're just an arrogant bully and—'

'Claire!' I shouted, jumping up and grabbing her arm to pull her away from him. 'Stop it! There's no need to be—'

'Actually there *is* a need, Sam, to tell this man exactly what you think of him.' She tried to shake me away from where I was grabbing her arm. 'And if you can't do it, allow me to help you out.' She turned back to Joe. 'How dare you put Sam down for wanting to go back to college and improve her prospects? What's wrong with you – are you afraid she'll turn out to be a better vet than you one day, is that it?'

'Claire!' I shouted again. 'Would you *please* just shut up?' My face was on fire. 'Joe, I'm so sorry – she's had a few drinks, she doesn't know what she's saying.'

'No I haven't!' Claire rounded on me. 'Don't apologise for me, Sam. It needed to be said—'

'Not by you, it didn't! For f—' I glanced at Nana, who was staring at us with her drink halfway to her mouth, her face a picture of shock. 'For God's sake, Claire, sit down and mind your own business.'

'I see your choice of friends is as lamentable as your choice of career,' Joe said calmly to me, then turned his back on us and walked away.

For a moment we all sat in stunned silence. Then I rounded on Claire. 'What were you thinking of, you stupid cow? He's my *boss*. Do you want to get me fired?'

'Sam,' Nana began, in a warning voice, but I ignored her, turning back to Claire again, my disappointment in her mounting with my anger.

'First you start being all superior about Hope Green—'

'Well, come on, you must admit it's pretty dire here. I can't understand what the hell you see in it.'

'You're my nan's *guest* – don't talk about her home village like that!' I was seething. Why did I think it was a good idea to invite her here? Claire belonged to my life in London, a life I never wanted to go back to. I might have known we couldn't pick up our friendship here, away from its roots. I should have seen it coming. 'And as for the way you spoke to my boss – you were even ruder than he is!'

'Come off it, Sam. You've done nothing but complain about him since I got here.'

'Yes, he might be bad-tempered at times, but I still respect him. A lot, actually,' I added. 'And I happen to love my job, which you've probably just ruined for me.'

'You've changed, do you know that?' she said, staring at me. 'You would never have put up with that kind of crap when you worked in London.'

'Maybe I *have* changed. But so have you,' I shot back. 'All you've seemed to want to talk to me about is my ex. How is that supposed to help me?'

'Let's face it,' she said, and was briefly distracted when Suzie the barmaid dumped her food in front of her in her usual offhand manner. Claire looked at her, and the food, with disdain. 'There's not much else worth talking about round here, is there? If you've got any sense you'll pack up and come back to London.'

We ate our lunch in silence. And then when we got back to the cottage, Claire packed her bag and left. I sat on the sofa, staring into space, cuddling Ebony, still too shocked and upset to talk about it, while Nana took up her knitting, muttering to herself about *coming down here with her highfalutin' ways from that dratted London*.

'I'm so sorry, Nana,' I said eventually, giving her a hug. 'I can't believe Claire behaved like that. I won't be inviting her again.'

'Not your fault, Little Sam,' she said. 'It's a shame you've quarrelled with your friend, she's spoilt the weekend for you. But it's nothing to do with me. I'm saying nothing.'

All the next day, I worried about facing Joe at work and what he would say, but when I arrived he and Natalie were already dealing with an emergency and as the day progressed, I realised he wasn't even going to mention the incident with Claire. His moody silences and glares were no different from normal. Perhaps he was used to angry confrontations with people. But I wasn't.

I was still upset and shaken, going over everything Claire had said. And the more I thought about it, one thing kept jumping out at me. Why on earth had she talked so much about Adam, prodding away at me about him, asking if I'd spoken to him, whether I still had feelings for him? Even if she had seen him recently, and even if she thought he looked lonely, shouldn't she be on my side about this? That's what real friends did, after all. What was that all about?

Well, I wasn't going to call her, and she wasn't calling me either. So perhaps I'd never find out.

CHAPTER EIGHTEEN

For the next couple of days, Joe and I continued to keep our usual professional coolness around each other. At the end of the week, I was just thinking about getting ready to go home from work when the surgery door suddenly burst open and a young fair-haired girl wearing riding jodhpurs and a jumper bearing a horse design came flying in, crying her eyes out. It took me a few seconds to recognise her as Ruby, Joe's daughter.

'What's the matter, love?' I said.

'I want my dad!' she sobbed, running towards the consulting-room door.

'Hold on!' I said. 'Let me see if he's there—'

Of course, I knew he was. But he was with a patient, and I had the feeling that if he was interrupted mid-procedure by his little girl, who might merely be upset about some childhood falling-out with a friend, I'd be bound to get the blame for it. But before I'd even got to the door, it opened abruptly and Joe stood there, frowning.

'Ruby!' he said as the child threw herself at him, crying even harder. 'What on earth's the matter? I heard you from inside the consulting room.'

'Daddy, come quickly!' she said, choking over her words. 'It's Hugo! He's hurt – it's really bad – his leg's all wobbly and he can't get up.'

'What?' Joe grabbed his bag immediately while at the same time trying to make his apologies to the woman whose border collie he'd just finished treating. 'What happened? Why didn't Mandy call me?'

'She tried, she kept trying, but she couldn't get through.'

'The line's been really busy,' I said helplessly, somehow managing to feel guilty even though I knew it wasn't my fault.

'And your mobile was off, Daddy. So I just got on my bike and rushed straight here. *Please* hurry up, Hugo's just lying on the ground.' She started to cry again.

'Right. Val, you'd better come with me,' he told the nurse who'd been assisting him with the border collie. 'Sam, book Mrs Reynolds an appointment for another follow-up for Bessie in a week's time. And give her one of the advice sheets on post-op care, OK?' He started to stride towards the door, followed by the sobbing Ruby. 'No!' he told her abruptly. 'You'd better stay here until I get back. Sam can look after you.' He turned back to me and added quietly, 'Please. If you don't mind.'

'Of course I don't mind.'

'I want to come!' Ruby protested, but I held on to her hand and gently pulled her back. It would be better if she stayed here, like her dad suggested. I sat her in my chair while Joe and Val made their exit. Joe gave me a small smile before he left.

'Sorry about this,' I told Mrs Reynolds, who was clutching her dog anxiously as she looked from one of us to the other. 'Bit of an emergency, I'm afraid.'

'Can't be helped, dear. I hope everything will be all right.' She smiled sympathetically at Ruby before walking out the door with her dog behind her.

'All right, sweetheart,' I told the tearful child. 'Try not to worry. You know Daddy will do everything he possibly can to make Hugo better.'

I felt sick at the thought of the pony's injuries. Memories from years back that I thought I'd learned to live with were resurfacing, and my head swam with horror and dread. But I couldn't let Ruby see that. I pulled up a chair and sat next to her at my desk.

'We were just doing some practice jumps,' she told me, sniffing. 'Just me and my friend Chloe. Mandy was watching us. But just as Hugo was about to take a jump, two great big rooks flew down into the ring. They were making a lot of squawking noises and it must have scared him. He kind of stumbled into the edge of the jump and fell down.'

'You were riding him at the time?' I said. 'Jumping? You didn't say that!' My head swam again and I had to swallow the bile that had risen in my throat. 'Are you hurt?'

'No, I'm all right,' she said. 'I just kind of rolled off him. It's Hugo who's hurt!'

'You might have some bruises tomorrow,' I warned her. 'Are you sure you're all right? Would you like a drink of water, or a cup of something?'

'No!' she cried. 'I told you, I'm all right, it's Hugo! Oh, I hope his leg isn't broken. I wish Daddy had let me go with him.'

Ruby started to cry again. I held her hand and gave it a comforting stroke. I *knew* her fears. I knew how a fracture, for a horse or pony, could be a death sentence. But I was aware that I needed to keep the little girl occupied until her father came back. I gave her a couple of sheets of paper and a pen and suggested she wrote a few lines about what had happened. I pretended it was a 'witness report' that might be useful for the insurance. In fact, it quietened her down to have something to concentrate on, although of course the tears continued to flow. I tried to talk to her about school and her friends while she worked, but she just shook her head, bent over the paper and continued scribbling away.

It was over an hour before we heard Joe's Jeep pull up outside. Ruby instantly threw down her pen and ran to the door to meet him.

'Is he all right?' she cried. 'Is his leg broken?'

'No.' Joe took a deep breath and gave her a hug. 'It's a ligament tear and luckily not a major one. It's painful for him at the moment so he's not putting his weight on the bad leg.'

'He'll have to be rested,' warned Val, who'd followed him in, 'but with some of your dad's magic medicine he'll soon be back to normal.'

'Oh, Daddy, thank you!' Ruby said, bursting into a fresh onslaught of tears as she hugged him back. 'I thought it was really bad.'

'Has she been all right?' he mouthed to me over the top of her head. Concern laced his eyes and I suddenly felt the urge to run to him just like Ruby had. The memories from long ago had really addled my grip on the situation.

'Very upset,' I whispered back. I closed my eyes for a second, trying again to suppress the memories. 'Did you realise she was riding Hugo at the time?' I added.

'Yes, Mandy told me.' He held Ruby at arm's length now and looked her up and down. 'And you're sure you're not hurt?'

'I'm perfectly fine, I keep telling everyone, I was just worried about Hugo,' she said, sounding exasperated. She turned to me and added politely, 'Thank you for looking after me, Sam.'

'That's all right, sweetheart. I'm glad Hugo's going to be OK.'

'Kids are tougher than we think,' Val said, after Joe had left with Ruby to make sure she got home all right. Then she looked at me. 'Well done for calming her down, Sam. Are you all right? You look a bit pale.'

'I'm fine,' I lied. I got to my feet, ignoring the buzzing in my head. 'I'll see you tomorrow.'

All the way home, I kept taking deep breaths, trying to stop the sounds and images bombarding my brain. Hoofs pounding, adrenalin surging, a jump up ahead – a high one. A sudden crash of thunder, a horse's squeal of terror. The sound of bones breaking. People running, shouting. My own screams …

I shuddered, walking on, trying to think of something else – something positive. The baby. Little Ebony, happy and healthy now and enjoying playing outside. The summer ahead of me, picnics on the beach, with David perhaps, or my new friend Izzie and her children. I couldn't let the old horrors undo me now, not when I'd managed to confront them so well just recently at the riding stables with Joe. I squared my shoulders, took a deep breath and told myself: *It's not all about you, Sam.*

I saw Ruby the very next day at the village fete, completely by coincidence. The fright the incident had given the poor girl had of course been upsetting in itself so I was surprised and touched when she ran up to me, eager to tell me that she'd been to see Hugo that morning and he was already looking better.

'I'm so pleased to hear that,' I said.

She was with her friend Chloe, a tall, quiet girl of about twelve who Ruby clearly seemed to look up to.

I left Nana sitting in the tea tent with a couple of her cronies and went with the two girls to queue up for ice creams. The whole time we were waiting, Ruby babbled away excitedly to me about how many rosettes she'd won in competitions at the riding school and how, after Hugo had recovered completely, she was going to continue working with him for the next gymkhana she'd set her heart on winning. It was nice to have the chance to chat to her without her father being around. She was a boisterous young lady and I immediately felt protective of her.

'He'll be out of action for a while yet,' I warned her.

'I know. But Hugo won't forget what to do. He's a really smart pony – isn't he, Chloe?'

Her friend smiled and nodded. 'Yes, he's great. And Ruby's a really good rider, too,' she told me. 'Better than me.'

Ruby beamed with pride. 'Have you got a horse, Sam?' she asked as I paid for their ice creams.

I quickly blinked back the memories again. 'No.' I handed them their cornets. 'I ... haven't, sadly.'

'But can you ride?'

'I used to be able to. Not any more.'

I tried to change the subject, asking about school, but she was already pleading: 'Come to the stables with me one day! Please, Sam ...'

'I'll see,' I prevaricated, giving her a smile and explaining that I needed to get back to Nana.

I found her in the tea tent, still, with Maggie Stammers, both of them giving vent to their feelings about Billy Henderson's habit of hoisting his trousers up and 'wriggling himself about inside them' while talking to people. I was glad I'd missed that, I thought in amusement. I helped Nana to her feet and we did a slow tour of the rest of the attractions, having a go on the hoopla stall hosted by Paul the vicar and the tombola stall being run by the preschool committee. When we came to the Knit and Natter group's stall, Nana insisted on buying me a selection of little white cardigans and jackets – a couple of which I suspected she'd actually made herself and donated to the stall. Carried away by the excitement of having my first things to put in the bottom drawer in my room ready for the baby, I bought a beautiful lacy shawl, which was apparently crocheted by Nora before she became ill.

'All our proceeds this year are going to the hospital's cancer unit, because of Nora,' Nana told me. 'She'll be tickled pink that you've bought her shawl.'

'Are they for you, then, these things, Sam?' asked the lady who served me – another friend of Nana's. She was giving me a knowing look, and I was grateful that someone else interrupted her before I could answer. Although I'd asked Nana not to spread the news about the baby too much until I'd told Joe, I knew how gossip got around in such a small village. It'd be awful if he found out before I'd told him myself.

Later, that evening, I decided to call Adam. I'd been thinking about doing so ever since Claire's visit. I wasn't sure whether to believe what she'd said about him being sad and lonely, but it had been niggling at me enough to make me want to check. Claire and I still hadn't spoken to each other since she'd abruptly left after our row, but I was continually mulling over how much she'd gone on about Adam while she was with me. What did it have to do with her anyway? They hardly knew each other – at least, they didn't when he and I were together. I was pondering this as I waited for him to answer the call, so when – instead of Adam's voice – it was Claire who responded. I thought for a minute I must have dialled her number by mistake.

'Claire?' I said, confused, wondering whether to hang up.

'Oh.' She sounded as surprised as I was – and definitely not pleased to hear from me. 'Sam.'

'I thought I'd dialled Adam's number.'

'Hang on.'

There was a pause and I heard music playing in the background. It sounded like Adele, and unless I was mistaken, I could also make out the sound of a cork being popped out of a bottle. And then Adam's voice: 'Hello Sam. This is a surprise.'

I swallowed back my shock. So I hadn't misdialled. Claire was there, with Adam. And she obviously hadn't checked the caller display; otherwise I doubt she'd have answered his phone. What the hell was going on? It was one thing saying she'd bumped into him a couple of times, but altogether another thing to be spending Saturday night drinking wine and listening to Adele with him. For God's sake, she was forty-two, a happily married woman with a son and a mortgage – why wasn't she at home where she belonged?

'Are you at home?' I said. My voice came out slightly shaky. 'Or in a pub or something?'

'No ... um ... just having a quiet one at home,' he said, sounding distinctly uneasy.

'So what's Claire doing there?'

'Oh, she just … um … popped in for a chat.' I wasn't imagining it. He sounded … kind of false. Like someone trying to hide something. 'So, how are you, anyway?' he went on. 'Haven't heard from you for ages. How is country life treating you?'

'It's … um … good.' I couldn't even remember what I was going to talk to him about now. All I could think of was that Claire was probably sitting next to him on the sofa, topping up his wine glass, smirking at the thought of my surprise. 'I was just calling to see how you are. But I'm obviously interrupting something.'

'No, not at all. We're just—'

'I don't want to know, thank you!' I snapped. The lyrics of 'Hello' were playing in the background and it was suddenly more than I could bear. 'I'll leave you to it.'

'Is everything all right, though?' he said, sounding suddenly anxious. Or guilty, perhaps? 'Claire told me you had a bit of a scare – with the baby.'

'I'm fine.' My finger hovered over the End Call button but still he persisted.

'And the job's going well? Claire says your boss is a bit of a miserable sod.'

Claire says this, Claire says that. It seemed Claire had already told him everything there was to know, even though she and I weren't even talking to each other. I wondered whether she'd told him about our argument. I had a sudden, horrible picture of the two of them discussing me together, comparing how much I'd supposedly hurt them both and consoling each other over a drink. Was that what was going on here? An unholy alliance of my ex-boyfriend and my ex-best friend? I couldn't even bring myself to answer him. There was a long silence between us. I noticed the music move to another Adele track, similarly full of heartbroken sorrow.

Eventually Adam coughed and said, awkwardly, 'Well, anyway, nice to hear from you, Sam. Let me know when the baby arrives, won't you.'

'It's not due till December!' I said crossly. What did he care, anyway?

'Of course, I know that,' he was saying – but I hung up before he could carry on with his protests.

I sat staring at my phone, trying to calm down. Even though Adam and I were finished, we'd been together such a long time and he was the father of my child. Of course he needed to move on, and it was always going to feel weird knowing he was with someone else, but for that person to be *Claire* was unthinkable. It's something you just don't do – seeing your best friend's ex. And now we weren't even on speaking terms it was even worse. Surely she wasn't playing up to Adam just to spite me? To get back at me for calling her a stupid cow in front of Joe and Nana?

But ... what was I thinking? She couldn't actually be seeing Adam, or even flirting with him – she would never be unfaithful to Nick, I knew that much about her. I really mustn't read something into this. Maybe she really *had* just popped round for a chat, I thought desperately. She surely wouldn't risk her marriage, just to hurt me ... Would she?

But it was no good, no matter how much I tried to analyse the situation, I couldn't help thinking how much the whole thing stank. There was something going on, and I didn't like it one bit.

'Are you all right, Sam?' Nana asked, looking at me with concern as she bustled in from the kitchen where she'd been feeding Ebony. 'Was that your Adam you were speaking to?'

'He's not *my* Adam,' I reminded her, a little too sharply. But he wasn't Claire's, either. Was he?

CHAPTER NINETEEN

All through the following week, I debated with myself about whether to call Claire and challenge her. I needed someone to talk it over with so when I saw Izzie one lunchtime and she had happened to mention that she wasn't working the next weekend, we made plans to have a day at the beach. I'd been thinking about making a trip out, but with everything that had been happening since my return to Hope Green, I hadn't got around to it just yet. The fresh sea air will do me a world of good, I thought to myself.

We agreed to take both our cars – as Izzie would need to bring her double buggy – which allowed us to bring Nana and Izzie's own mum, Jen, along to share in the fun too. Nana was so excited. I'd promised myself I'd take her out for trips like this once the summer was here so it was the perfect opportunity. We made up a picnic – which needless to say included a home-made walnut cake and a batch of cookies for the children – and met up with Izzie down at the beach.

Because of its difficult access, Hope Green Bay was a fairly quiet little beach, but as Izzie pointed out, this was better for the children as there were none of the expensive distractions like the shops or funfair rides along the coast where the holiday resorts were. It was pleasantly warm without being uncomfortably hot. We spent the day in blissful calm: the baby slept under a sunshade, while the other two children played in the sand under the watchful eye of Nana and Izzie's mum, who were sat in two fold-up chairs. Nana and Jen were good friends, having known each other over the many years they'd lived in the village, and were perfectly happy chatting away together.

As the day came to a close, the two ladies were indulging in a lively discussion about the judging of the Best-Kept Village competition, so I took the opportunity to pull Izzie to one side.

'I'd like your opinion on something a bit personal,' I told her quietly, and I explained the situation as briefly as I could. She gasped when I told her about Claire's confrontation with Joe and frowned at the description of my phone call to Adam.

'You want me to be honest?' she asked when I'd finished. 'It does sound dodgy to me. I reckon you're right – she's having a bit on the side with your ex.'

'You don't think I'm imagining things?' I said, my heart sinking. I'd been hoping she might say something to that effect. 'I mean, I'm still mad at her about what happened when she came to visit, but I honestly never thought she'd do something like this. She always seemed so happily married.'

'Maybe you didn't know her as well as you thought.' Izzie glanced at me sympathetically. 'I wouldn't start accusing her of anything, though, if I were you. Give it time. If she were really doing it to hurt you, she'd want you to find out, wouldn't she? She'd tell you. Or he would.'

'He sounded really awkward, talking to me.'

'Yeah, he would, wouldn't he! Men, eh?'

She proceeded to tell me about how her own relationship ended in more detail. But then the baby woke up and needed feeding, and the kids were getting tired, so the whole subject of men and infidelity was dropped. I wasn't sorry – I'd had a lovely day at the beach, but in a way, I'd spoilt it by bringing up the subject: now I knew Izzie agreed with me, I was more sure than ever that something was going on behind my back – possibly with the sole intention of Claire and Adam hurting me.

As we were packing up to go, I heard a sudden shout of 'Hello, Sam!' from behind me and, looking round, I saw Ruby running across the beach towards me, followed, unfortunately, by her father.

'Hello!' I smiled at her and nodded at Joe when he caught her up. 'Did you walk down here?'

'Of course we did,' Joe said in his usual abrupt manner. 'We could do, what with us not having the amount of people and clutter *you've* brought with you.'

'Oh, Daddy, they've had a picnic!' Ruby said, sounding wistful, and I wondered why on earth her mum hadn't come with them and brought their own picnic.

'Yes, well, all you wanted was a swim, wasn't it?' Joe threw a couple of towels on to the beach. To my surprise, he then proceeded to strip off his shirt and shorts so he was just in his swimming shorts. I tried to look away out of modesty, but as he ran towards the sea I couldn't help snatching a glance. 'Last one's a rotten egg!' he called back to Ruby who, giggling, tossed her own clothes on to the pile and ran after him.

'Bye, Sam!' she yelled back at me as she jumped into the waves. 'Please don't forget to come and see Hugo with me! I'm down there every day after school.'

Even from where I was standing on the beach, I could see Joe turn back and give me a glare at this, as if it was my fault his daughter wanted to be friends with me. Well, he'd have to put up with it, I decided, because that was all the challenge I needed. I *would* go to the stables with Ruby. Apart from anything else, being with the ponies would be good therapy, perhaps helping me to get over the flashbacks that had started troubling me again.

I was still watching them both diving into the surf when Izzie nudged me.

'What are you staring at, or shouldn't I ask?' she whispered. 'He's got a good body, I'll give him that.'

I flushed. 'Didn't even notice,' I said, turning away sharply. 'It's a pity he hasn't got a nicer temperament instead.'

I was busy at work that week, often finishing late, and I didn't get a chance to go to the stables until Thursday, driving down as soon as I finished work. I could hear Ruby's and Chloe's voices even before I got out of the car and I followed the sound of their laughter all the way to Hugo's stable.

'Sam! You came!' Ruby said, looking up from where she was brushing Hugo. She dropped the brush into her bucket and ran to give me a hug. It was so unexpected that I felt a rush of warmth and pleasure as I hugged her back.

I watched her work with the pony and listened to her chatter on about how well his bad leg was mending. She was such a nice little girl, I thought to myself, but I felt there was something almost desperate in her efforts to befriend me. I was sure that, as well as Chloe, she must have plenty of friends her own age at school to make up for not having any brothers or sisters. So what was it that made her want to form an attachment to someone like me? What was missing? Flattering though it was, I couldn't help thinking it was unusual. She didn't know me all that well, and I was, I supposed, just about old enough to be her mother.

'It's so nice that you're here!' she said, looking up at me with shining eyes. 'When Daddy says Hugo's ready for riding again, will you come and watch me?'

'Of course I will,' I said.

'And especially when I'm in the gymkhana!' she added excitedly.

I closed my eyes as the unwelcome images flooded my mind again, of pounding hoofs, a startled neigh, the screams ...

'But Ruby, surely your mum will want to come and see you in that, won't she?'

There was a sudden silence. I opened my eyes. Ruby had turned away from me, dropping the brush, and to my horror I realised she'd started crying. Chloe, rushing to put her arm around her, turned back to me, her eyes wide with shock.

'What have I said?' I asked, my heart in my mouth. 'Ruby, love, I'm so sorry – what did I say?'

'Nothing. I'm all right.' She shook Chloe's arm off her and went to pick up her brush, but then changed her mind. 'I think I'll just go home, Chlo.'

'Won't you tell me what's wrong?' I pleaded, but Chloe frowned and shook her head at me. I felt dreadful, without knowing why. 'Can I give you both a lift, at least?'

'We've got our bikes,' Chloe said. 'We'll be OK, thanks.'

Feeling dismissed, I watched in silence as they collected their bikes and rode off. The scenario had disturbed me so much, it was several minutes before I could drive myself home, and I spent the rest of the evening worrying about it. It was obvious the mention of her mum had upset poor Ruby, but why? I could only assume I'd been right in thinking her parents' marriage was on the rocks. Perhaps her mother had decided to leave. I wondered whether I should mention to Joe about what happened, but if his marriage was falling apart, then surely I'd be the last person he'd want to talk to. There must be something I could do to help, though. But how could I, without finding out what the problem was?

The next morning I went into work early. I needed an answer, and there was only one way to get it. Joe had only just arrived himself, and he looked up at me with irritation when I followed him into the consulting room.

'Did Ruby tell you I went to see her at the stables yesterday?' I asked him straight out.

'No.'

He stared at me, and I took a deep breath. I could just leave it there. If Ruby hadn't told him about the incident, maybe he didn't need to know, and I didn't need to face his disapproval. But on the other hand, if I didn't find out what I'd done wrong, I could unwittingly keep on upsetting Ruby every time I saw her.

'I think I said something to upset her,' I said, a little shakily. 'I'm so sorry – I have no idea what it was, she wouldn't tell me.'

'Don't go down there with her again, then,' he retorted. 'Perhaps you're not very good with children.'

I gasped. 'Ruby *wanted* me to go! She practically begged me! In fact, she wants me to watch her riding when Hugo's better. She even wants me to see her in the gymkhana, which frankly I'd have thought was her mother's place, if you can't go.'

He spun round, his face suddenly contorted with anger. 'You didn't say *that* to her, I hope?'

'Yes, I did – but not quite in those terms, obviously …' I stared at him. 'Why? What—'

'Ruby's mum,' he said, more quietly, his face looming threateningly close to mine now, his voice trembling slightly, 'would like nothing better than to watch our daughter compete – among other things. She's perfectly well aware that it would be "her place", as you put it. Unfortunately, she's never going to have that pleasure and privilege, ever again. She's only got a few weeks left to live.'

My hands flew to my mouth as I realised my error. I recoiled in horror – and embarrassment. 'Oh my God, I'm so sorry, Joe. That's … just awful. If there's anything I can do …'

But he turned away and banged his instruments down on the table aggressively, ignoring me.

I slipped out of the room and fell into my chair, tears in my eyes, wishing the ground would swallow me up. If only I'd not uttered those words to poor Ruby, or indeed put my foot in it so badly with Joe himself.

'That wasn't your fault,' Val said, having clearly overheard the whole exchange. She put a mug of tea in front of me and a comforting arm around my shoulders. 'He should've told you. Or I should've done, at least.'

'I wish somebody had,' I said tearfully.

'He won't talk about it.' She sighed. 'I only found out a little while ago because I had to go to their house one evening to pick something up, and the nurse – the one he's hired to look after Andrea, his wife – was just leaving. Like you, I pretty much put my foot in it, saying something quite innocent. It seems it's only when someone says the wrong thing that he lets them know the situation – and in quite terse words too.'

'That's ... well, obviously I'm terribly sorry for him, and for his wife of course,' I said, wiping my eyes, 'but it's hardly sensible, is it? To keep everyone in the dark and then snap at us for saying the wrong thing?'

'I know, but I don't think he can help it, Sam. He's going through hell. The nurse thinks Andrea should be moved to the hospice soon and of course, that, to Joe, means admitting it's nearly the end – and another huge step for Ruby too. He's done his best to keep her life as normal as possible in the circumstances. The pony is part of that. It gives her something happy ... and *alive* ... to love and devote herself to.' She sighed again. 'I'm so sorry, Sam. I really do wish I'd told you myself now, but it's very awkward when he's determined to keep it a secret.'

'Yes, I can see that.' I took a sip of tea in an attempt to pull myself together. 'Please don't feel bad – you were in a difficult position. It does make it easier to understand his mood swings, though.'

'I know. Poor chap,' she said and shook her head before adding, 'Come on, let's just do our best to get on with the job, Sam. That's the only way we can help.'

She was right, of course, I thought as I turned on the computer. I'd certainly have to be more understanding and tolerant of Joe Bradley's bad moods from now on, and more of an understanding friend to young Ruby too. But even as I thought this I realised the answer to what I had been wondering this whole time: it wasn't a *friend* Ruby wanted at all, it was a mother substitute.

CHAPTER TWENTY

All that week I could think of nothing but Joe's tragic situation, but as the next weekend came, I had another problem to contend with.

'Ebony hasn't come back yet,' Nana said, staring anxiously out the back door. 'She's been gone all night, Sam.'

We'd tried, so far, to keep her in at nights, but the previous evening no amount of calling her or walking around the garden in the dark, shaking packets of cat treats, had achieved the desired result.

'I'm sure she's fine.' I tried to reassure Nana. 'She's getting more confident about being outside now, and it was a warm night. She probably got excited chasing after some creature in the moonlight and now she's curled up fast asleep somewhere. She'll wake up in a minute and realise she's hungry.'

'I hope so,' Nana said, not sounding any happier. 'Would you go out and give her another call, Sam?'

I circumnavigated the little garden again, peering into shrubs and under the leaves of plants. 'Ebony!' I hollered, shaking the packet of treats every few steps. 'Come on, Ebony, where are you, baby?'

A neighbour's big white cat jumped down from the fence, obviously liking the promise of the cat treats, and followed me round the garden. I laughed. 'Where's that little rascal Ebony, eh?'

But the white cat just looked at me disdainfully and walked off again.

'No luck?' Nana asked when I went back into the kitchen.

'Not yet. But don't worry. She'll turn up.'

Nana couldn't concentrate on her paper or her crossword puzzle. She kept getting up from her chair, walking to the back door, looking out and shaking her head.

A little later the doorbell rang and I got up, expecting it to be David calling for me for our usual Saturday morning walk with the dogs. But it wasn't. It was Joe, standing on the doorstep and looking like he'd rather be anywhere else in the world but there.

'Oh, er, hello. Is everything all right?' I said at once, my first thought naturally of terminal illnesses and hospices, my second of Hugo and his leg injury and finally, rather less nobly, I wondered about anything I might have done wrong with the appointment system.

'Yes. Um, that is, no, not really. I, er … look, it's just, well, the thing is …'

I stared at him. Joe Bradley, mumbling awkwardly and shifting from foot to foot on my doorstep, unable to meet my eyes? What on earth? Was he still angry with me for what I'd innocently said to his daughter about her poor mum?

'Joe, I'm really sorry about upsetting Ruby—' I started, hoping to head off any more embarrassment. But before either of us could get any further, there was a shriek from inside the house.

'*Ebony!*'

I turned, abandoning Joe there on the doorstep, and ran down the hallway into the kitchen. 'Is she back? What's wrong?' I called, but before the words were even out of my mouth, I could see only too well. 'Oh no!' I said. 'Is it still alive?'

'Only just, I'd say,' came Joe's voice from behind me, making me and Nana look up in surprise. 'Sorry, please excuse me walking in,' he added. 'I thought – when I heard you scream – that I might be able to help.'

'Thanks,' I said. 'Um, perhaps it *would* be best if you picked it up, if you don't mind. I'm wary of doing even more damage than Ebony's already done.'

It was a baby rabbit, lying very still where Nana had made Ebony drop it on the kitchen floor, its breathing very faint and shallow, its eyes glazed.

'I can't imagine how she managed to catch it,' Nana said shakily. 'She's not very big herself.'

'But now we know why she stayed out all night,' I pointed out.

'It might have been injured already,' Joe muttered as he lifted the poor thing on to a clean towel I held ready.

'Perhaps another cat got it first. It's a jungle out there, isn't it, Ebony?' He glanced at the little cat, who was watching crossly as Nana held her back from her prize.

'Do you think it can be saved?' I asked, looking at the rabbit's limp, bloodied body.

'No,' he said. 'Afraid not, and it wouldn't be kind to try. I'll take it straight back to the surgery and euthanise it, if it even survives that long.'

'Thank you, Joe.' Nana sighed. 'Perhaps the bell on Ebony's collar isn't working.'

'It might give the birds a fighting chance,' Joe said. 'But not rabbits so much, maybe, if Ebony's learning to sit quietly watching their burrow.' He looked at Ebony again and gave her a warm smile. 'You're a crafty little girl, aren't you? Too clever by half!'

I walked back with him to the front door. 'Thanks,' I said. 'I'm sorry to have got you lumbered with that.'

'No problem.'

'But … was there something you wanted to tell me?' He hadn't, after all, turned up to shuffle awkwardly on my doorstep, just to make himself available in case a fatally injured baby rabbit happened to appear.

'Um, yes.' He still wasn't meeting my eyes. 'It's just … I wanted to say—'

But just at that moment, David appeared at the cottage gate with Apollo and Brian. 'Morning, Sam! Ready to walk these two off their paws again?' He stopped and stared at Joe, who stared back.

'Right,' Joe said abruptly, holding the towel with the moribund rabbit close to his chest. 'I'll be off then and will despatch this little chap. Bye.'

'But you haven't told me what—' I called after him as he walked away.

'Nothing important,' he replied without even looking back, seeming oblivious to the fact that I was now going to spend the rest of the weekend wondering what it was all about.

'What was *he* doing here?' David asked in a tone of voice that was, for him, almost aggressive.

'Helping us with a half-dead rabbit,' I told him. 'Courtesy of Ebony. She stayed out all night hunting – Nana was frantic with worry.'

'Oh dear. Now your troubles start, eh, Peggy?' he said in a kinder tone to Nana. And he launched into a long and rather too vivid description of the number, size and ultimate condition of various frogs, grass snakes and rodents his own KitKat had brought into the house over the years.

The subject of Joe was thankfully forgotten and Nana seemed quite relieved to see us off on our walk with the dogs. But as we walked I was finding it hard to concentrate on anything David was saying. It had unsettled me to have Joe coming to the house, and I felt very anxious at the thought of what I could have done wrong to solicit a visit from him.

Eventually David asked me if I was feeling all right.

'Yes, sorry. Just a bit of a headache.' I lied, and then had to backtrack quickly when he made such a fuss about my health; that I ought to get more rest, not work so hard, go to bed earlier, eat more, and so on, until I wanted to hit him. He could really be suffocating with his concern.

'I'm fine, give it a rest, for God's sake!' I snapped, and then had to endure the strained atmosphere of his hurt feelings for the rest of the walk. Sometimes, I thought, nice though David was, it was just so wearing having to bear the burden of his feelings for me.

By the time I went into work on Monday morning, I was dreading facing Joe. Apart from anything else, I knew I'd have to tell him soon about my pregnancy – if he hadn't already guessed. I was halfway through now, and feeling great, but getting bigger by the week. Fortunately the weather was very warm and I'd got some light, floaty tops to wear to work that I hoped simply looked cool and didn't shout 'maternity'. I ought to tell Joe myself, but perhaps I'd wait until I'd found out what his visit on Saturday had been all about.

When I arrived at the surgery, Natalie told me Joe had gone to see a sick cow at one of the farms, and by the time he arrived back, his first patient, a scruffy-looking old black dog, was waiting for him with his elderly owner. Joe looked a little flustered but greeted us all surprisingly politely, apologising profusely to the lady with the dog. After they'd been seen and had both hobbled out, he seemed to want to chat: he was leaning on the reception desk – in a way that was both awkward and familiar at the same time – and telling me and Natalie about the dog's condition. I'd have liked to talk to him then, while he seemed to be in a reasonably good mood – if only Natalie hadn't been there, ears flapping.

The rest of the morning was busy and, later, when there was a gap between Natalie leaving and Val arriving, I had to help out with a working sheepdog who'd been brought in as an emergency with a cut paw.

'Thank you, Sam. You were very helpful,' Joe said after we'd finished treating the dog.

I nearly fainted. It was probably only the second or third time Joe had ever spoken to me quite so gratefully and politely.

'Oh,' I said. 'No problem. Glad to help.' And then, realising I finally had a chance to bring up the subject, I added, 'Joe – was there something you wanted when you called at my place on Saturday?'

He shook his head. 'It's not important right now.'

'I see.' I took a deep breath. 'Well, look, while we're on our own, I just want to say that I'm obviously really sorry about your wife. I mean, that goes without saying, of course, but I'm so sorry. I didn't know and I ended up upsetting Ruby. I'd never have wanted to do that. If I'd only known ...'

I stopped, aware that it now sounded as if I were criticising him for not telling me about his personal life.

'Well, I'm sorry anyway,' I repeated, feeling increasingly more uncomfortable, as he still hadn't responded. I was probably just making things worse, I thought, if that were even possible. And I still hadn't worked up the courage to tell him about my pregnancy. I was just about to go back out to the waiting room to see if the next patient was there yet, when he suddenly asked: 'Do you have to go straight home after you finish here tonight?'

'Er – no, not if you need me to help with something,' I said.

'No. I just wondered if you'd have a quick drink with me at the Horse.' He was looking out of the window while he spoke. It was bizarre, almost as if he were inviting someone outside in the street, rather than me, to go to the pub with him. 'I can explain then. Why I came round on Saturday, I mean.'

'Oh.' By now I was pretty much lost for words. A drink after work? What the hell ...? Was it going to be a sweetener for telling me the job wasn't working out? That I'd done something terribly wrong (quite apart from upsetting his daughter)? 'Um, well, yes, OK, sure.' And then, embarrassingly, I suddenly remembered. 'Oh no! I'm really sorry – I can't. My parents are coming down from Norfolk today, and of course, they want to see me. I don't see them too often and it would look pretty rude if I didn't—'

'No worries,' he said surprisingly calmly. 'Let's make it tomorrow instead.'

'You've got an evening surgery tomorrow,' I reminded him.

'Right. Well, how's the diary looking for lunchtime?'

'Tomorrow lunchtime?' I could barely scroll through the appointment system for surprise. 'Well, you have a free hour scheduled between one and two. Unless there's an emergency, of course.'

'OK. Tomorrow lunchtime it is, then.' He nodded. 'Have a good evening with your parents.'

It seemed that just as I'd found out the reason for Joe's stroppy moods – and just as I'd forgiven him, in my head, because after all who could blame him for being unhappy, with his awful home situation? – he'd undergone a personality change and become more polite and reasonable.

I didn't have a chance to think much about it, though. As I returned home from work, Mum and Dad were waiting for me at the cottage. Mum threw herself at me, enveloping me in a hug as soon as I walked through the door.

'Darling! Look at you!' She held me away from her, studying me intently. 'You look wonderful! You're positively blooming!'

She sounded slightly manic. I smiled and hugged her back, agreeing that I was feeling fine, and she ushered me gently on to the sofa, sitting next to me and grabbing my hand in a girly let's-be-friends kind of way, suggesting we have a talk about the baby while Dad and Nana were sitting outside.

I was surprised that Mum was suddenly so excited about the baby, but I then understood why as soon as she told me that her friend Sharon Overton was expecting her first grandchild too. I got the feeling we were in some kind of competition, and I didn't seem to be winning. I was, apparently, being silly for not wanting to find out the baby's sex. Sharon's daughter Julia already knew she was having a boy. I was even more ridiculous, it transpired, for not having a place of my own. Sharon's daughter had a beautiful three-bedroom house on a new estate just outside King's Lynn. She was also married to a bank manager – which obviously helped – but when I pointed that out to Mum, she sighed and reminded me that she and Dad would help me financially if I wanted to move somewhere more 'suitable'.

'I'm not saying you should move back to Norfolk,' she added quickly. 'It's very nice that you want to keep an eye on your nan, and I suppose Dorset is all right, in its way. But for heaven's sake, Samantha, you can't live in your grandmother's spare bedroom for ever.'

'I know. I'll look into renting something locally, after my maternity leave, when I know whether I can go back to work part-time, or—'

'Here in Hope Green? Surely there's far more suitable property available somewhere a bit more *civilised*? Dorchester is supposed to be very nice, for instance. Dad and I noticed some adverts for new town houses going up there, and you'd still be close enough to your nan ...'

'There's nothing uncivilised about Hope Green!' I shot back. I'd always known Mum was a terrible snob, but it infuriated me to think she was ashamed to admit to her stupid friend Sharon Overton that I lived in a cottage in Hope Green. 'I don't want to live in Dorchester, thank you very much. Or anywhere else. I love it here.'

'Really?' She looked at me with irritation. 'There aren't even any decent shops for miles around! Where are you proposing to buy things for the baby?'

'Online,' I said, 'like everyone does, these days. And there *is* a shop, as you know – it sells everything—'

'Sharon's taking Julia out shopping in London, for all the essentials,' Mum said, sounding so wistful that for a moment I almost felt sorry for her – until she added: 'And she's ordered one of those top-of-the-range Bugaboo prams for her. Apparently all the celebrities have them. I thought perhaps I'd—'

'Mum, I know you're trying to help, and I'm really grateful. But a pram isn't supposed to be a status symbol.' Especially not for the grandmother, I thought to myself. 'And I wouldn't even *want* a top-of-the-range one. It'd look out of place around here. I was going to look on eBay for a good second-hand—'

'Second-hand, for my grandchild? Absolutely not! How could I ever face Sharon—'

I sighed. I'd had to bite my tongue to stop myself from saying *stuff Sharon and stuff her bloody daughter*.

'Honestly, I really do appreciate everything you're doing to help me,' I said firmly. 'But I'm not entering into some kind of ridiculous contest with Julia Overton about who's going to have the best stuff for their baby.'

'I see. And you're insisting on living here in this village, even with a baby?' she said, as if doing so was as bad as child abuse.

'Absolutely. I can't think of anywhere nicer to bring up a child.'

She tightened her lips. 'Well, your father won't be pleased.'

I couldn't imagine my father caring less, not that it was going to make any difference. I was beginning to wish they hadn't come.

When the doorbell rang I was quite relieved – whoever it was. Perhaps now we could change the subject. But when I opened the door to find David smiling at me, with Mabel and Tess tugging on their leads and salivating all over the doorstep with excitement, I almost wished I'd hidden in the bathroom instead.

'Coming out for a walk?' he said.

'Sorry, David, I can't tonight. Mum and Dad have come down from Norfolk and they're not staying long so—'

But Nana had hobbled in from the garden, and greeted him with pleasure. 'Oh, hello David. Come in and meet Sam's parents.'

Before I could stop her, she was pulling David into the house, with the dogs coiling themselves enthusiastically round our legs. She called out to Mum and Dad to 'come and meet Sam's friend David'.

To say it was a difficult encounter would be an understatement. Mum was trying to shake David's hand even as he tried frantically to stop the dogs jumping up at her legs. She kept giving me indignant looks, and I knew what those looks were saying. *Why haven't we been told about this?*

'Live in the village, do you? And what do you do for a living?' Dad was interrogating the poor guy as if he were a prospective suitor.

'I ... err ... walk dogs,' David said.

'He's also building up a freelance copywriting business,' I said, noticing the look on Mum's face. 'And he's a real help to Nana and me, doing odd jobs for us, helping her with shopping and stuff ...'

'Yes, he's done all that work in the garden, painted my shed and cleared out the attic too.' Nana agreed, smiling at David.

In the silence that followed, I noted quietly to David that I could see the dogs were desperate for their walk. He seemed as relieved to get away as I was to see him go. I knew exactly what was coming, and, sure enough, as soon as he had walked out the door, my parents cross-examined me about who he was, how long I'd known him and how often I saw him.

'He's just a friend,' I said wearily for what felt like the twentieth time, but Mum took no notice.

'I presume this is why you're so determined to stay here in the back of beyond, instead of making any attempt to *better yourself*,' Mum hissed at me when Nana was out of earshot. 'Samantha, I really cannot allow you to consider marrying a *village person* who *walks dogs*.'

I didn't want a full-blown row with her or for us to part on bad terms, so I just spelt out, as calmly as I could, that I had no intention of marrying anybody but if I did, it really wouldn't be up to her to allow it or not.

'I'm nearly twenty-eight, Mum, not seventeen,' I reminded her, and she sniffed and gave me a look that said quite plainly that nevertheless, she still considered me a juvenile.

When they left we hugged goodbye. But there was disappointment in my mum's eyes and a leaden feeling of resentment in my heart. Mum was being just as bad as Claire, with her dismissive attitude to my choices in life. I wondered whether she and Dad were going to issue me with some kind of ultimatum: that the money they were helping me with was dependent on me changing my lifestyle. Well, as long as I kept my job, I'd just have to manage without it, but I hated the feeling that they didn't approve of me. It felt as if no one, other than Nana, would give me their blessing.

CHAPTER TWENTY-ONE

By the time I arrived at work the next day, my annoyance with my mother and even my constant nagging anxiety about Claire and Adam had faded to a dull niggle at the back of my mind, overtaken completely by the worry about going out to lunch with Joe. I was sure this sudden invitation couldn't mean anything good. If Joe was pleased with me, he'd just come out and say so, as he'd already done before, even if that was a rare occurrence. No, the reason he'd been uncharacteristically polite must be because he felt awkward about the fact that he was going to fire me. Perhaps he'd say I'd failed to impress him during my three-month trial and he'd found someone better? Someone more qualified, more able, less 'frivolous', less ... *pregnant*. Oh my God! I sat up straight at my desk as the realisation suddenly hit me. That was it! He'd noticed, of course – what an idiot I was, thinking the loose cotton tops would fool anyone for long, let alone someone who dealt with pregnancies on a daily basis – and OK, I knew pregnant cows and sheep and cats were a bit different but even so …

Joe was going to tell me he didn't want a pregnant woman working for him. But he couldn't actually *do* that, could he? It would be illegal. Should I be calling a solicitor or an employment tribunal or something? I started trying to Google it, but kept getting interrupted by patients arriving at the desk. It was no good, I'd just have to wait to see what it was he wanted to say.

Just after one o'clock, he came into the reception area and nodded at me. 'Let's go, then,' he said, holding the door open for me.

Natalie normally covered reception during my break, during which I often popped home to have lunch with Nana. Needless to say, when she realised Joe and I were leaving the premises together she looked up with eyes as wide as saucers.

'Call me on the mobile if there's anything urgent,' Joe told her as we left.

We crossed the road to the Horse without any further discussion and settled at a table in the far corner of the bar. He slid the bar menu across to me.

'Choose whatever you want. My treat.'

I swallowed my surprise. 'Just a ham sandwich, thanks,' I said. What would he have said if I'd ordered a steak? 'And an orange juice and lemonade.'

There was another uncomfortable silence after he came back from ordering the food.

'Right,' he said finally, fiddling with his cutlery. 'Well, look, I expect you guessed, really, why I came round to see you on Saturday.'

'Um, no, I didn't, actually.'

'No? I thought it would've been obvious. I should have said it straight away, but there was the situation with your cat catching the baby rabbit. And then you had another visitor ...'

'Oh yes, David. With the dogs. We often walk them together on a Saturday.'

'Right.' He frowned. 'So unfortunately I've left it longer than I should have done, which makes it worse, I realise that.'

'So what is it?' I just wanted him to get it over with, now.

'An apology, obviously.' He finally met my eyes, for what must have been the first time in days. 'I had no right to snap at you. It wasn't your fault Ruby was upset. I should have told you about my wife. Unfortunately I find it very hard to talk about, but I realise it would avoid a lot of distress for everyone if I explained the situation from the start.'

'Oh,' I said, hoping I didn't sound as shocked as I felt. I'd been so sure I was in for some kind of criticism at the very least, if not the sack, or a discussion about my pregnancy and its impact on my work. An apology was the last thing I'd been expecting. 'There's no need to apologise. I do understand. Obviously I was really upset that I'd put

my foot in it, and …' I hesitated, then went on in a rush,
' … upset for you, too – and Ruby. It must be absolutely
dreadful for you all.'

'Thank you. Yes, it is.' He sighed, and almost as if he'd
suddenly decided he might as well let it all out now, he
went on in a rush: 'Andrea had the original cancer a few
years back, and we thought at one point that the surgery
– and all the treatment afterwards – had worked. But the
cancer came back. It had spread to her lungs. This past
year has been … pretty tough.' He wiped a hand across
his face. 'She's on so many drugs now, she barely knows
whether Ruby or I are there.'

'How awful.' I could feel my eyes prickling with tears.
It was no wonder the poor guy was difficult at times. 'I
really am so sorry.'

'No, *I'm* sorry,' he insisted. 'When I spoke to Ruby on
Friday evening about what you'd said to her at the stables
and explained that you didn't know about her mum, she
told me off.' He smiled ruefully. 'She said it was my fault,
that she'd told *her* friends, so that they knew the score and
didn't say the wrong things, so why hadn't I done the
same? So I promised her I'd say sorry to you.'

'She seems like a great kid,' I said gently. 'You should
be very proud.'

'You're right, she is.' He sighed again. 'And it was wrong
of me to make you feel it was your fault she was upset.
She seems to like you – she asks after you all the time.
And she's mentioned that she'd like you to watch her riding
when Hugo's fit again.'

'I'd love to. I'm so glad Hugo's on the mend. I can see how important he is to her.'

'Yes, he's helped her enormously.' Joe smiled. 'He's a good pony, very gentle, and intelligent too. She loves him to bits – they've formed a really special bond. And it looks as though he'll be fit enough for her to ride him at the gymkhana. She's so excited about it, and she desperately wants you there for that. Would that be OK with you?'

'Of course!' I closed my mind, as firmly as I could, to the images that flooded my mind: the jump, the fear, the screams ... 'As long as you're happy with it.'

He shrugged. 'It's hard for me to be there for her all the time. I just hope I can make it up to her somehow. I'll have to be daddy *and* mummy to her before too long, and I know it won't be easy.'

'No, of course it won't, I can imagine.'

I didn't know what else to say. It was such a surprise that he was talking to me about his personal life at all, never mind letting down his guard to this extent, confiding his feelings to me. I felt like I was finally seeing something of the real Joe – the one we only saw glimpses of at the surgery when he was treating sick animals or tenderly caring for those who were past saving. I suddenly felt a warmth towards him that overcame all the previous hurts and annoyances.

'The thing is,' he suddenly went on, staring at the table, 'it's reached the point now – with Andrea's illness – where I just want it to be over. For her sake. Does that sound terrible?'

'No, it doesn't, Joe. I'm sure anyone would feel the same in your situation.'

I did it instinctively – I reached out across the table and laid a hand on his. It was only when he looked up at me and then back down at my hand, that I'd realised what I'd done. I expected him to shake my hand off immediately, but for a moment he just continued to stare at it, his expression unreadable.

But at that moment Suzie the barmaid appeared at our table. 'One ham sandwich on granary, no mustard, one sausage and onion baguette,' she announced flatly, hovering with the plates as if she didn't know what to do with them.

And I jumped, moving my hand away from his like it was burnt.

'Enjoy your food,' Suzie said, plonking it down in front of us and walking disinterestedly away.

'Thank you for this,' I said, after an awkward moment of silence.

'You're welcome. It's the least I could do.'

I picked up half of my sandwich and began to nibble at it. In truth, I'd lost my appetite the moment I'd seen him staring at our two hands. My heart was racing. Did this – the way he was opening up to me, the sudden new closeness we seemed to have achieved – did it *mean* anything?

'I'm well aware, Sam, that I'm not always the easiest person to work for,' he was saying now, picking up his own lunch and putting it down again. He gave me a proper smile, as if to signify that I was allowed to laugh, and I did, though a little awkwardly, a little breathlessly.

For a few minutes we both sat in silence, making half-hearted attempts at our sandwiches. I had no idea what to say. Then I gave another little self-conscious laugh and admitted, 'I honestly thought this lunch was going to be about something else.'

'Such as what?'

'I thought I'd probably done something wrong. Or that you weren't satisfied with my work.'

'Don't be ridiculous,' he said. 'Didn't I tell you how well I thought you'd settled in?'

'Well, yes, but—'

'I'm not the type to ladle out praise every five minutes, but if you really need that kind of reassurance, then ...' He stared at me as if he was trying to think of the right words. The air seemed to resonate with expectation. 'Then I can tell you,' he went on, leaning closer to me, his voice becoming more earnest, 'you should know that you're absolutely perfect.'

His face by now was quite close to mine. I found myself staring at him. There was something about him today – something about the anguish he'd been pouring out, the sorrow in those dark eyes, and now the emphasis he'd put on that word: *perfect*. Later, I asked myself over and over again what the hell I'd been thinking. I leaned in towards him and lifted my face to his. But instead of his lips meeting mine, as (if I was totally honest) I'd imagined happening a hundred times, he moved abruptly away, sat back in his chair, dropped his baguette on his plate and added quickly, with a splutter: 'I mean, perfect for the *job*, obviously.'

'Oh.' My face burned hot with embarrassment. What an idiot – what on earth must he think of me now? But somehow I managed to stutter back: 'Thank you. I'm glad you're pleased with my work.'

'I am, and perhaps I should have made that more clear.' He now didn't sound even the slightest bit ruffled. It was almost as if nothing had happened. Perhaps he was so used to women trying to kiss him across pub tables that he just ignored it and moved on. 'As far as I'm concerned, I'm more than satisfied with your three months' probation and I'm happy to make your employment permanent.'

Ah. Now, of course, despite my intense mortification, I needed to tell him about the baby.

'Thank you, that's great,' I said, trying to avoid his eyes. 'But as I'm sure you've noticed by now, I will be needing a few months off at the end of the year, and possibly to talk to you about going part-time afterwards.'

I patted my stomach, to make my meaning completely clear and risked a glance to see his expression.

He was staring at me as if I'd spoken in tongues. 'You mean – you're *pregnant*?' he said.

'Yes. The baby's due early in December.' I paused. 'I thought perhaps you'd realised.'

'No. I hadn't.' His whole tone had changed dramatically. 'You've kept it well hidden, obviously.'

'Well, of course I'll keep working for as long as I can, right up till a week or so before the birth, I hope, and—'

'Right. Thank you for letting me know, I suppose.' He pushed back his chair and, to my surprise, started to get to his feet. 'I'll go and pay for the food.'

'You're going?' I said. 'You haven't finished.'

'I've had enough. I'll get back to work.' He threw down his serviette. 'Don't rush. Sorry for boring you with my problems.'

'I wasn't bored, Joe!' I gasped. I couldn't believe the closeness I'd thought we'd developed earlier had been replaced by such coldness.

'Look, it's obvious now that you've got enough on your plate in your own life, without having to listen to my worries. To be honest it's always a mistake to let personal lives intrude into working relationships. Let's just keep it professional, shall we?'

He turned and walked away, leaving me open-mouthed, bewildered and on the verge of tears. What the hell was *that* all about? Was he annoyed that I hadn't told him earlier about the pregnancy? Or was it, after all, my stupid, *stupid* move there, attempting to kiss my boss in the middle of his lunch? My *married* boss, about to endure the loss of his poor dying wife? How on earth had I expected him to respond, for God's sake?

Burning with humiliation, I finished my drink and, leaving the rest of the sandwich on the plate, crept back to the surgery.

I sat down at my desk without looking at Natalie, who I knew would be staring at me and waiting for me to spill the beans. I had to concentrate on my work. I had to not think about what just happened.

And I'd have to see Joe, and talk to him every day. But just at that moment I had no idea how I was going to do it. It was unbelievable that less than half an hour earlier, I'd felt so close to him, and now it seemed as if he couldn't bear the sight of me. I felt so stupid and upset with myself. I couldn't imagine how I'd managed to read so much into a few confidences over lunch, when I knew perfectly well that Joe was about as interested in me as he was in the dirt underneath his shoes – and anyway, did I even really *like* the man? He'd been rude and horrible to me more times than I could count! Was it normal for a pregnant woman's hormones to mess her around as much as this?

With all these thoughts going through my head, I managed to get through the day – only just – and walked home slowly, trying to decide how to word my letter of resignation. Although I loved the job, these emotional ups and downs were taking too much out of me, and more to the point, I was sure they weren't good for the baby. It would be better for me to look for another job. A temporary hotel receptionist's post would be less stressful by far.

As I rounded the bend in the road just before home, I glanced up and froze on the spot. There was a car parked outside Meadow Croft – a car that was instantly recognisable to everyone in Hope Green: the distinctive shade of turquoise and the huge dent on the outside rear door. It belonged to Dr Williams, the local GP, and it could only mean one thing: something was wrong with Nana.

I ran the last few yards down the road, almost crying out with alarm as I saw Irene Parks coming out of her cottage next door. She was looking down the road and shaking her head.

'Ah, Sam!' she said as I reached the front gate. 'I've been trying to call you.'

My phone! I gasped out loud at my own stupidity – I'd turned it to silent mode before going to lunch with Joe and forgotten to turn the sound back on again.

'I tried the surgery phone a couple of times but it always seemed to be busy, and I didn't want to leave your nan...' Irene was going on.

'What's wrong?' I cried. 'Is Nana OK?'

She put her hand on my arm. 'Don't worry, Sam,' she said soothingly. 'Come in and sit down; don't start upsetting yourself. The doctor's here, it'll be all right.' And then, as if to contradict herself, she added, to my horror, 'The ambulance is on its way.'

I rushed indoors, cursing myself as I went. If something terrible had happened to Nana, while I'd been ... oh my God, while I'd been *flirting* with my surly, stroppy boss over lunch ... I'd never forgive myself. Or him, I added to myself fiercely, even though I knew it had really nothing to do with him. At that moment, as far as I was concerned, I couldn't care less whether I ever saw or spoke to Joe Bradley, ever again.

PART 4

A NEW START

CHAPTER TWENTY-TWO

Nana sighed and tutted with exasperation as I put the blanket over her legs and tucked it around her feet.

'Leave off with all the fussing, for crying out loud!' she said. 'Anyone would think I was cold – it's August, not bloody Christmas; I can see the sun pouring through the windows. I'm not feeble in the head as well as the legs, you know.'

'I know, Nana. Sorry.'

I lifted the blanket off again. It was hard to know how to help her; she was so cross and upset about being incapacitated.

'No.' She sighed. 'I'm sorry, sorry for snapping, sorry for being a bad-tempered old bag. I don't want you taking any more time off work to look after me. I'll be all right, you know, Little Sam. Just leave a flask of tea and the biscuit tin by my side …'

'I'm not leaving you until you can get about all right again,' I said.

I hardly cared, anyway, about the couple of days I'd taken off work since Nana's emergency dash to the hospital. Compared with the fear I'd felt when I'd pushed past Irene Parks to get into the cottage and found Nana lying on the sofa half-conscious, her face grey with pain, my worries about work had faded into insignificance. Dr Williams had apparently had to help her up from where she'd fallen off a stool on to the hard kitchen floor.

'She was trying to reach something on the top shelf of the cupboard,' Irene told me.

'The big cake tin,' Nana muttered. 'Wanted it to make you a birthday cake for tomorrow, Sam.'

'Oh, *Nana!* You didn't have to! You should've waited,' I cried, kneeling down beside her.

'Lucky I was in my back garden and heard the crash when she fell. She'd knocked herself out, poor thing,' Irene went on.

The doctor gave me a sympathetic smile. 'I think her left ankle might be fractured. And she's going to be black and blue with bruises, I'm afraid.'

I wanted to drive her to the hospital myself, but Dr Williams said I wasn't in a fit state – the shock had made me feel shaky – and the ambulance arrived before I could argue the point, so I went with her instead. She was kept in overnight as she'd bumped her head in the fall. It wasn't until the next day, after I'd been back and brought her home, that I suddenly realised I hadn't even told anyone at work.

'Oh, Sam!' Natalie said, sounding flustered when she answered my call. 'I'm sorry, I can't talk now. We're in the middle of cancelling everyone. We got Kerry to come in early as we couldn't get hold of you.'

Kerry was the weekend receptionist. But why had she had to go in early, and why were they 'cancelling everyone'? I couldn't make sense of it, and Natalie had hung up without even asking me why I hadn't turned up at work. It wasn't until the afternoon, when Val called me back, that I found out. Joe's wife had deteriorated further overnight and he'd had to move her to the hospice. He'd taken the day off and had instructed the girls to rebook all the non-urgent cases and refer anything urgent to the big vets in town. Ruby would be home at home all day now as it was the school summer holiday, and apparently Joe's mother had been staying for some time, to look after her. I could barely imagine how hard this development would have hit the little girl. No wonder Joe hadn't gone into work. My own circumstances with Nana's broken ankle seemed suddenly less serious.

'Don't worry, Sam. Stay with your nan until you're sure you can leave her,' Val said gently. 'Kerry's going to cover for you.'

I could hardly tell her, given the circumstances, that Kerry might have to cover for me permanently. My determination to hand in my notice was wavering now there was some distance between Joe and myself, and anyway, it seemed churlish to harbour a grudge against a man whose life was currently being turned upside down.

Unfortunately Joe's wife passed away a few days later. I'd gone back to work that Monday, only to find that he had again called in to cancel his appointments. It had happened in the early hours of the morning.

I'd never even met her, but I felt consumed with sadness for the man I'd wanted nothing to do with just a few days earlier, and for his poor little daughter's loss of her mother.

On the day of the funeral, we closed the surgery completely. Nobody in the village would have wanted it any other way. Joe might have been unpopular in the beginning, but word had eventually got around and people turned out in force for Andrea's funeral. The church was almost as full as it had been on Easter Sunday, and I felt that this was Hope Green's way of showing Joe and Ruby its collective love and support.

'They may not have lived here long enough for us to get to know her, the poor soul,' said Maggie Stammers, leaning over from her seat behind me in the church. 'But at the end of the day, she was part of Hope Green, same as Joe is himself.'

Sitting further back in the church was 'miserable' Nora, flanked on either side by women from the village who hadn't had a good word to say about her until they found out she was ill and were now rallying round her. Nora had been given a good prognosis now that she was having treatment, but she'd taken retirement from the post office and her previous assistant Frances had been given her job, much to everyone's satisfaction. I thought how typical it was of village life here that even the most unlikeable characters were looked after and cared for when hard times struck. Even old Billy Henderson had turned up looking relatively smart and clean for the funeral, and I was relieved to see he was sitting quietly on his own and didn't appear to be eyeing up any unwilling ladies.

The family sat in the front row with their heads bowed. Joe had his arm around Ruby, as did her grandmother on her other side, while Paul the vicar quietly read a moving eulogy. My heart ached for them all, and as they followed the coffin out to the churchyard I couldn't believe that I'd been considering handing in my notice. How could I when the last thing he needed was work complications at the moment?

I thought back to a few days earlier, before we'd heard about Joe's terrible news. It surprised me how sure I had been that I wanted to leave it all.

'I can't put up with it – with *him* – any more,' I'd said to Nana. 'It's making me too stressed, it's not right, it'll affect the baby.'

'What a load of rubbish.' Nana had brushed me off.

I'd stared at her, taken aback and hurt. But, now that she'd started, she went on, saying that I cared more about my own feelings than Joe's, that I should know better than to expect him to be full of the joys of spring, what with his poor wife 'probably taking her last breaths on God's earth even as we speak'.

If only I had known how true her words were.

'I know. I feel really sorry for him, I've told him that!' I protested, telling her that I'd listened to him pouring out his heart and thought we'd reached an understanding. 'He even told me he was pleased with my work, that I was "perfect" for the job …' I swallowed. No way was I going to admit to Nana that I'd tried to kiss him. 'But then, when I told him I'm going to have a baby, he snapped my head off and walked out on me.'

'But what is he? Your husband? Your boyfriend or something? You get all emotional and upset over his moods …' She shook her head at me. 'No. He's your boss, and the only thing that ought to matter to you is that he's pleased with your work. If he wants to act like a spoilt child, well, let him. He's probably just disappointed that you're going to be taking maternity leave and he'll have to find someone to cover you.'

'There was no need to be so unpleasant about it.'

'No. But there's no need for you to be so upset about it, either,' she said.

'I'm pregnant.' I sniffed. 'I get emotional.'

'I know.' She smiled. And by the time she'd reminded me that I loved my job, and more to the point, that I needed it, needed the maternity leave, needed Joe to want me back again afterwards, I was beginning to feel that the decision to hand in my notice had been a silly, hysterical overreaction.

But seeing Joe and his family at the funeral really cemented it for me, and I made a promise to myself: I'd work for Joe for as long as he wanted me and I'd never again make the mistake of taking anything he said – good or bad – to heart. Val was right when she'd told me the poor guy really couldn't help it.

Nana's wonderful brand of down-to-earth common sense had once again pulled me through. She hadn't been able to make it to the funeral, what with her ankle being strapped up and all, but if she'd been here I could just imagine what she'd be saying about Joe: 'Anyway, I'm only your grand-mother, it's nothing to do with me, I'm saying nothing.'

I smiled despite myself.

CHAPTER TWENTY-THREE

I kept my promise over the next few weeks, accepting Joe's heavy silence and his dark and distant moods for what they were – the grief of a man who found it hard to share his feelings.

The warm summer slowly gave way to a chilly, wet autumn. The carpet of red and brown leaves that lay underfoot was so soggy and slippery that David and I had to watch our step as we walked the dogs in the woods, and the sea, when we ventured as far as the beach, was as grey as the sky.

My pregnancy was advancing fast and most of my pre-maternity clothes were no longer any use to me, but I was still feeling fit from all the fresh air and exercise. And despite everything, I was glad I hadn't resigned from the vets. I tried to concentrate on staying calm and efficient in my work. It gradually got easier, and Joe and I seemed to slip back into a quiet, impersonal, professional relationship. But my pregnancy was never mentioned by either of us, and neither, thank God, was the fact that I'd made that embarrassing move on him during our lunch. If I occasionally pondered the fact that he was now a widower, a single man, and I was still attracted to him, I shut the thought down quickly and crossly. How could I even think like that, when the poor man was grieving? It didn't seem decent.

By October, my mood had become as gloomy as the weather. When I was at home, I moped in my room, tormenting myself constantly about Claire and Adam. I thought, often, about calling Claire to try to find out the truth about the situation, but then I remembered how rude she'd been when she came to Hope Green. She hadn't spoken to me since. Why should I be the first to break the silence?

I was miserable, too, about David. It was all very well telling myself I'd made it clear that we were just good friends, but I knew he was still hoping I'd change my mind, perhaps after I'd had the baby. I knew I wouldn't. Kind, funny and endlessly patient though he was, I just didn't feel that way about him. He still felt like an older brother to me.

It wasn't fair. It would be better for him if we stopped seeing each other, but I couldn't bring myself to say that to him.

And when I wasn't stressing about either of *those* issues, I was brooding about Mum and Dad. I'd hated the way Mum had been comparing me with her friend Sharon's daughter. But was it really such a crime that she wanted

what she saw as the best for me and my baby? Even if I
didn't agree with her views, I supposed I could have been
a bit more gracious about my parents' generosity. If they
wanted to buy a nice pram for their grandchild, and if
Mum would get so much pleasure from a trip to London
to look at ridiculously expensive baby clothes in the West
End shops, was I actually just being mean by refusing? In
the end, I gave in. I called her and said I would like to
meet her for a day in London. She immediately became so
excited by my change of heart that she'd started asking
whether I'd thought any more about moving to Dorchester.
I'd had to cut her off sharply and assure her of my decision
to stay in Hope Green.

Even Izzie had commented that I seemed to be quiet
and preoccupied.

'Sorry,' I told her. 'I've just had a few things on my mind
lately.'

She'd given me a sympathetic look. She knew about the
Claire and Adam issue, of course, and I'd also talked to
her about my mum's visit. But I suspect she thought I
should snap out of it; even I knew I probably should. I
had the baby to look forward to, and everything was going
well, wasn't it? Surely I wasn't starting to regret my decision to move down here?

I'd even found it hard to get excited when, the previous
month, Izzie had told me that seven new children from
outside the village had been enrolled at the preschool
already, and that there had been some more enquiries
about filling the remaining vacancies after half-term. She

expected me to be thrilled, stressing that it was all due to my idea of advertising outside the area. And I *was* pleased, of course. It meant the preschool's future was assured for now, and the new children might then stay in the village when they moved up to 'big' school. Izzie had told some of the other mums that it was all because of me, and I was now being met with people in the street and in the shop who came up to me and thanked me, and they all asked if I'd be helping on the preschool committee in due course. It was what I'd been hoping for: an active involvement in the village. But somehow I couldn't shake off my autumn blues.

I knew that I wasn't going to settle until I'd somehow got closure on the business with Adam and Claire. I hadn't even had occasion to email him recently as, apart from the earlier scare, it had been a very straightforward pregnancy. There was one way I could find out the truth, I realised, without having to talk to Claire at all. I'd call on Adam while I was in London, take him by surprise and demand to know what was going on. He'd never been very good at concealing the truth. He even used to find it hard to keep Christmas and birthday presents secret when we were together. I'd probably get my answer just by the expression on his face. At least then I'd know and I could move on.

Meanwhile I had a very important date: the riding school's gymkhana. I'd been going to the stables to see and chat to Ruby at least once a week since her mother's death and I'd been struck by how brave the little girl was being.

'I try not to cry,' she'd told me, not long after the funeral. 'And it's hard, because I miss her so much and so does Daddy. But she was too ill, wasn't she, Sam, and she couldn't get well again, so it's better for her to be in heaven with the angels.'

I'd given her a hug. 'Mummy would be so proud of you, sweetie.'

And when she clung to me then, her eyes full of tears, I think I would've promised her the earth if it would make her happy. So facing my own fears to watch her in the gymkhana was really not a lot to ask.

It took place on a Saturday afternoon. I hadn't expected Joe to be there but he turned up, straight from the Saturday clinic, just in time for the first competition, and sat down next to me.

'Good of you to come,' he muttered.

'I promised I would.'

My voice was trembling slightly. Watching the first child taking a jump had started my flashbacks again. I had to clench my fists and dig my fingernails into my palms to force myself to stay put. I felt Joe staring at me and I knew that if I looked round and met his gaze, I'd give myself away, so I kept staring at the jumps, trying to remind myself why I was there.

When it was Ruby's turn to compete, I tried my hardest to put my own fears aside. For a ten-year-old, she was a superb rider. The last jump worried me, though. It looked quite high for little Hugo. I sat on my hands, bit my lip and didn't even realise I'd been holding my breath until he'd cleared the jump and Ruby trotted him out of the ring, to a round of applause from the spectators. According to the announcer, she'd completed her clear round in an excellent time. She had a grin as wide as her face.

'Well done, Ruby!' Joe called out. 'Brilliant!' He turned to me, frowned and added in a different tone: 'Are you all right?'

'Yes, I'm fine, thank you,' I said a little sharply. I'd forgotten I was still trying to hold my breath and now my heart was pounding like mad. But it was all right. Ruby was OK; Hugo was OK. There'd been no problem with the jump, no screams, no horrific scene of people running into the ring with white faces, no ambulance sirens, no … awful, crippling, life-changing *guilt*.

'You don't look fine,' he persisted, staring at me. 'You've gone very pale. Do you feel faint or something?'

'No.' But actually, I did. I was beginning to gasp for breath. I lowered my head and closed my eyes, suddenly engulfed by nausea, and felt myself starting to sweat and shiver – and the next thing I was aware of was Joe grabbing my hand. My eyes flew open with shock, but then I realised, of course, he wasn't being affectionate – he was checking the pulse at my wrist.

'I thought you were a vet, not a doctor,' I managed to say.

'I know enough to recognise someone having a panic attack,' he replied. 'Try to slow your breathing, Sam. In through your nose – slowly, count to five. Out through your mouth. That's it. You'll feel better in a minute. Don't try to talk.'

Slowly, slowly, the pounding of my heart, the painful tingling in my fingers, the shaking and sweating began to settle. My head cleared and I realised how close to me Joe had moved, to check I was OK.

'Has this happened before?' he asked.

I nodded. 'Not recently. But it used to happen a lot. Years ago.'

'So do you know what's brought it on today?' He sounded so gentle – almost the way he did when he was treating a sick animal – that my eyes suddenly filled with tears and I just nodded again.

'I was frightened,' I said quietly. 'Watching Ruby jumping, I was scared she'd have an accident.' I took a deep breath and, sitting there on the hard bench beside the show ring at the riding school, I finally gave myself permission to let go, to unleash the memory that had haunted me since the age of eighteen. 'I had a riding accident myself,' I told him.

He frowned. 'Were you badly hurt?'

'No.' The tears were overflowing now, and I didn't try to stop them. 'Only a broken wrist.' I'd raged about that, at the time – the injustice of it. I should have come off worse. It should've been me, not Strawberry, my beautiful red roan mare, who suffered such terrible injuries. 'But my horse ...' I swallowed and shook my head. 'She had compound fractures of both front legs. It was impossible ... they couldn't ...'

I managed to take a deep breath, and Joe waited, silent. I was grateful for that.

'She couldn't be saved,' I whispered eventually. I'd screamed at them – all of them – the vets, the other riders, my parents. Screamed and screamed until my throat gave out, but I knew, really, there was no choice. There was only one kind thing they could do for Strawberry.

'I'm so sorry,' Joe said. He paused. 'Is that what stopped you trying again to get into veterinary college?'

'Yes.'

'But we have to come to terms with animals dying – sometimes in horrific ways like that. Even the ones we love. You would have coped.'

'You don't understand!' I snapped. 'It wasn't just that I couldn't get over losing Strawberry – it was *my fault*. The whole thing was my stupid fault.'

'What, you misjudged a jump? Come on, that was an accident, surely. You can't blame yourself, these things happen—'

'I shouldn't even have been riding!' I'd raised my voice. The next child was coming into the arena, and people had turned to look at me. 'I was being selfish, a bloody-minded, stupid girl who thought she knew it all,' I continued more quietly.

I'd set my heart on competing at the county show, but I'd been getting terrible stomach pains for a few days. I tried to ignore it, took painkillers and eventually told myself I was imagining it – because it was the same kind of pain, in the same place, as the pain of my appendicitis. And how could that possibly happen again now I'd had the appendix removed ... My mum noticed me wincing with pain a couple of times and said I ought to see the doctor. She told me a horror story of someone she knew who'd had adhesions from her appendectomy scar and had to have further emergency surgery. Well, I wasn't going to risk going down *that* route just before a major competition. On the morning of the event the pain was still bad. I swallowed the painkillers and told myself to put it to the back of my mind, to concentrate on winning, and then I'd go to the doctor's afterwards.

'I don't know what happened,' I whispered now. 'It was a warm, humid kind of day and there were a few rumbles of thunder in the air. Perhaps Strawberry was reacting to the atmosphere, getting a bit nervous. I should have been more attuned to her. Normally I knew exactly what she was feeling, all the time; we worked, moved, as if we were ... just one body. But I was too distracted by the pain. When there was this sudden, loud clap of thunder, I wasn't prepared; I hadn't sensed her alarm before it happened, the way I should've done.'

The timing couldn't have been worse. We'd been about to take the most difficult jump on the course, the one I was convinced would win me the competition. I urged her forward, but too late I saw her head come back, her ears twitching, heard her snorting in protest.

Joe looked at me sadly. 'She didn't make the jump?'

'I should never have pushed her to try. She'd been too spooked by the thunder, and I ... I wasn't aware. I wasn't *with* her. I shouldn't even have been riding. I was too preoccupied with my own pain.' I stopped and wiped my eyes. 'I've never ridden a horse since. And as for becoming a vet, well, that just went out of the window. The way I saw it, if I let my own horse die, how could I possibly look after other people's animals?'

'But you know that's not true, don't you? You must know that now. It wasn't your fault. Horses get spooked—'

'It took me a long time to accept that it was an accident. But yes, eventually I forgave myself enough to work in a vets, even if it *was* only as a receptionist.' I glanced at him, but he didn't react. 'I think I'm still a work in progress. I'm beginning to trust myself looking after animals again.'

'As long as nobody undermines your self-confidence,' he said, nodding to himself like he'd just realised something. And then, with an abrupt change of tone, he added: 'So what was your own problem? Did you have to have surgery for scar adhesions?'

'No. It just turned out to be a lot of inflammation around the surgery site. A course of strong anti-inflammatories and it all settled down.' I sighed. 'It wasn't serious.'

And the truth was, of course, that I'd *wanted* it to be worse. I'd needed to punish myself for Strawberry's death. A fractured wrist, a sore tummy, they weren't nearly enough. Instead I dropped out of the A-level re-sits. I abandoned my ambition, gave up on my dream. It served me right, I thought. I needed to suffer.

Of course, I didn't say all this to Joe. We sat in silence for a few more moments until I felt calmer and more in control, then I told him to say goodbye to Ruby for me and apologise to her. I'd wanted to watch her compete in the rest of the gymkhana, but I was too exhausted to stay any longer.

As I got up to leave, he said, so quietly that I had to turn back to catch it, 'Maybe you should see someone. A counsellor or—'

'A psychiatrist?' I said with a sneer. 'No, thank you. I'll survive.'

I regretted my tone as soon as I walked away. He was probably only trying to help. He'd looked so concerned, as if he actually cared. But I should know better, really. Why would he care about my ancient memories, when he had so much grief to cope with, himself?

It was funny, though. Somehow I felt better just for having told him about it.

CHAPTER TWENTY-FOUR

By the day of my planned shopping trip to London, Nana was recovering well and managing to hobble around the cottage carefully with a walking frame, but I still felt anxious about leaving her alone for a whole day.

'Don't you worry about me,' she told me firmly. 'Go off and have a good day with your mum. You know she's dying to spend some money on that baby. I've got my little Ebony here to keep me company, and old Nosy Parker next door will be popping in and out like a cuckoo in a clock, to make sure I haven't popped my clogs.'

'Don't say that!' I protested, giving her a kiss goodbye. 'I'm glad she's keeping an eye on you.'

I hadn't told her about my plan to call on Adam. And I didn't tell Mum, either. I couldn't imagine what she'd say if she knew I was plotting to catch him out in a relationship with Claire.

The shopping went well. Mum was in a good mood, her credit card at the ready every time I so much as paused to look at anything cute in the size 'birth to three months'. She only mentioned Sharon Overton and her bloody daughter about half a dozen times, and I tried not to let it rile me, for the sake of a harmonious outing. A pram was ordered, the model an amicable compromise between 'celebrity' and 'supermarket', and also a crib and a car seat, to say nothing of all the other bits and pieces my baby was apparently going to need. By the time we stopped for a late lunch, I was feeling shattered but happy. We'd made our peace, and Mum seemed to have taken on board the fact that Dorchester was a taboo subject, for now, at least.

'Thanks so much, Mum. I don't think there's anything else I need now,' I said, stretching my aching legs under the restaurant table.

'What?' Mum protested, consulting her list. 'You haven't even got a changing mat yet! Or a baby bath! Or any of those nice fluffy white towels with hoods in them and ears like rabbits—'

I smiled. 'I'll order those online.'

'Well, all right, if you're sure. There's a lovely website Sharon's daughter uses—'

She stopped herself, and we both laughed. I was glad we'd been able to. But I'd had to look down at the table as I fibbed about needing to get back to Hope Green to make sure Nana was all right. The truth was that I knew Adam would be at home on a Saturday afternoon, glued to the TV, watching his favourite team play – whether he had anyone with him or not. Perfect timing for a surprise visit.

I felt ridiculously nervous on the journey to Hampstead. I'd travelled this way so many times before – going to see Adam when we were together – but now it felt odd, and wrong, to be doing it. I kept trying to picture his face when he saw me on the doorstep. Was he going to look shocked, or even horrified, especially if Claire was there again? And what exactly was I going to say, if she was? I couldn't begin to work that out. I just knew I wanted the truth. It wasn't until I was ringing the doorbell that it occurred to me that Adam's mum or dad might open the door – it was, after all, their house – and this thought unnerved me so much that I nearly turned round and bolted straight back to the station. How could I face them? I hadn't spoken to either of them since the break-up. They probably hated me. Or would they want to talk to me about being involved with their grandchild? Of course they would! Why hadn't I even thought about that? Flushing hot with panic, I'd just turned to walk back down the path when the door opened and there was Adam, in his old trackie bottoms and T-shirt, his face a picture of amazement.

'Sam!'

'Adam.'

We stared at each other. As a conversation opener, it wasn't exactly inspiring.

'What are you doing here?' he said. He sounded anxious. And then he glanced behind him into the house, and that was it. I was convinced.

'I was in London. So I thought I'd pop round. Can I come in?' I couldn't seem to manage more than a few words at a time, and they came out in jerky splutters. I wanted this over with.

'Of course.' He held the door open and stood back to let me pass. He had to; I was too big by now to squeeze by him. I felt his eyes on me. 'I'll put the kettle on, shall I? You look tired.'

'Of course I'm bloody tired. I'm nearly eight months pregnant,' I snapped. I peered into the lounge. 'Are you on your own?'

'Yes. Mum will be sorry she missed you. They're in the Cotswolds for the weekend.'

'Lovely.' I followed him down the hallway towards the kitchen. 'So am I interrupting anything?'

'No.' He turned to me, frowning. 'I was just watching the Chelsea match. Are you all right?'

'Yes. I just want to know …' I pointed back towards the hallway. 'Who were you looking round at, when you opened the door to me?'

'What?' He was standing in the middle of the kitchen, holding the kettle as if he didn't know quite what to do with it. 'I wasn't looking at anyone – just the TV. You turned up just as the other team scored.'

'Oh.'

I hesitated. So maybe Claire *wasn't* there. I'd just have to get him to tell me about it. And I didn't quite know how to start.

'Actually,' I said, rubbing my tummy, 'don't bother with tea. I'll just have a glass of water, please.' The baby was kicking, hard. The shopping trip had taken too much out of me and I really should have gone straight home. I pulled out a kitchen chair and sunk into it. It felt so peculiar, being here now, being with Adam, remembering how we used to be.

'Adam,' I said, quietly, without looking at him, 'What's going on?' I wouldn't be able to bear it if he and Claire were deliberately trying to hurt me.

'What do you mean?' But it was there again, that anxious tone to his voice. I knew him too well, knew when he was trying to hide something.

'I mean, I'm not bloody stupid. I called you, and Claire was here. You were drinking together and listening to Adele. *Adele*, Adam! You and I went to see her together, live – it was special! We used to sing along together to "Someone Like You". I know something's going on. Claire was funny with me when she came to visit. She talked about you non-stop, asking me if I still had feelings for you, saying she'd seen you. I had a big bust-up with her and we haven't spoken since.' I was off on a rant now, but he seemed to be rooted to the spot, blinking at me, still holding the kettle. 'So I'll ask you again. What exactly *is* going on between you, Adam, because for one thing, she's a married woman, she's got a little boy, and I can't believe you'd just ...' I was running out of steam. 'And I just think,' I went on shakily. 'I really do think, to be honest, that you might have had the decency to let me know.'

Finally, he put down the damned kettle with a clunk and came to sit opposite me. He sighed. 'I'm sorry, Sam,' he said.

So I was right. I clenched my teeth. My *best friend*! Well, she used to be. How could she? How could *he*? He tried to touch my hands across the table and I shook him off, angrily.

'What about her marriage?' I snapped. 'And her son?'

'It's not what you think,' he said, with another sigh.

'Right. I suppose you're just good friends, is that what you're going to say?'

'Yes, actually, we are. But I'm sorry I haven't told you about Sophie.'

'Sophie?' I shook my head. 'Who the hell's Sophie, and what's she got to do with it?'

'Claire's sister Sophie.' He shifted in his chair, looking really uncomfortable now. 'We're ... well, I *was* going to tell you, I really was. It's all moved a bit faster than ... well, the thing is, you see – we're engaged.'

What?! I sat up straight with shock. I certainly hadn't seen *that* coming. And then he suddenly smiled at me, and I saw it in his eyes. The look I remembered from our early days together. He was in love.

'You're right,' he went on. 'Claire's been round here a few times. We bumped into each other, back in the spring, soon after you and I split up. I told her I was feeling a bit down. And well, over a coffee, she mentioned that Sophie had been on her own for ages. So Claire invited me round to her and Nick's place to make up a foursome for dinner.'

'How nice,' I said faintly. I felt sick. I wasn't sure if I was more sick about the idea of all this going on without anyone telling me about it, or about having jumped to the wrong conclusion.

'And then, after the second time, well sometimes Claire and Nick got a babysitter and came here instead, with Sophie. And even after Sophie and I started dating, we made our dinners with Claire and Nick a regular thing. So that night you called, they were here, of course, and I was cooking, so I yelled out for someone to answer my phone, and Claire picked it up.'

'And even then, you didn't think to tell me about Sophie. You were too busy enjoying your cosy little "foursome".'

He dropped his head. 'I didn't know how to tell you. By then, you and Claire had fallen out. It all just felt too awkward, to be honest.'

'Better to keep me in the dark. Imagining all sorts.'

'I'm sorry, Sam. If I'd known you were thinking that about Claire and me ... well, I mean, that's obviously ridiculous. She and Nick are crazy about each other.' He hesitated. 'Claire wants to make up with you, you know. She feels bad about what happened on her visit. She was in a difficult position: she wanted to tell you about Sophie but I'd asked her not to.'

'She was completely out of order when she came to Hope Green,' I said. 'I don't know what she told you and maybe I'd better not go into it. But I can't see how we can get past it. And now, I feel ...' I sat back, rubbing my tummy again. It felt as if the baby had hobnail boots on today. Perhaps he'd tuned into my distress. 'I don't honestly know *what* I feel, now. I mean, I understand you need to move on. I suppose I should say I'm happy for you, but I think I need time for it to sink in.'

'I wish I hadn't kept putting off telling you. I don't want you to think it'll change anything – you know, about my responsibility to you and ...' He nodded at my bump, as if he couldn't quite bring himself to mention it. 'It won't, obviously. I won't let you down about that. Sophie's absolutely insistent that I should be a responsible father to your child, as well as any we might have ourselves.'

'*What*?!' I'd been sipping from my glass of water, but at this I spluttered a mouthful all over the table. 'Any *children* you might have? *You*?'

'I know.' He shrugged and gave a silly nervous laugh. 'I bet you thought you'd never hear me say that, eh?'

I couldn't even respond. If he'd gone on to say he and Sophie were going to buy a country cottage and get two dogs, I think I'd have had to murder him. But he was already babbling on about how they were saving up for a deposit on a little flat in Bethnal Green, that he'd had a promotion, and Sophie was 'going places' in her career in law.

'Well, good for you,' I said through my teeth. 'Congratulations, and all that.'

I got up and turned to head for the front door.

'Don't just leave like this,' he said, following me. 'You look tired, you've got a long journey.'

'I'll be fine. I'll sleep on the train.'

'But Sophie's coming round later. Maybe you could stay and say hello.'

'Adam,' I said, weighing my words carefully, 'I'm glad you're happy. I mean that. If I seem less than thrilled about it, well, it's just been a bit of a surprise, OK? But I really don't want to sit down and talk about weddings and babies with your fiancée. Sorry.' I opened the front door. 'Say hello to your parents. You can go back to the football now.'

Of course, I didn't sleep on the train at all. I spent the entire journey back to Dorset going over and over everything in my mind. I didn't really know why I still felt upset. After all, it was a relief at least to know that Adam wasn't involved with Claire. I suppose I felt stupid now for suspecting it, as well as being a bit miffed at not being told about Sophie. So did I begrudge Adam his new romance? Did I envy them their little city flat and their marriage plans? No, it wasn't what I wanted, anyway. But I couldn't get over his comment about having children. How could he have changed so suddenly, so drastically, since we split up? It was almost obscenely ironic. It seemed to me that he had wanted children after all – just not with me! But whether he liked it or not, that was what was happening. And although it had turned out he wasn't the man I wanted to raise my child with, the fact of the matter was that he and I were going to be in each other's lives for at least the next eighteen years. Any children he had with Sophie would be half-siblings to my little one. It was a lot to take in. And there was something about his newfound happiness that made me ache with a kind of loneliness and regret.

I needed to pull myself together, I told myself sharply as the train pulled into my station. I'd moved to Hope Green to make a new life for myself, and looking back, having thoughts about loneliness and regret, was definitely not the way to go about it.

CHAPTER TWENTY-FIVE

I was glad to be busy at work, and although Joe was still quiet and we didn't talk about our personal lives at the surgery, I did feel that the ice had thawed between us a little since my panic attack at the gymkhana. I couldn't stop thinking about how gentle and caring he'd seemed that day, and sometimes I caught him looking at me with his head to one side, as if he was considering saying something, but then he'd suddenly blink and look away again. I remembered how close I'd felt to him on the day he took me to lunch, back in the summer, when he'd opened up his heart to me about his wife. But tempted though I was to somehow try and get back to that, I was too afraid of being knocked back again, the way I had on that previous occasion. The result was that I'd begun to feel awkward and uncomfortable around him and avoided having too much close contact in case I gave myself away.

Meanwhile, the weather had deteriorated further as we moved into November, with heavy and persistent rain that made the lanes run with muddy water and turned the fields and woods around the village into bogs. Whenever Joe had to go out to visit one of the farms, he came back with his boots caked in mud, and the Jeep was constantly splattered with it. Unfortunately, he'd had to visit the pig farm a couple of miles up the lane on a fairly regular basis. Geoff Noakes, the pig farmer, was apparently a notorious drunk and Joe had already told me he was worried about how he was going to cope with one of his sows giving birth in a few weeks' time.

'Last time he had a litter of piglets arrive in the winter, he damned nearly let them all die of cold,' he said crossly. 'Went off to the pub without turning on the heat lamps. I wouldn't be so worried if his son was there to help, but he keeps going off on what he calls "business trips". Says he's looking to "diversify".' He shook his head, as if this was the most ridiculous thing he'd ever heard. 'Now it looks like Poppy, the sow, might have a difficult delivery. She's got a small pelvis. I just hope Geoff's going to have the sense to call me when she goes into labour. If he's had a drink ...' He sighed. 'Frankly, he shouldn't be in charge of the farm on his own. It's far too much for him even when he *is* sober.'

'But perhaps that's why the son's talking about diversifying?' I suggested. 'Maybe he's going to talk his dad into giving up the farm and doing something different.'

'You could be right.' Joe nodded at me thoughtfully. 'Although it's hard to imagine what else Geoff could do. He's been a farmer all his life, and a drunk ever since his wife walked out on him.'

He sighed when he mentioned the wife leaving, and I imagined he probably felt some sympathy for the pig farmer, knowing how it felt to be left on his own. But I knew better than to comment. As usual, I just turned back to my work, and Joe went to treat his next patient.

Then a couple of days later, a lady who lived close by in the village came in with Cookie, her chocolate Labrador bitch who'd recently given birth to puppies.

'Hello, Mrs Evans,' I greeted her. 'How are those puppies getting on?'

'They're doing great, thanks!' she said, taking out her phone to show me some pictures.

'Oh my God, they're just adorable!' I gushed, staring mesmerised at the little balls of furry mischief climbing over each other to get to their mother.

At that moment Joe walked out of the consulting room, came up behind me and peeked at the photos over my shoulder.

'They certainly are,' he agreed, smiling at Mrs Evans. 'Have you found homes for them all yet?'

'Five down, two to go,' she joked.

'And I'm sure the last two will be snapped up quickly too,' Joe said politely. 'Labs are so popular, and these are little beauties. Well done, Cookie!' He stroked her head. 'Come on in, and let's have a look at her. I presume that little bit of mastitis settled down OK?'

As Joe turned to lead the way into the consulting room, I handed Mrs Evans back her phone, not realising how loudly I'd sighed as I did so. She gave me a surprised look.

'Sorry,' I said quietly. 'It's just that they're my favourite dogs. It was always my dream to have one of my own, and Cookie's puppies are so beautiful.'

'Well, if you want one, let me know quickly,' she said, smiling. 'As I've just said, there are only two of the litter left who haven't been claimed.'

I smiled back but didn't respond. Joe was waiting in the consulting room doorway and I knew he wouldn't thank me for holding up his schedule any longer. However, a little later when I was taking Mrs Evans' payment, he came out again just in time to hear her say: 'Don't forget, Sam. Let me know if you decide you want one of the puppies.'

Joe stared at me, and kept on staring after Mrs Evans and Cookie had left. 'You're seriously thinking of getting a puppy?' he said.

'I'd love to. But I realise it's not exactly a good time.'

'No, it's not.' Despite the way he was frowning, he was perfectly calm as he began to list on his fingers the reasons why I wasn't fit to own a dog: 'Apart from anything else, you're living with your grandmother, and you've already got a cat, and—'

'And I'm having a baby,' I snapped before I could stop myself. 'I *am* aware that it's not exactly the perfect environment to bring a puppy into. You don't have to tell me.'

His expression darkened. 'Good,' he said, turning to walk away.

But I couldn't leave it alone. I was so confused by my feelings about him by now that I couldn't bear any perceived criticism from him at all.

'I didn't actually say I was *going* to get a puppy,' I said. 'It's just what I'd *like* to do. There's a difference.'

For a minute he just stared at me again.

Natalie, who'd come out of the room after him and was rummaging in one of my desk drawers for something, looked up at me with her eyebrows raised.

'We all need our dreams, Joe,' I finished a little shakily, looking away from him. I wished I'd kept my mouth shut.

But to my surprise he just sighed and said, as he turned back to his room: 'Yes, you're quite right. We do.'

'Poor thing,' Natalie whispered as his door closed behind him. 'He's still heartbroken over his wife.'

'I know,' I said, staring at the closed door.

'Although, recently I don't think he seems as cross as usual,' she added thoughtfully. 'Just sad.'

I kept thinking about the chocolate Labrador puppies when I went home and found myself wondering whether it might actually have been good for Joe to adopt one himself. It might have been just the thing to help him and his daughter deal with their grief. But I wasn't going to be the one to suggest anything so personal to him. If he reacted in any kind of negative way, I was more likely now than ever, to burst into tears.

There was a barn dance being held in the church hall that Saturday evening, and David had asked me to go with him.

'You should go, it'll do you good,' Nana urged me. I think she was worried about me. Although I'd tried to stay cheerful at home for her sake, my sombre mood was hard to shake off.

'I can't imagine that I'd be able to join in,' I said, lumbering after her into the kitchen. I felt as enormous as an elephant. Even Nana was getting around better than me now, to be honest, despite her ankle and her knees.

'You could sit and watch the fun. David wants you to go.'

'I know he does!' I said irritably. 'But I don't want to go with *him*.' I sighed. 'Sorry, I'm being a miserable moo, I know. But I thought I'd made it clear to David that I'm not interested in him as a boyfriend, and I'm worried that he's still hoping I'll change my mind. It isn't fair. I think I need to stop seeing him altogether.'

'That would be a shame, Little Sam. You're good friends.'

'I know. Oh, why is everything so difficult?'

'Is it the one you *don't* want that you're getting so upset about?' Nana said, giving me one of her looks. 'Or the one you do want?'

'I don't know what you mean,' I said, turning my back on her and ignoring her mutterings about being only my grandmother and saying nothing.

I didn't go to the barn dance. David was cross about it because he'd got me a ticket and had automatically expected me to agree, which just made me even more determined not to go. We ended up having an argument, the first one we'd ever had. I suppose I took out some of my frustrations on him, but I didn't expect him to react quite the way he did.

'I just can't seem to get anything right, for you, can I?' he exploded. 'Nothing I do seems to please you. I don't know why I bother.'

I opened my mouth to say that I wasn't asking him to bother, but he'd already turned and opened the door. He'd gone off down the path before I could try to apologise. Then I decided I didn't really want to apologise anyway. It was his own fault for having such expectations. But falling out with him just added to my miserable mood. I began to wonder if my future really *was* in Hope Green. If it hadn't been for Nana and the baby coming so soon, I might even have looked at Mum's bloody townhouses in Dorchester – and that was saying something!

There was one piece of good news though, although I wished I felt more amenable to being cheered up by it. Izzie came round on the Sunday morning to tell me that an announcement had been made at the end of the barn dance by the Chairman of the Parish Council.

'We've won the Best-Kept Village competition!' she said, throwing her arms around me in her excitement. 'Apparently the result was delayed this year because we were running neck and neck with East Pentleford. The judges decided to make another unannounced visit to both villages and apparently they were so impressed by the "community spirit involved in the repainting of the preschool building",' – she grinned at me – 'and the flower tubs, *and* the fact that we were pulling out all the stops to get more children here, to keep the place open, that they decided to award us first prize again!'

'That's wonderful!' Nana said. 'I bet they were all abuzz with the news in church this morning. I should've gone.'

'It's horrible weather outside, Nana,' I reminded her. 'I didn't want you going out in it.'

'Never mind, Peggy,' Izzie said. 'I wanted to be the one to give you and Sam the good news. And will you tell David, Sam? I thought he was coming to the barn dance last night, but he didn't turn up. He'll be pleased to hear the news. It's you two we have to thank for that final decision, after all.'

'I'd rather you told him, if you don't mind,' I said. I saw a look exchanged between Izzie and Nana and I sighed. 'I'm not sure when I'll see him next, OK? But thank you for coming out in this rain to tell us. It is good news. I'm pleased.'

I tried my hardest to smile and look suitably thrilled. Only a few weeks ago I'd have been over the moon about the competition result.

'Are you all right?' Izzie asked as I saw her out. 'Are you getting anxious about having the baby?'

'No. I'm fine, honestly,' I said, apologising yet again for being distracted.

After she'd gone I sat down and stared into space for ages, the hiss and crackle of the fireplace being the only thing to calm me. Even Izzie thought I was being a misery guts. If I didn't snap out of it, I'd lose *her* friendship too. It was bad enough that I still wasn't reconciled with Claire, and that, since finding out that Adam had moved on to the extent that he was getting married, it had felt like my old life was a completely closed chapter. That was what I'd wanted, I supposed, but it all felt so sudden and final. And now I'd fallen out with David too. Was there something wrong with me? Did I even *know* what I wanted? Why I was moping around like a moody teenager? I was about to become a mother, for God's sake – it was about time I grew up, I told myself crossly.

Perhaps it was the gloomy November weather. The rain, the dark afternoons – maybe I had seasonal affective disorder. Or perhaps Izzie was right: I was subconsciously worrying about having the baby and I'd feel better after he (or she) was born. But even as I tried to convince myself of this, all I could envisage was a long, lonely future as a single mum, everyone in the village avoiding me because I'd turned into a grumpy old woman. Of course, if only I could have admitted it, what I really wanted to envisage was … something else altogether. Something I was pretty sure was never going to happen.

CHAPTER TWENTY-SIX

I didn't hear from David for a couple of days, during which time I felt more and more guilty about upsetting him. I knew I needed to have another serious conversation with him about whether we could actually remain friends, and putting it off was just making it worse. Twice I picked up my phone to ask him if we could meet up for a chat, and twice I put it down again. But then, the following evening, just as I was psyching myself up to try again, he phoned me.

'Oh, I was just going to call you,' I said, before realising how pathetic that sounded. 'Um, look, would you like to have a quick drink tonight at the Horse? I need to—'

'Sam, I can't,' he gasped. 'There's something wrong with KitKat. How do I get hold of the out-of-hours vet service?'

'You just dial the normal surgery number and it transfers automatically,' I said, everything else immediately forgotten. 'But what's wrong with him?'

'I don't know. He's been sick twice, and now he's lying on his side, panting, and he yowls like hell if I touch him. I'm really worried. Do you think it's something serious?'

'Call the surgery number. Try not to panic. I'm coming straight round.'

I walked as fast as my huge belly would allow, all the time thinking about poor KitKat and how David must be feeling. It didn't matter any more whether he was angry with me, whether he was expecting too much of me or trying to control me – he was still a friend, and he needed help.

I was just about to turn into his road when I saw two familiar figures approaching. It was Joe and Ruby, swinging hands and amiably chatting as they walked along. Joe gave me a small nod, but Ruby was much more excited to see me.

'Hello, Sam! Guess what! I've just been to my first rehearsal for the school Christmas play. I've got one of the lead parts.'

'Oh, wow, that's great, Ruby,' I said. I glanced at Joe. 'I'm so glad I bumped into you, are you free? I'm on my way to see David. His cat seems to be very poorly. I told him to call the out-of-hours bu—'

'Oh, Daddy!' Ruby said. 'Poor cat! Can't you look at it?'

'I haven't got my bag with me,' he told her. 'The emergency vet will be better equipped.'

'Of course,' I said, trying not to feel too downhearted. 'Don't worry.'

Not that he seemed worried anyway …

'I'm just about to go there now,' I added, too distracted to think about what I was saying. 'He lives in the first house round the corner here.'

'Oh, Daddy, please!' Ruby said again, tugging at his arm. 'At least have a look at the poor cat! The other vet might not be here yet.'

Joe looked at her and shrugged. 'OK. If they're not here yet. I'll see whether it looks serious, at least …'

'Thank you,' I said, leading the way. 'It's very good of you.'

David, whose face was creased with distress as he opened the door to me, blinked in surprise when he saw who was standing behind me on the doorstep.

'I happened to bump into Joe and his daughter on the way here,' I explained quickly as we went inside. 'Is the emergency vet on her way?'

'No.' David sighed. 'Apparently she's out on another house call but she'll come straight here afterwards.'

'I'll have a look at the cat, then,' Joe said.

'OK. Thank you,' David said. Neither looked the other in the eye as they spoke, I noticed. 'I shut him in the kitchen in case he tried to run out when I opened the front door, although to be honest, I don't think he's up to running anywhere.'

David led us through and as soon as he opened the door the smell hit me.

'Lilies,' I said, nudging Joe and pointing to the jug on the draining board. By the look on his face, I knew he'd already noticed them.

David shrugged, and looked a bit embarrassed. 'They're for you,' he said quietly. 'I'd been planning to come round later to give them to you.'

He gave me a meaningful look, and I realised the flowers were supposed to be an apology. 'But David,' I began, 'you shouldn't have lilies in the house, with a cat—'

'Has he come into contact with them at all?' Joe barked from where he was already examining KitKat, after having pretty much shoved David out of the way to get there. The poor cat was lying on his side in his bed, panting heavily.

'Um … I don't think so.' David looked at me. 'I didn't know—'

'Think, man!' Joe ordered him. 'Have you put the flowers down in a place where he could have brushed against them?'

'The pollen is highly toxic to cats,' I said gently. 'If he got any on his fur and licked it off, that would probably explain what's wrong with him.'

'Oh my God, I didn't know,' David said again, looking wide-eyed with panic. 'I suppose … well, yes, I laid the flowers on the table when I first came home – he could have jumped up and walked around them, you know how curious cats are …'

'And he's been vomiting?' Joe interrupted without looking round.

'Yes, and he seems to be in pain. He's been lying on his side like that, yowling—'

'The poisoning can lead to kidney damage,' Joe said abruptly.

I saw the look on David's face and put a sympathetic hand on his arm.

'Will he be all right, Daddy?' a quiet voice came from the corner of the room. I'd almost forgotten Ruby was here.

'Hopefully,' he said. 'I'll take him straight into the surgery now for a blood test to check his kidney function. We'll have to keep him in on a drip for at least forty-eight hours.'

'Are you going to wait for the emergency vet? You're off duty. We're closed,' I reminded him.

'I want to save this cat's life,' he barked back at me. 'We can't afford to wait. Are you going to come and help with the blood test? Or are you too busy?' He turned round, finally, looking from me to David with an expression that I could only describe as disdain.

'No, of course I'm not too busy,' I replied at once, knowing that David, because of his problem with needles, wouldn't be much help.

Joe was bending over KitKat again, gently soothing him, his voice entirely different from the way he'd spoken to us.

'All right, boy. Yes, I know, you're in a bit of pain, aren't you? But we're going to give you some medicine that'll help. OK, calm down now, I'm not going to hurt you.'

'I'll get his carrying basket,' David said. 'And – thank you. I ... I really appreciate this.'

'Just throw the damned flowers away. And wipe up all traces of pollen before he comes home again,' Joe barked as David scurried outside.

I was glad he hadn't said '*if* he comes home'. But even so, his tone was unnecessarily harsh.

'Not everyone is aware of the dangers of lilies,' I pointed out quietly to Joe. 'He's terribly upset, you know.'

'Well, I'm sorry he's upset. But my priority is the cat.'

'Of course.' I glanced at Ruby, who was looking upset too. 'Daddy will do everything he can to make him better,' I told her.

'I know,' she said. 'He's the best vet in the world. I want to be a vet when I'm grown up, too.'

'That's a wonderful ambition,' I said, giving her a smile. 'Now, here's the basket. I'm going to help Daddy put KitKat into it.'

Given KitKat's reputation, to say nothing of his pain, I was expecting him to resist handling, but he was obviously too sick to put up a fight and allowed himself to be lifted into the basket with only a low growl of discomfort.

'Call the emergency vet and tell her she doesn't need to come any more,' Joe instructed David as he carried KitKat to the front door. 'And then you can join us over the road if you want to.'

'Of course I *want* to!' David protested. 'I'll be right behind you,' he added to me, as I followed Joe out. He gave me a tortured look. 'I'm so sorry, Sam, for the trouble. I can't believe I didn't know—'

'Don't be silly. It's very common, but lots of people don't realise. I've got to go, David. See you in a minute.'

In fact, we'd barely got the surgery door open and turned the lights on when David arrived, out of breath from running down the road after us.

'Perhaps you wouldn't mind sitting in the waiting room with Ruby to keep her company?' I suggested, not wanting to draw Joe's attention again to his needle phobia.

'Of course.' He tried to smile at Ruby. 'I hear you've got a pony? What's he like?'

I joined Joe in the consulting room and closed the door behind us.

'Just hold him still for me,' he instructed as he took out a syringe for the blood test. 'He's not going to attack you, he's gone past that. He's a really sick cat.'

My eyes involuntarily filled with tears. 'Poor KitKat.'

'Yes, well, if *David* had paid a bit more attention to the care of his cat and a little less to plying you with flowers …'

'That's not fair, Joe!' I gasped. 'He loves his cat. And obviously, if I'd known he was buying lilies I'd have warned him about them.'

'Right. Well, you're bound to defend him, I suppose.'

'Yes, I suppose I am, in this instance anyway.'

There was no response. Joe was busy drawing KitKat's blood and I watched his face, his concentration, as he did so, struck as usual by his tenderness with his patients.

'There you go, boy,' he said gently. 'Now we'll get him set up with an IV line, Sam, and—'

'Someone ought to stay here with him until the morning,' I said. 'I'm happy to do that. David will probably want to stay too.'

'Absolutely not,' he returned without looking at me. 'I'm going to stay here myself. You go home. You need your rest, and *David* wouldn't be any help whatsoever.'

I was too shocked that he'd even mentioned me needing my rest, to argue. 'What about Ruby?'

He glanced at me. 'Would you mind taking her home? My mother's there.'

'Of course,' I said. 'And thank you. You've been very good, giving up your evening like this. I know David's grateful.'

'I'm not doing it for him. I'm doing it for his cat.'

'Fair enough.'

David and I were quiet as we walked Ruby back to her home and her grandmother. Ruby chattered away about KitKat, about Hugo, about her own dream of being a vet, and about her school play, and we just listened, glancing at each other from time to time.

'Are you annoyed with me?' he said, finally, as we turned to walk home again. 'I know you must think I'm stupid, but nobody's ever told me that, about lilies—'

'No, David. I don't think you're stupid at all and I'm not annoyed with you; I'm upset about KitKat. But I feel really bad about arguing with you the other day. I was going to call you, as I said, to apologise and suggest we had a chat.'

'It was my fault,' he said earnestly. 'I shouldn't have assumed—'

'No, you shouldn't.' I sighed. 'But David, I think you always do. I think you always *will*, as long as we're such good friends. And you know, I've told you, that's all it's ever going to be.'

'Ever?' he repeated, very quietly.

'Ever. I'm sorry, I really am. I just ... think of you as another big brother.' Despite trying to say it as gently and kindly as I could, it still felt like sticking pins in a baby. 'I *have* always warned you,' I reminded him again.

'Yes. You've always been very fair.'

We walked on in silence for a few minutes. I could only imagine what he was thinking and how much I'd hurt him. Why had he kept on hoping for more?

Although really, I supposed I knew the answer before he'd even said it.

'The trouble is, I'm in love with you,' he whispered sadly.

'I'm so sorry,' I said again, my eyes filling with tears. 'I love you too – as a friend. But ...'

'But there's someone else, I suppose.'

'No,' I said, a little too quickly. 'There's nobody.'

I think we both knew I was lying. David seemed to be mentally squaring his shoulders and taking it on the chin, saying he understood, that he still wanted to be my friend – if I'd let him – and he promised not to pressure me or take anything for granted in future. But I had my doubts we could work purely as friends. How could we?

I'd got the difficult conversation out of the way, but I didn't feel any better about it. And now I had to say goodnight to him knowing I was leaving him doubly upset, about his cat as well as about me. What sort of a friend did that make me? I went home feeling even more miserable than before, and tossed and turned for most of the night, thinking about how much I'd hated having to hurt David, and how he would inevitably blame himself if poor KitKat didn't make it.

The next morning David arrived at the surgery almost as soon as I'd called him to tell him the good news: KitKat was going to be OK.

I'd come into work early and found Joe asleep in the chair in his consulting room, just where I'd left him, only this time his head was back and he was snoring very gently. I'd gone in to the kitchen to make us both a hot drink, and by the time I returned he was on his feet, checking KitKat's cage.

'You didn't need to come in so early,' he'd said without turning round.

'Couldn't sleep,' I replied. 'How's the little guy?'

'Rallying, thank God. The blood we took last night did show evidence of kidney damage – as expected – but hopefully we've caught it in time.'

'Are you taking more blood today to check how he's responding?'

'Not yet. I'll leave him on the drip until tomorrow and rerun the blood tests then.'

'He looks more comfortable, at least.'

'Yes, he's on pain relief, and Zantec to soothe his stomach lining. There's not a lot more we can do for now.'

'I'll call David. Can he come in and see him? I'm sure he's been lying awake all night worrying.'

And by the looks of him, he had been awake all night. He hadn't shaved yet and his hair was sticking out to the side at an unnatural angle. But David was relieved, of course, to see KitKat looking more comfortable, and even more relieved when I told him that Joe wasn't around as he had gone back home to shower.

'No wonder Joe thinks I'm a complete idiot.' He sighed. 'I mean, it's been pretty obvious he dislikes me, ever since he tripped over the dogs, but he probably despises me now.'

'That's ridiculous,' I protested. 'He just wanted to get on with treating KitKat as quickly as possible.'

'You always defend him,' he said, giving me a sad look. 'Even though he's been rude and unkind to you so many times.'

'Yes, well, he's my boss, and he's an exceptionally good vet,' I said, turning away from him.

'OK, if you say so.' David shrugged. 'I know the score, Sam. I'm not stupid. But, well, I have to admit it was good of him to take care of KitKat the way he did, especially staying with him all night.'

'Yes, it was.'

I still couldn't look at him. We stood, side by side, looking at KitKat in his cage for a while longer without speaking, before David said goodbye in the same sad tone of voice.

'I'll be back to see KitKat again later,' he said, and I found myself hoping I'd be at lunch. Was I always going to feel uncomfortable around him now? Would I ever be able to look into those sad brown eyes without feeling like a mega bitch?

When Joe returned, I told him how grateful David was.

'Well, I'm glad his cat's looking like he's got a fighting chance of survival,' he muttered. It seemed like just the mention of David's name was enough to annoy him.

'I don't think many vets would have done what you did, staying here overnight rather than letting the emergency vet handle it,' I went on. 'Although I'd have been happy to stay here with him myself, of course.'

Apparently it was the wrong thing to say.

'Of *course* you would,' he said, in a sarcastic tone almost like a sneer, 'for *this* cat. But as you seem to have a habit of forgetting, Sam, you're not qualified, not even as a nurse.'

'I know, I just meant I could have kept an eye on him and—'

'In fact,' he went on, ignoring me, banging a file down on my desk with such force that I jumped, 'I don't know why I've been allowing you to handle animals at all. If anything went wrong, I'd probably be sued or even lose my licence to practise, for letting an unqualified *receptionist* help with procedures.'

He almost spat the word 'receptionist' at me. I took a deep breath, determined not to weaken, or show him that he was upsetting me yet again. I thought I'd got past that stage, but what the hell was this suddenly all about? There was no one else in reception at the time. I could speak my mind, and I decided I was damn well going to.

'I know you've been having – you're *still* having – a horrible time in your personal life,' I said, trying to keep my voice level although I could hear it trembling. 'But I don't accept that gives you any excuse to talk to me in that tone. You know perfectly well that I've only helped you with animals when you've asked me to, because you needed me to. And it's only ever been helping to hold a patient still, or handing you items of equipment. I don't see how that could possibly be construed as causing a problem.'

'All the same,' he said brusquely, turning away, 'I think it's probably a bad idea.'

I spent the next day or so wondering whether he was going to do something drastic. Hire another nurse, perhaps, so that he didn't have to ask me to help out any more? Tell me I wasn't allowed to touch animals in future? Ban me from his consulting room?

Once again, just as I'd thought things were better between us, he was suddenly being unpleasant to me again. What on earth had I done wrong now, that all of a sudden, he didn't want me doing the very part of the job I enjoyed the most?

CHAPTER TWENTY-SEVEN

The baby was due in just over three weeks' time, and I didn't think it physically possible for me to get any bigger. I'd been slowing down quite a bit by this point and had definitely begun to adopt the 'pregnant waddle' I'd heard so much about. I'd told Joe I would carry on until two weeks before the due date, or even longer if I could, and he had a temporary receptionist lined up to do my maternity cover, who I'd promised to spend a few days training before I finished. There had only been one occasion since his outburst when I'd thought he'd need an extra pair of hands, but when I offered, he replied without even looking at me that I shouldn't.

So when Geoff Noakes, the pig farmer whose sow Joe had been worried about, called the vets to speak to Joe about Poppy's labour, I simply put the call through without asking too many questions. Joe had made it perfectly clear that he didn't need my help, so instead I quizzed Val on what was happening.

'Poppy's been straining a good while now and no sign of delivery yet.'

'And what did Joe suggest?' I asked her, eager to know.

'He talked to Geoff about manual intervention – delivering the piglets by hand,' she said. 'It's pretty rare to get a problem with pig farrowing. We haven't heard anything since, so hopefully Geoff's managed to deliver them, but Joe says he'll call at the farm before he heads home.' She gave me a look. 'He's worried Geoff might've started his nightly binge and won't look after the litter properly.'

'Yes, I heard about him being a drinker. I presume his son's not there, then?'

'Apparently not. Sorry, Sam, I've got to scoot. I'm going to my daughter's in Sherborne. Aren't you going home yourself?' She looked at her watch. 'It's past five o'clock.'

'I know.' I yawned. 'I just want to make sure tomorrow's appointments are all set up OK.'

'Well, don't overdo it. You look shattered.' She smiled. 'Not long now.'

'No, thank God!'

It was quiet after she left. There was no evening surgery that day and Joe was obviously working on something in his own room. Ten minutes later, with my coat on ready to go home, I tapped on Joe's door and asked if he wanted me to switch the phone over to the emergency line before I left.

'Yes, you might as well,' he said, getting up from his desk and stretching. 'I'm just about to head off myself. I promised Geoff I'd call in—'

Before he could finish, the phone started to ring. I pulled a face and muttered 'Sorry, I should have switched it over sooner,' but he shook his head and picked up the call, waving a hand at me, to indicate I should go.

'Yes, Geoff, I'm on my way,' I heard him say as I headed for the door. And then, in a different tone of voice: 'Christ! Right, I'll be with you in five minutes!' He rushed out of the room, pulling on his coat, his face creased with anxiety.

I hesitated by the door, and he paused, looking at me.

'It's an emergency,' he said. 'Sorry, but can you call Val, see if she can come back? She'd better meet me at the farm. Geoff's on his own there and we might need someone to help. He sounds pissed,' he added half under his breath.

'Yes, of course.' I pulled my phone out of my pocket and started looking for Val's number. 'She's not answering,' I called Joe, waddling after him. 'I'll keep trying, but I know she was going to her daughter's—'

'Leave her a message. Tell her it's urgent.' He jumped into the driver's seat of the Jeep. 'Or try Natalie, if absolutely necessary,' he added grimly as he started the engine.

'OK. But meanwhile why don't I come with you?' I yelled through the open window.

He stared at me. 'You? In your condition? Just make the phone calls, please, Sam.'

'I'll make the calls while you're driving.' Determined, I went round and opened the passenger door. 'I'm better than no one, surely? At least while we're waiting for one of the others to turn up.'

I got into the Jeep and sat down, pressing Val's number on my phone again as I did so.

Joe was frowning at me. 'You only help if absolutely necessary, OK?'

'OK.'

Neither of us mentioned the fact that he'd effectively banned me from doing anything to help with the animals at all.

It was dark, and once again it had been raining heavily all day – a gloomy, miserable, wet November evening – and the wipers were going at full speed as we drove down the hill and turned into the narrow lane leading to the pig farm. I gritted my teeth and held on to the dashboard as the Jeep bounced and juddered over the ruts and potholes. I'd left messages on both Val's and Natalie's phones but so far there'd been no response. I didn't mind. I wanted to help. Although I'd been tired until this all happened, I'd suddenly had a burst of energy now and, perhaps unrealistically, felt that I could cope with anything.

'What's gone wrong with the birth?' I asked, to stop myself from gasping as Joe swung the Jeep round another bend in the lane.

'Farrowing. It's called a farrowing,' he said. 'I don't suppose you came across many of these at your posh London vets.'

'No, I didn't, I'm afraid,' I said, trying to keep my voice level. 'But if you explain what's happened, I might be of more help.'

He sighed. 'Well, the sow, Poppy, has a small pelvis. As you know, I've been a bit concerned but I hoped she'd manage to deliver the piglets OK. It's been going on too long so I suggested Geoff tried to deliver them manually. But apparently he's been trying to do it with a sprained wrist – idiot, he didn't tell me that, or I'd wouldn't have let him try. And needless to say, he's had a few drinks, just to make matters even more dangerous. The man's a liability. The sooner his son gets back here, the better.'

'So Poppy's still in labour?'

'Yes, and now it's an emergency because there are two piglets trying to come out simultaneously. Geoff can't get them out, and Poppy's getting hysterical.'

'Poor thing,' I sympathised, automatically putting a hand on my bump. 'What will you have to do?'

'Tranquillise her to calm her down, give her some oxytocin, and see if I can get those two piglets out. Once they're delivered, the others should come out without a problem. Hopefully.'

We were pulling into the farmyard and I could see light through the window of the pig shed.

'Infra-red lights,' Joe explained as he yanked on the handbrake and flung the door of the Jeep open. 'At least that idiot Geoff has remembered that the piglets are going to need to be kept warm. Poppy will be in the farrowing pen at the end of the shed,' he said, and then added, 'Come on!' impatiently as I lumbered out of the Jeep after him. As I slammed the door shut he turned back, frowning at me, and in a completely different tone of voice said, 'Sorry.

Are you sure you're all right to come with me? You could stay in the Jeep and keep trying to contact Val.'

'I'll come,' I insisted. 'I want to.'

I was pleasantly surprised by his apology, but for once I did understand his impatience. It sounded as though Poppy and her piglets could be in serious trouble, and the only help he had on hand was an alcoholic farmer with a bad wrist and a heavily pregnant *receptionist*.

I waded through the mud after Joe, thanking God I was wearing boots, although they weren't quite as serviceable as the wellies he was striding in. Just as we were approaching the pig shed I had to stop for a minute with a bad pang of indigestion. Shouldn't have had that spicy salami at lunchtime, I thought to myself ruefully. It happened again a bit later, when we were in the pen with Poppy and I was watching Joe giving her an injection.

'You all right, girl?' Geoff barked at me. 'What the hell's she doing here in her condition?' he added quietly to Joe, without waiting for me to answer.

'I didn't have a lot of options, unless you wanted to wait for the emergency vet,' Joe retorted, pointing at the farmer's bandaged wrist. 'You're as good as useless, with only one hand, and in *your* condition – and don't try to pretend you don't know what I mean.'

Geoff looked down at the ground, suitably chastened. Joe turned to me.

'I didn't want to have to ask you, Sam, but if you're sure you're OK to help, I need you to wash your hands at the sink in the yard – the same as you just saw me doing, soap and water – and then put a pair of gloves on. I'm going to try to pull out the piglets next time Poppy strains, and as soon as they're out I'll hand them to you. I don't want Geoff dropping them. Dry them off – Geoff will show you how – and put them on the straw under the heat lamp. Then we'll have to wait to see if Poppy can deliver the other piglets herself. Once they're all out we'll put them all on a teat and make sure they suckle OK. Got it?' He stopped, frowning at me again. 'Are you sure you're all right?'

'Yes, I'm fine. I'm ready,' I said. As he turned back to Poppy I took a couple of deep breaths. I'd had another sharp pang of stomachache and was hoping it was going to settle down.

'My son's on his way back from Devon,' Geoff said, looking at his phone. 'So I'll have some help when he gets here.'

'Good.' Joe was watching Poppy. 'OK, she's calmed down. We're in business.'

The next couple of hours felt like the longest in my entire life. There were moments of excitement and elation when Joe pulled out the first little pig by its head, followed immediately by the next one by its feet and then when each subsequent piglet arrived, as he'd hoped, without any more intervention. And there were some tense moments for me, as I carefully took the wriggling piglets out of Joe's hands, dried them and placed them on to the warm straw, trying to hide the fact that, instead of my stomach pains subsiding, they were gradually getting worse. And the fact that I finally had to acknowledge to myself that this wasn't indigestion, and had nothing whatsoever to do with spicy salami.

At last all nine piglets were happily feeding from their exhausted mother, and Geoff's son Neil had arrived back from his business trip, to take over.

'I wish I'd come back sooner,' he said quietly to Joe. 'I should've known Dad couldn't cope. I didn't even know he'd sprained his wrist, the old fool.' He sighed. 'But I wanted to make sure the deal was in the bag.'

He went on to explain that he was buying a small fruit farm for his father to manage instead of continuing to struggle looking after the pigs. 'We're selling up here. It's too much for Dad, and I can't always be around to help him. He can't cause too much damage to a few fruit trees, and he can get pickers to help out in the season.'

'Well, I'll be sorry to see you go, but it makes sense,' Joe said, shaking Neil's hand.

'Want a cup of tea, Joe? And you, young lady?' Geoff asked as we walked back with him through the farmyard. 'I reckon I can make tea with one hand, if nothing else.'

'Actually, I think I need to … um … get going,' I said.

My voice was shaking. The strain of keeping quiet about what was happening to me, as well as my shock at realising it was happening so early, had made me feel weak and sick.

Joe nodded. 'Yes. You must be shattered. You've done well tonight,' he said. 'Thanks for coming.'

At any other time, I'd have been thrilled to have received this praise and gratitude from him. But at that moment, I was racked by another spasm of pain.

'Joe, I think I'm in labour!' I gasped.

'What!' He swung round, staring at me in disbelief. 'Are you sure? Have you had a contraction?'

'I've been having them ever since we arrived here,' I admitted.

'Why the hell didn't you say?' Joe began, but he seemed to check himself, shaking his head, and instead pointed to an upturned oil drum and said, surprisingly gently: 'Sit there for a minute. Breathe. That's right. I take it you've done one of those childbirth courses?'

'Yes.' Although I'd already realised how different the reality was from the theory. Especially if you happened to be assisting at a pig farrowing at the same time.

'Good.' He waited until I said the pain had receded. 'How many weeks are you?'

'Thirty-seven,' I said, panic rising in me again. 'It's OK, though, isn't it? Not too early?'

'No, it'll be fine, but we should probably get you to hospital. How often have the contractions been coming?'

'Not too often at first, but now they're getting closer together. I haven't exactly been able to time them.'

'Right. Are you OK to get up and walk to the Jeep?' He held out his hand and I took it, grateful for it.

'I don't expect you to drive me,' I protested. 'Honestly, I'll call—'

'What's the matter?' he asked sharply. I'd stopped, staring down at my legs and feet.

'I think my waters have broken,' I said shakily.

'Right,' he said again. 'Get in the Jeep. I'm taking you straight to the hospital, OK? It's too late to mess about calling anyone else.'

'OK,' I agreed. 'Thank you.'

And as we pulled out of the farmyard, back on to the muddy, winding country lane, I found myself thinking this was the most surreal situation I could imagine. Instead of waiting impatiently for my baby to arrive at forty weeks or even later, it seemed like I was going to be giving birth three weeks early, and instead of the calm and unhurried approach to the birth that I'd anticipated, I was on my way to hospital in a Jeep with my boss, after spending the evening helping to deliver piglets. I hoped things would start to go more to plan once we arrived at the hospital. I just wanted to be safely settled in the maternity unit with all the right people on hand to help. It was probably just as well I didn't know how far from the truth that would turn out to be.

CHAPTER TWENTY-EIGHT

The rain was coming down in torrents as we bumped and bounced down the rutted lane. Joe frowned as he focused on the road, glancing at me only once or twice when I winced with another contraction. Each time I tried to breathe through it the way I'd been taught.

'Well done,' he said calmly, turning off on to another narrow lane. 'Sorry about the rough ride, but until we hit the main road there's not a lot I can do about it. This is the quickest way. It's a shortcut but not many people know about it.'

It certainly wasn't a road I'd ever been down before. It hardly deserved the name *road* at all, being more of a dirt track through the fields. Without a four-wheel drive, I doubted many people would have risked it, especially with the road conditions the way they were that night.

We made slow progress. Joe had just negotiated a particularly boggy part of the lane when suddenly the pain really started to hit. Although the contractions had been pretty bad up till then, I'd been managing to cope quite well, but the next one almost overwhelmed me, and as soon as it finished another one started building up.

'Oh my God!' I gasped. 'It's got worse! Much worse! I feel like I'm going to faint. I can't do it! I need drugs, or gas and air, or something! I can't – oh no, another one's starting!'

'OK, try not to panic, it's all right,' Joe said soothingly. 'It's normal, Sam, all quite normal, you're doing brilliantly. Just stay calm and concentrate on your breathing.'

'This is what they talked about in the classes, right?' I yelled at him, wanting someone to blame, someone to scream at. 'The transition stage? Please don't tell me I'm about to have the baby?'

'It'll take a while yet, don't worry,' he replied. 'First babies hardly ever come that quickly, remember.' But even as he spoke, he started to accelerate, and the Jeep jumped and rocked as it struggled through the mud. From what I could tell, we might as well have been driving through a ploughed field. 'Good girl, that's right, keep breathing,' he said, glancing at me again. 'We're nearly there.'

But I didn't believe him. We were miles from anywhere, in pitch darkness and pouring rain, surrounded by fields, on a lane that was almost impassable. Why the hell had I offered to come out on this call tonight? I must have been mad. I'd had that strange burst of energy and determination at the time, wanting to do something useful. Wasn't that supposed to be a sign of impending labour, or was it just another of Nana's old wives' tales? Why hadn't I listened to her instead of just laughing as usual when she finished up with her usual stock phrase about saying nothing and being only my grandmother?!

'I'm scared! I can't do this!' I cried as another fierce contraction took hold of me. And then: 'Why have you stopped?'

'It's just stalled for a minute. It's fine, don't worry, it'll be OK,' Joe said, giving me a quick smile, as if that was going to reassure me. I watched him try the ignition, and then heard the sound of the Jeep's engine splutter, shudder and finally die again. He flung open the door and went round to the boot. I could hear him rummaging with tools, and then the bonnet was flung up in front of my vision as he started fiddling with the engine.

'Oh no, please, no!' I moaned to myself, rocking myself back and forth in the seat. 'This can't be happening! Oh my God, I can't do this any more!'

'Keep concentrating on your breathing, Sam,' Joe called. 'You're doing great. Don't worry, I'll soon have this fixed and we'll be on our way.'

Don't worry? Doing great? I wasn't – I was falling apart. Much as I'd like to say I was brave and strong and calm in the face of such daunting circumstances, I was completely losing control, the lessons from the antenatal classes having gone completely out of the window. I moaned, I cried, I banged my fists on the windscreen and shouted swear words at Joe that I was ashamed, afterwards, to think my baby might have heard from inside me. Despite keeping up a constant stream of platitudes about everything being fine, Joe seemed to be taking for ever fiddling under the bonnet, and I had a horrible feeling that his knowledge of the insides of an engine was considerably smaller than that of the insides of a pig.

And then, just as I thought it couldn't get any worse, everything changed again and I knew precisely what it meant.

'I need to PUSH!' I screamed at the top of my voice, winding down the window so that the rain poured in. 'Joe! What the hell am I going to do? The baby's *coming*!'

Flinging the bonnet shut, he opened the passenger door, took one look at me, and to my shock, lifted me, without too much apparent difficulty despite my vast girth, and laid me carefully on the back seat.

'OK, Sam, you need to calm down and listen to me now,' he said, and because his voice was so quiet, so gentle and persuasive, I did. I listened. 'I've already called an ambulance, in case I couldn't get the Jeep started. I didn't want to frighten you, but you were right, it was obvious the baby was coming quickly.'

'An ambulance?' I shrieked. 'It'll never get down this lane!'

'Well, they may be able to get in from the other end – it's only another mile or so to the main road from here. In the meantime, I'm sorry but I need you to take off your trousers and underwear.'

Fortunately I was in no frame of mind to imagine how I'd have felt if he'd said those words to me at any other time. I was too frightened, the urge to push out the baby was coming over me in waves and getting harder to resist.

'Oh, God, I need to push!' I shouted again, terrified.

Without another word, he yanked off my boots, jeans and knickers. Being half-naked in the back of Joe's Jeep might have featured in some of my secret fantasies, but right then, none of that mattered. At that moment, Joe wasn't my boss and I wasn't his employee. I wasn't even a stupid girl who'd got a crush on a man who couldn't care less about her. All that mattered now was getting this baby out, and how it was actually going to happen – in the back of a Jeep.

'Are you going to deliver my baby yourself – right here?' I squawked.

'I think, actually, you'll deliver it yourself,' he said calmly. 'You're doing so well – you've been contracting so quickly and efficiently, I reckon this little chap – or chappess – will just come sliding out without any interference from me whatsoever.' While he was talking, he took things out of his bag: plastic sheeting, towels, antibacterial wash, disposable gloves. At least I'd had the good fortune to find myself in labour in the presence of a man so well prepared for such an event. 'You're going to be absolutely fine, Sam,' he said. 'I'll be right here to help.'

I tried to calm down, to breathe properly and listen to his words of reassurance. I reminded myself how much I trusted him. He was a brilliant professional, and surely human birth wasn't so *very* different from dogs and cows, was it? He'd help me. It was going to be all right. I'd get through this. But at that moment another overpowering urge came over me and I gasped, automatically grabbing hold of his hand.

'Another contraction?' he said.

I nodded, unable to speak.

'OK. Sorry, I'm just going to have a look …'

At that moment I didn't think I'd have cared if the entire population of Hope Green had queued up outside the Jeep to have a look.

'I need to push! NOW!' I spat at him again as if it was his fault.

'OK! Yes, the head is right there! Push away, Sam.' His voice wobbled a bit. 'You're about to have your baby. You're nearly there. Give it all you've got, girl.'

I'd be lying if I said it was the beautiful, spiritual experience some mothers wax lyrical about. It was frankly horrible. I was scared, uncomfortable; it was bloody painful and yes, I made a fuss. I cried for my mum, my nan, the ambulance, the hospital. I swore at Joe for being a man, ranted at God for making it so bleeding difficult to have babies, raged incoherently at Adam, even though he wasn't even there, because it was all his fault in the first place, and yelled at the rain because – well, I just wanted to yell.

'I know, I'm sorry,' Joe said, surprisingly gently considering how deeply I was digging my nails into his hands. 'I wish I could do more to help, but honestly, believe me, you're doing an absolutely great job. It's painful because it's been so fast. But it'll soon be over. Here we go – the head's nearly out! Yes, Sam, that's it, keep it going, push!'

And then came the moment, the moment when I finally understood what all those mums go on about. My baby son, slithering into Joe's hands, his perfect little fingers curled into fists, his perfect little mouth open in a howl of protest.

'Is he all right?' I panted, trying to raise myself up on the seat to look at him. 'I mean, because of being a bit early – will he be all right?'

Joe held him up to show me. 'He looks absolutely perfect,' he said. He wrapped him carefully in a towel and laid him on my chest.

'Oh my God! He's so beautiful!' I said, bursting into tears. 'I've got a baby boy! I can't believe he's here!'

For a moment, Joe didn't say anything. I looked up at him, just in time to see him wiping his eyes. I felt a strange sensation, like we were alone in a bubble, just the three of us, sharing something so precious it could never be equalled as long as I lived.

'Thank you,' I said quietly. 'Thank you for looking after me – us. And sorry for shouting and swearing at you.'

'I probably deserved it,' he said, giving a little laugh, but the tears were still glistening in his eyes. 'For getting us stuck in the mud. I should have just called an ambulance from the farm instead of trying—'

'They'd probably have got stuck too,' I said. 'You … you've been amazing, Joe.'

We stared at each other. I could hardly believe what I'd just said to him, but when I looked down at my baby's soft, downy head, I felt I just had to say it again. 'Amazing. I'm glad you were with me.'

'You're pretty amazing yourself,' he muttered. He coughed and turned away. He was half in, half out of the Jeep door, rainwater dripping off his hair. I smothered a giggle. He laughed too and it broke the spell. Probably just as well.

'Who'd have thought it?' I said wonderingly. 'Only a few hours ago we were both at the pig farm.'

'Yes. Nine piglets and one human baby in one evening – not a bad score,' he joked. Then he stood up straight, listening. 'I can hear the ambulance. It seems to be getting through. OK – *Mum* – let's get you and this baby boy off to hospital.'

He insisted on coming with me in the ambulance and accompanying me up to the postnatal ward, and it was only when a nurse smiled at him and offered her congratulations that it occurred to us that he was being mistaken for the father. We both laughed a little awkwardly.

'He's my boss,' I explained. 'But he delivered my baby.'

'Oh my God!' the nurse exclaimed. 'You gave birth *at work*?'

'No.' I was laughing, some kind of euphoria having taken over now. 'In the back of a Jeep.'

'I'm a vet,' Joe said quickly. 'Sam and I were out at a pig farm, and … well, we got stuck in the mud.'

'Oh my God!' the nurse said again. 'Well, thank goodness he was with you!'

'Yes.' I stopped laughing and looked up at Joe. 'Thank goodness.'

The baby was weighed, checked over and given back to me to feed while Joe went off to the hospital shop, reappearing later when the baby was tucked up in his little crib next to my bed. He'd bought sandwiches and biscuits for me.

'You must be starving,' he said, and I realised I was. I hadn't eaten since lunchtime. 'And ... I bought this too,' he added looking slightly sheepish. 'His first present.'

It was a soft toy, a bright blue pig. I burst out laughing, as did Joe.

'Just so you never forget the circumstances of his birth,' he said.

'As if I'm likely to! Thank you. That's ... sweet of you.'

We looked at each other for a moment. I was acutely aware that something had changed between us. A short while ago we'd shared the most intimate thing possible together, and I couldn't see, now, how we could ever go back to the cold and sometimes hostile relationship we'd been used to.

'I suppose I should go,' he said, without moving.

'No, you don't have to.'

'You need your sleep.'

'I'm too excited. I can't stop looking at the baby and thinking—'

'You can't keep calling him "the baby"! Haven't you chosen a name for him?' he asked, smiling. He actually had a lovely smile. How had I never noticed? Probably because he'd hardly ever smiled at me before.

'Nothing definite. I was thinking of Thomas or Joshua. What do you think?'

'Mmm. I like them both. Use one for his first name and the other for his second? Or should you check with his father? Does he get a say in it?'

'No. He said it was up to me. I'm the one who's going to be bringing him up.'

'Right.' He gave me a strange look, and then went on quickly, 'Well, I probably should get going. I need to get on to the RAC to go and sort out my Jeep. I'll have to go home by taxi.'

'Yes, of course.' I glanced down at my baby and smiled again. It felt as if all I could do was smile, in wonderment, at both of them.

Joe still made no move to go.

'I've been in this room before,' he said suddenly, very quietly. 'Andrea was in that bed opposite, ten-and-a-half years ago, when Ruby was born.'

'Oh.' I looked at him in confusion. 'I thought you'd only moved to this area recently.'

'Yes. But only from the other side of Dorchester, so this was still our nearest hospital.'

'I see.' How selfish of me. I'd been so engrossed with my own happiness and excitement, it hadn't crossed my mind that the hospital would of course hold memories for him – sad ones now – because of his wife. I reached out for his hand – it felt completely natural now to do so. 'I'm sorry.'

'Why?' He smiled again. 'Ruby's birth was one of the best days of my life. The other times Andrea was in hospital, she had to go to the cancer unit in Poole. I hope I never have to go back *there* again. Not that it isn't a wonderful unit, but—'

'The memories.' I nodded sadly. 'I understand.'

'We moved here because we needed a house we could adapt for her after she was so ill – with a downstairs bathroom and a room for her bed,' he explained quietly. Then he shook his head and gave me another smile. 'But let's not talk about that now. Today is a happy day,' he said brightly. 'For you, and for David, of course. I presume he's on his way?'

I frowned. 'No. Why would he be?'

'Well ...' He stared at me. 'Haven't you called him? Did you want me to—'

'No! He doesn't have to know about it yet!' Even the mention of David, at this moment, felt like an intrusion into the happy bubble that had encompassed me, Joe and the baby. I didn't want Joe to talk about him.

'Really?' Joe was still staring at me. 'Have you broken up with him, then? Won't he still want to know about his baby?'

'*His*?! For God's sake, it isn't *his* baby! What on earth made you think that?'

'Well, I just assumed.' Joe looked as shocked as I was. 'I mean, sorry, but you *are* a couple, aren't you, so—'

'No! No, we're not! We're just friends; we go for walks, well we *did* but ...' I trailed off, remembering that David and I might not even go for walks any more, might not even be friends any more.

'You're not in a relationship with him at all?' Joe still sounded like he couldn't believe it. He was staring at me, wide-eyed with surprise.

'No!' I said. 'The baby is Adam's. My ex. He's going to help support him financially, but apart from that, he probably won't be involved at all. He's getting married soon, actually. To my friend's sister. My ex-friend,' I added sadly. 'Claire, the one who was so rude to you when she came to visit me – remember? We haven't spoken since.'

'Oh.' He was frowning slightly now. 'I see. I seem to have got it completely wrong.'

'It doesn't matter.' I smiled. To be honest, nothing seemed to matter much to me at that moment. After the emotional turmoil of the last few hours, what Joe and I been through together, all that really mattered was the here and now. And he was the one who was here, now. I reached out for his hand again, our eyes met and he stroked my fingers – just once, very slowly, very lightly. For some reason it made me want to cry. Those damned hormones again.

'Well, I really *must* go. Have a good night's rest. I'll see you …' He paused. 'It'll be strange not seeing you at work,' he said quietly, as if this had only just occurred to him. 'Would it be OK if I come round sometime, when you're home? I'd like to see how you're getting on with him.' He smiled at the sleeping baby.

'Yes, of course. That'd be nice.' I felt a funny kind of warmth creeping up my neck. 'Thanks again, Joe, for everything. And for the toy pig! I'll call it Poppy, obviously.'

'Obviously,' he said with a grin.

He walked away, turning back for a moment at the door of the ward and giving me a little wave.

It felt kind of … strange … after he'd gone.

CHAPTER TWENTY-NINE

I was discharged home the next day. The baby and I were both fine, and according to the nursing staff, it had been a straightforward delivery – which wasn't exactly what I'd have called it! Nana had been disgusted to hear I wasn't being kept in for a full week's rest like they apparently did 'in her day', but was nevertheless excited to hear I'd be home so soon.

'I've told David to come and pick you up,' she said, and my heart sank a little. Seeing David, while my mind was still so full of yesterday's events with Joe, was going to be difficult.

But he arrived on the ward smiling, carrying the car seat for the baby and a bag Nana had presumably packed with a set of clothes and a warm blanket for him. And a posy of flowers tied with a blue ribbon, for me.

'Not lilies this time,' he said, and I smiled back, but inside I was trying to fight my exasperation. I didn't want him bringing me flowers. What was the point, when I was on my way home? Why, even now I'd spelled my feelings out to him so clearly, did he have to keep on doing so much for me? Why be so bloody *nice* all the time? It wasn't natural! I shook my head, ashamed of my thoughts but unable to stop them.

'Thanks,' I said. 'Now, I'll just get Thomas dressed ...'

'Thomas.' He nodded. 'Nice name.'

'Yes,' I said, looking down at the baby. 'His name's Thomas Joseph.'

I'd decided during the night. It sounded better than Thomas Joshua. And why wouldn't I want to name him for the man who helped him into the world? I could see from David's face that he'd understood the reason for the name straight away. But still he smiled, still he carried my bag out of the hospital for me and helped me into the car as if I were made of porcelain. I couldn't stand it. I knew now, with more certainty than ever, that I could never have survived a relationship with this man, and it was my fault, not his. He would eventually have irritated me to death. The way things were going, he still might.

'Sam,' he said quietly when we finally pulled up outside the cottage, 'I want to say something to you.'

'OK.' I sighed, dreading that he might yet make another plea for me to reconsider.

'I've decided it would be best, for us both, if we have a bit of time apart from each other. It's hard for me, seeing you all the time. And anyway, you'll be busy with the baby.'

'Right.' I felt bad now. 'I understand.'

'I mean *really* apart from each other,' he went on. 'I haven't told you this yet, but I've been offered a three-month temporary contract with one of the clients I've done some freelance work for. It'll mean working in London, so with the commute as well, I'm not going to be around much.'

'Oh. Well, I'm pleased for you, obviously.'

'Yes. It's a good contract, and it might bring me in more work, too. I hesitated, because of the dog-walking, but I'll still be able to do the weekend walks. So – now, I think I'll definitely accept it.'

'Of course you should.'

'I'll be out of your way. Leave you free … for Joe.'

I flushed hot. 'What? Joe isn't … I'm not … He just happened to deliver the baby. We don't even—'

'If you say so,' he said lightly, with a flicker of a smile. He suddenly leant towards me and kissed me very quickly on the cheek. 'I want you to be happy,' he added in a hoarse whisper, before getting out of the car to open my door for me. I realised it was probably my hormones again, but after he'd gone I had to wipe away the tears.

Nana soon had me smiling again, though.

'Trust you to do things in a completely unorthodox way, Little Sam!' she complained as soon as I was indoors and settled down.

'Everything turned out fine, though!'

'I know, but I was worried out of my life. Having the baby in the back of a car, for goodness' sake.'

'A Jeep.'

'Whatever. And Joe Bradley delivering it! You must have nearly died of embarrassment.'

'Not at all, surprisingly enough. I couldn't even think about being embarrassed. Thomas was coming so fast.'

'Thomas? Who's Thomas?'

'Your great-grandson! You haven't even looked at him yet!' I teased her, indicating the baby, who was still lying peacefully in his car seat. Nana sat down in her chair and I placed him on her lap.

'He's beautiful, Sam,' she whispered, and then started chattering about getting him into a routine, and where we would put his things, and how we'd manage his feeding times.

I interrupted her at once – now that Thomas had come into the world, I suddenly felt less bad for not taking her old-fashioned advice. Routine wasn't good for newborns, I told her.

'All right, all right,' she said. 'I know my ideas are out of date, I'm only your grandmother, I'm saying nothing. We'll do everything your way, Little Sam.'

'But I do want you to be involved!' I protested. 'I might have been given different advice, but I'll still always listen to you, Nana.'

And of course, it was a definite advantage to have an ever-ready extra lap and pair of arms available for cuddles.

I settled down surprisingly quickly to caring for Thomas. Mum and Dad visited on my second day home, bringing more lovely things for him, as well as the inevitable comparisons with how bloody Julia Overton was getting on. And then, on the third day, someone very unexpected turned up.

'Claire!' I gasped as Nana showed her into the living room.

'Hi Sam,' she said quietly. 'I'm sorry I didn't call first. To be honest I thought you'd probably hang up on me.'

'I wouldn't have!' I protested. Or would I?

She handed me a neatly wrapped little parcel. It jingled when I shook it, making me smile.

'I thought it might be an appropriate time to offer an olive branch,' she said. 'I'm really sorry – for everything. I was a total bitch when I came down in the summer. I was missing you so much, I wanted you to come back to London. But I could see how settled you were here, and I guess I resented it. And all I ended up doing was destroying our friendship completely.'

'I've missed you too, you daft cow,' I said, holding out my arms to her. 'Come here. Let's start again, shall we?' Then I laughed. 'I can't believe I thought you were having an affair with Adam. I presume it was him that told you I'd had the baby? I phoned him from the hospital with the news. I was pleased he finally sounded excited to hear about Thomas! He's coming down at the weekend, with Sophie, to see him.'

'That's good. I'm glad. But no – actually it wasn't Adam who told me.' She gave me a sly look. 'It was Joe.'

'Joe?' I felt myself flush at the very mention of his name. 'How …?'

'Apparently you mentioned the fact that we weren't speaking. He thought it might have been partly his fault, that he'd overreacted to me being so obnoxious to him in the pub. It wasn't, obviously. But anyway, in the hospital he got the opportunity to nab your phone while the nurse was with you, or something, and he found my number.' She paused, looking at me curiously. 'Are you and him an item, now, or something?'

'No!' I said, flushing again. I couldn't seem to stop myself. 'Didn't he tell you? He delivered the baby.' I started to tell her the story, but she was still giving me that look, and in the end I laughed and admitted: 'Well, I suppose it's kind of brought us together.'

'Yes. He sounded …' She hesitated. 'Well, he sounded, on the phone, as if he cared a hell of a lot about you, Sam.'

I couldn't answer. What I'd shared with Joe on the night of Thomas's birth was still too fresh, too special, and thinking about it still overwhelmed me a bit. I held Thomas close to me and breathed in his delicious baby smell.

'Would you like to hold him?' I asked Claire as she sat down next to me.

And just like that, we were friends again.

The following day, Joe turned up.

'I hope it's not too soon?' he said as Nana showed him in (raising her eyebrows at me). 'If I'm intruding …'

'Of course you're not.' I couldn't stop grinning at him, and he was grinning back. It was weird. Had we actually been … *missing* each other?

He sat down in the armchair opposite me. Nana bustled off out to the kitchen, muttering about making tea, and Joe and I sat looking at each other in silence for a while.

'Thomas is asleep,' I said unnecessarily, pointing to him in his Moses basket. 'Thomas Joseph,' I added. 'I've called him Thomas Joseph. Because of what you did. Helping me, when he was born.'

He stared at me. 'Well, I'm very flattered.' He smiled. 'I've never had a baby named after me before. Not even any of the foals or piglets I've delivered!'

'Don't remind me about piglets being born,' I said with a groan. 'That's a memory I'm trying to suppress.'

'You were brilliant,' he said. I looked at him in surprise. Brilliant, me? The *receptionist* who shouldn't even have been allowed to help out? But he was going on, in a quiet, earnest voice: 'You were struggling with your own labour pains that evening but you didn't say a word. You just got on and did everything asked of you, as you always do, frankly.'

'Well, I've always *tried*—'

'No, let me finish. I've been working myself up for ages to say this to you. I tried to say it before – that day we went to the pub for lunch – but I blew it. It was supposed to be an apology for the way I'd spoken to you, but instead I went on and on about my own circumstances, and then when you told me you were pregnant, I just assumed it was David's and, well, I know it was none of my business, but I just didn't get it! I couldn't believe he was the right man for you. I mean, I know he's a good-looking guy, charming and all, and some girls would have fallen for that. But I didn't think *you* would, somehow.' He glanced up at me quickly, and looked away again. 'You've got too much spirit for him. He's too ... too *bland*, for God's sake!'

'That's unfair,' I said quietly. 'He's a really nice guy.'

'Yes. As a friend, I'm sure he is. But I thought ...' He shook his head. 'Sorry, I'm not making much sense. As I said, it was none of my business and I was horribly rude to you that day. And, well, on several other occasions too.'

'I knew what a tough time you were going through.'

'That's no excuse!' he retorted, with a flash of his usual fierceness. 'You're not *just* a good receptionist, you've been extremely helpful with the animals too, and you definitely didn't deserve me biting your head off about wanting to become a vet. Especially now I understand what happened – the accident with your horse.'

'Oh, you were right, though. It was a stupid idea.' I shrugged. 'Now I've got the baby, I can't imagine trying to go back to college and everything. It'd be impossible.'

'Not stupid, or impossible. Just a bit impractical, perhaps, at the moment. *But* ...' He leant forward in his chair. 'Here's something for you to think about during your maternity leave. A more realistic option for a career, eventually, might be to train as a veterinary nurse instead.'

'But I'd still have to go to college. And I can't; I need to work.'

'You could study for your diploma while you work for me as an apprentice.'

I stared at him. 'Are you serious? Would you really want me—'

He smiled. 'Of course I'd want you. Not only are you good and reliable at your job but …' He dropped his head. 'Come on, Sam. You must realise. Why do you think I've always been so cool around you?'

'I presumed you didn't particularly like me,' I said, holding my breath.

'The opposite, for God's sake!' He met my eyes, unblinkingly now, and I stared back at him. 'But – well,' he went on. 'You know what my circumstances were. I couldn't allow myself to get close to anyone else. Even now, it feels … too soon. Kind of disloyal to Andrea, to be feeling what I'm feeling …'

It was as though I'd stopped breathing completely now. I tried to swallow, but couldn't. I cleared my throat, gasped for air, and managed finally to get out, 'What? *What* are you feeling?'

'Well. Put it this way. Since the other night – being together with you in the Jeep, when you had the baby – I've felt … something has happened between us. I'm probably talking out of my backside. You're probably going to swear at me, like you did back then, and tell me to get lost, and I won't blame you. It's probably just my imagination, but …'

'No. It's not.'

'Really? You've felt it too?' He paused, staring at me. 'You don't think it's just, perhaps, the whole thing of going through such an emotional experience together?'

'Perhaps.' I shrugged, but it was hard to stop myself from smiling. 'Perhaps we should just wait and see how we feel after everything has settled down a bit.'

'Absolutely.'

'You're still grieving for Andrea. Your emotions must be all over the place.'

'So must yours, after giving birth. Especially three weeks early, in a Jeep in the middle of the fields.'

He grinned. I grinned back.

'And, to be honest,' I said, 'I only broke up with Adam – my ex – earlier this year, and I'm not sure I'm ready, even if this … *thing* between us is really *something* …'

I tailed off. We went on staring at each other for a minute like idiots. And then two things happened almost simultaneously. Thomas woke up and immediately began to wave his fists in the air and bawl. And Nana came back into the room carrying a tea tray and eyeing me and Joe in a very suspicious manner.

'The baby's crying,' she told me, as if I might not have noticed. 'Are you going to pick him up, or do you want me to? I know I'm only your grandmother, but I'm not completely stupid, I can see you're otherwise engaged at the moment.'

'I'm not!' I said, laughing. 'Nana, don't be like that. Joe's been giving me some fantastic advice about my future career. And, well, I have to be nice to the man who brought Thomas safely into the world, don't I?'

I picked up the crying baby and placed him into Joe's arms. Nana watched him as he stroked Thomas's head and rocked him gently to soothe him.

'He looks like a natural,' she said, winking at me.

'He should be. He's already got a little girl.'

Joe looked up at us both, smiling. 'And don't forget how many piglets I've delivered recently,' he said. 'To say nothing of all the calves, lambs, kittens, puppies …'

'Well, I must say I'm glad you were with Sam when she needed you,' Nana said more seriously. 'Although God only knows why she thought it was a good idea to rush off to a pig farm like that, in her condition.'

'I know. It was stupid of me,' I acknowledged.

'Probably. But I'm glad you did,' Joe said.

There was another pause. Nana looked from one of us to the other, coughed very pointedly as if to remind us she was still there, and said, 'Well, I'll leave the pair of you to enjoy your tea, then,' and bustled out of the room again.

And even though Joe and I were sitting yards apart, both of us staring at baby Thomas and not at each other, I felt strangely like a teenager caught in the act of kissing her boyfriend outside the front door.

'I hope you didn't misconstrue—' I started to say to Nana after Joe had left.

'I didn't misconstrue anything,' she interrupted, turning to smile at me. 'But I certainly picked up some kind of feeling in the air.'

'That's all it is.'

'Well, it's nothing to do with me. I'm only—'

'—my grandmother!' I laughed, putting my arms round her. 'And you're far, far wiser than I'll ever be.'

'You know I've always liked Joe. It's you who seemed to have mixed feelings about him.'

'I've always liked him too, really, as I suspect you knew, since you have such amazing insight. I just didn't think *he* liked *me*.'

'He was struggling against it. Obviously. Didn't want to admit it to himself.' She winked at me. 'Don't you read any Mills & Boon, girl? Happens all the time.'

I laughed. But she suddenly went very quiet and gave me a warning look.

'Be careful, though, Little Sam,' she said. 'He's still grieving. He might not know what he's saying or doing right now.'

'I know. I realise that.' I smiled at her. 'I'm not about to behave like a silly teenager now, Nana. I'm a mother. My baby comes before everything else.'

'Pleased to hear it,' she muttered. 'But it's nothing to do with me. I'm saying nothing.'

Joe came to see me regularly, often bringing Ruby with him. She loved being allowed to hold baby Thomas carefully on her lap. I'd been slightly nervous that the force of feeling that had overtaken Joe and me so powerfully since the baby's birth might gradually fade away again, but the thrill I felt every time he appeared at the door showed no sign of diminishing, and his answering smile told me he felt the same. Nevertheless, we'd agreed to take things very slowly, not least for Ruby's sake. The loss of her mother wasn't something the little girl would get over quickly, and she might well resent another woman coming into her father's life, however much she seemed to enjoy my company.

Soon it was December, and there were a couple of days when there was a hint of snow mixed in with the interminable rain and sleet. All the cottages in the village had lights and Christmas trees in their windows, and the village shop, decked out with tinsel, holly and things in shiny gift wrappings, looked like something out of a Dickens novel. And one chilly evening I was surprised to hear Ruby asking her father if I was going to spend Christmas with them. Joe raised his eyebrows at me, but I shook my head, smiling.

'Nana and I will be taking Thomas up to my parents in Norfolk, Ruby,' I explained. 'But perhaps I can come with Thomas another time, if that's OK with Daddy.'

So maybe we didn't have too much to worry about there, after all.

And eventually, just before we packed our bags to travel up to Norfolk for the family Christmas, I opened the front door one bitingly cold evening to be met by – not just Joe and Ruby, but also a very overexcited little chocolate Labrador puppy who was pulling Ruby into the house by her lead, sniffing around my feet and wagging her tail madly.

'Hello!' I said, crouching down to get better acquainted. 'And who do we have here?'

'We've called her Bailey,' Ruby said. 'She's a surprise. I've been *bursting* to tell you, haven't I, Daddy? But I've managed to keep the secret.'

'Secret?' I ruffled the little dog's fur and frowned up at Joe. 'Is she one of Cookie's litter, by any chance?'

'Yes.' He smiled at me. 'She's the one you were tempted to buy.'

'So ...?' I was a bit lost for words. 'Have you borrowed her, or what?'

Nana had come to see what was going on, and we were all making a fuss of the pup, getting her even more overexcited, so I suggested Ruby might like to take her into the kitchen to get her a bowl of water and calm her down.

'I bought her,' he admitted, looking at me sheepishly. 'I told Mrs Evans I'd have her, soon after she talked to you about the pups. I'd had a bad day that day. Ruby was missing Andrea terribly, and then when you said something about everyone needing a dream ...'

'You don't have to explain,' I said gently. 'I'm glad you bought her. I did think at the time that it would help you and Ruby to have a puppy yourselves.'

'But I bought her for *you*,' he said. 'I was going to look after her, and pass her over to you once you'd settled down with the baby.'

'Really?' I smiled at him. 'Well, that was sweet of you, but it's still not really ideal, is it? You were right, it's not fair, while I'm living with Nana and we have Ebony to consider. She's a bit nervous of dogs.'

'Actually, I'm afraid it was a daft thing to do, anyway. You see, Ruby's got so attached to Bailey. She's helped so much to comfort her, and I'm not sure I can just pass her over now.'

'Of course not! It's lovely for you and Ruby to have a new little friend. At least I can come and see her, and perhaps I can come out for walks with you sometimes when I take Thomas out in his pram?'

'Exactly. In fact, Sam, I'd like you to share her with us.' He gave me a very direct look. We were, after all, both passionate animal lovers. We knew there was something very serious about sharing a dog, something you couldn't do with just anybody. It was a commitment, of a kind – to the dog, even if not to each other. 'Ruby actually suggested it, although she doesn't know that was my plan all along.'

And without even thinking, I did what I'd been wanting to do for much longer than I'd admitted, even to myself. I reached up – I had to stand on tiptoe to do it – pulled Joe down towards me and kissed him. There just happened to be a bunch of mistletoe hanging over us so it seemed like too good an opportunity to miss.

'Excuse me, I'll just go and make some tea …' Nana said at once.

Then: 'Ooooh!' Ruby had appeared in the kitchen doorway without us even noticing. 'I hope Sam's going to be your new girlfriend, Daddy!'

And so did I, of course. Even if it had taken me an exceptionally long time, and having a baby in a Jeep in the middle of a muddy field, to make me realise it. Looking up at Joe now, I remembered how Adam used to tease me about my silly, unrealistic dream. Well, here I was, living in a cottage in the country. I had the child. I had the dog – or at least, a share of one – and ... perhaps I might even have found the man.

We all need our dreams, don't we? And it seemed that, here in Hope Green, mine might actually be coming true.

ACKNOWLEDGEMENTS

With thanks again to Sharon Whelan of Clarendon House Vets in Galleywood for checking several aspects of animal care in this story, as well as giving me advice on the set-up of a vet surgery and the receptionist's role. The internet is great but can't beat personal experience!

And as always, thanks to my editor Emily Yau for all her input, guidance and patience with me, and to my agent Juliet Burton for handling contracts and payments (which my brain can't cope with) and letting me get on with the writing!

Coming soon from Sheila Norton:

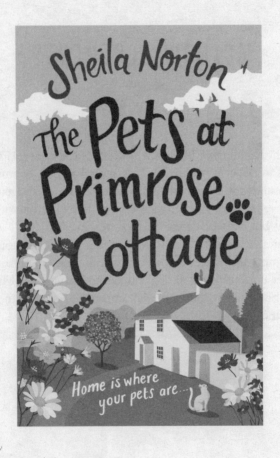